T0195875

Books by Lem Moyé

- *Statistical Reasoning in Medicine: The Intuitive P–Value Primer*
- *Difference Equations with Public Health Applications (with Asha S. Kapadia)*
- *Multiple Analyses in Clinical Trials: Fundamentals for Investigators*
- *Finding Your Way in Science. How to combine character, compassion, and productivity in your research career*
- *Probability and Statistical Inference: Applications, Computations, and Solutions (with Asha S. Kapadia and Wen Chan)*
- *Statistical Monitoring of Clinical Trials: Fundamentals for Investigators*
- *Statistical Reasoning in Medicine: The Intuitive P–Value Primer- 2nd Edition*
- *Face to Face with Katrina's Survivors: A First Responder's Tribute*
- *Elementary Bayesian Biostatistics*
- *Saving Grace – A Novel*
- *Weighing the Evidence: Duality, Set, and Measure Theory in Clinical Research*
- *Probability and Measure in Public Health*
- *Finding Your Way in Science. How to combine character, compassion, and productivity in your research career. 2nd edition*
- *Catching Cold Series*
    - *Vol. 1: Breakthrough*
    - *Vol. 2: Redemption*
    - *Vol 3: Judgment*

Catching Cold
Vol 3 - Judgment

LEM MOYÉ

Order this book online at www.trafford.com
or email orders@trafford.com

Most Trafford titles are also available at major online book retailers.

Print information available on the last page.

ISBN: 978-1-6987-1423-3 (sc)
ISBN: 978-1-6987-1424-0 (hc)
ISBN: 978-1-6987-1425-7 (e)

Library of Congress Control Number: 2023905858

Trafford rev. 03/21/2023

www.trafford.com
North America & international
toll-free: 844-688-6899 (USA & Canada)
fax: 812 355 4082

Let what you want to be, be you.

Lem Moyé

CatchingCold@principalevidence.com

CONTENTS

A DAY FOR LOSING JOBS

11:02 AM EDT April 4, 2017
Dover, Delaware
SSS headquarters
32 minutes post-detonation

Meredith Doucette lifted her head.

A severed hand bearing a wedding band on its pale, ring finger rested on her stomach.

The Triple-S CEO exhaled, collapsing back on the freezing, metal gurney. The falling drizzle, twisting and blowing in the fluorescent light, soaked the cold sheet covering her.

A face appeared above her.

She vomited into it.

"I am the CEO here," she sputtered. "Tell me what happ—"

"And I'm the czarina of the Russian empire," the towering woman said as she laughed, wiping her own face with a towel wet with rain and blood.

"You'll be going to surgery soon, Ms. CEO." She reached for a new cloth, cleaned Meredith's face, and wiped the CEO's head and neck with soft, gentle strokes.

"I don't know a thing, much less who you are. The doctor will see you soon, but right now we need to get you to the hospital to control your ble—"

The CEO's stomach clenched as a shooting pain flew up her left leg, the spasm leaving her breathless. Her mouth opened, but no sound emerged.

With a pinch of a needle in her arm, she closed her eyes.

●

The finger prods, like rifle butts, jabbed her awake.

1

"What's your name?" demanded the grating voice.

"I'm . . ." Meredith paused, fighting to collect herself. "I am Ms. Doucette, CEO of SSS."

She looked into the face of an overweight, pale man, his sweat dripping down on her.

He belched and then smiled, "I heard that story from an orderly. What a sense of humor after what's happened. Do you have any discomfort?"

Anger consumed her as the executive meeting and its tension jumped back into her. *No, I feel great. Where's my bicycle?* The CEO closed her eyes, taking a slow deep breath. *Why doesn't my arm hurt? And the leg pain is gone.*

She looked up to see the IV bottle dangling from the metal rod above her.

"Not really. Whatever you have given me is making a difference, and I'm thankful for that. What happened?"

The man nodded. "I am Louis Simmons, PA. There was an explosion on the twenty-ninth floor of your building. Looks like a bomb blast. Lots of shrapnel. Many people were hurt."

She saw him look at her hand that was now in an ice-filled plastic bag, sitting like a companion.

"Including you, I'm afraid."

"Please tell me, sir, who was injured."

Meredith watched as he shook his heavy head back and forth.

"Don't know much, and I couldn't tell you anyway. Not just to you. To anybody. HIPAA rules." He shrugged.

Meredith, heart pounding, struggled to sit up. "Listen to me. I've been the CEO of this company for years. Many of these people who were hurt were friends of mine. For some of them, I was the only family they had. I need to know now so that I can help—"

"Well, I may lose my job if I tell you too much."

She almost jumped off the gurney. "I probably already lost mine. This is a day for losing jobs. Let's just move on with it, shall we?"

The man stepped back. "If you were a real CEO, I wouldn't need to explain it to you."

She saw him turn and walk off. *What am I going to—*

"Ms. Doucette."

"Monica."

The head of SSS Safety came into view above her. Short black hair and large brown eyes sat above a dour mouth.

"You're okay, dear?" the CEO asked.

"Yes. Just a cut on my leg that may need a stitch. How do you fee—"

The CEO watched as Monica looked down at the hand and gasped.

Meredith did her best to smile. "What? You think it's going to drag you off to hell or something? Monica, I need you to focus. Someone said that it was a bomb. How bad?"

"It destroyed the twenty-ninth floor."

"Injuries."

"Dead and injured."

Meredith closed her eyes.

The CEO's head pounded. "The deaths, Monica."

"We only have preliminary information," the safety director said, closing her eyes. "Dr. Stennis died, as well as the entire clinical trial leadership team."

"Jasper?"

"Surviving so far, but his left leg was in pieces under his wheelchair." The safety leader shivered.

"You're doing fine, Monica," Meredith said, trying and failing to get her right hand over to reach and console her.

"The doctors said that they were going to amputate." Monica looked up and down the outdoor makeshift corridor that held several patients. "He's in surgery now."

Meredith shook her head. "That wasn't even the leg that has hurt him for so long." She closed and then opened her eyes. "How about Nita?" she said, referring to her chief financial officer. "Is the baby okay?"

"Yes, and Nita's alive but—"

"And?"

"She took the brunt of the shrapnel in her face. She will need multiple surgeries. And—"

"Yes?"

"She's blind, Ms. Doucette."

Meredith passed out.

SINGING OUT OF THE WINDOW

"I get nervous up here," Olivia said, shivering.

"I bet you do." Kevin Wells drove the new blue Infiniti up the highway into the Superstition Mountains, forty miles east of Phoenix.

"What happened to us a year ago was a 'one-off', but I still think on it."

He turned to his girlfriend, expecting her eyes to be fixed straight ahead, unblinking and lost in the horror of what Siphod had attempted that afternoon.

But she seemed easy, flowing, lost in the scenery.

Lots had changed in the past months. He raised his eyebrows.

"This is so Jon." She turned to her boyfriend.

"How does he seem to you, Kev?"

"I don't know. I've never seen him without money woes before."

"The decision to release the vaccine production process was a masterstroke? Where is he going to build?"

"Well, the DeLeon Institute will—"

"No." She smiled. "He really chose that name?"

He watched, smiling as she turned her head toward him.

"Well, one of his bankers suggested it." Kevin sighed. "Anyway, you can't blame him. These last years he has been running and ducking for cover. With nobody chasing him anymore, he's decided to show the world who and where his team works." He shrugged. "Cathartic for him, I suppose."

"Well," she said, smiling. "It's been three months since the release of Emily and Luiz's vaccine work, and judging by the donations, the planet's been grateful." She sighed. "It's taken the world in a . . ."—Kevin watched as she sought the right word—"a healthy direction. For one time, who knows, maybe the last time, people worldwide celebrate a success that was not tailored to be some geopolitical bank shot."

"And, it works," Kevin said, nodding. "Effective vaccines are now ready just after the emergence of a suspicious viral strain before an epidemic can pick up steam."

His throat was blocked, but he had to get it out. "Decide when you're leaving yet?"

"On the day like this, talking with you, I'm never leaving."

"I know, sweetheart, I know, but you're committed to your project."

He felt for her right hand and grasped it. "I love my Kevin," she sang out the window. "Yes, I do, yes, I do."

She looked back at him. "Yes, I do."

Lifting his brown hand up, kissing it, she said, "It may only be a fact-finding mission, but I need to know—"

"Here's the turnoff."

Kevin signaled the right turn, parking with the four other cars that had already arrived.

"Tomorrow," Olivia said, opening her door, "I leave in the morning."

LOVED A LIFETIME

"It's the last time that we're together." Jon unbuttoned his denim jacket.

"Most of us anyway. Where's Rayiko?" Nobody's seen her for days."

Makes me feel strange too, Luiz, but I'm kinda alright. Oh," he looked down at his phone.

Email.

Rayiko.

"I better read this."

"Hey, no problem, man. I'll be thinking about what the next set of troubles is that you'll get us into."

Jon laughed, walking away, head in his phone.

> To: Jon DeLeon
> From: Rayiko Snow
> Date: May 3, 2017
>
> By now, you know I'm gone.
>
> I don't have much time. You will carry me around in your heart for some time. You know I know this. But also know that you are in mine. There's not a day I don't long for you.
>
> As for the rest, we only had that one night, but I feel that you and I used it to love for a lifetime.

Take care of yourself. Jon, You can't help but do well. Don't destroy yourself in the process.

R

Jon read the note again and again and then walked toward Luiz and the road.

SAYING EVERYTHING WITH NO WORDS

"Here they are," Jon said, pointing to Kevin's car pulling off the road. He raised his hand.

"Well," Luiz said, elbowing him, "there are only rocks and sunshine here. I think they see us."

Kevin and Olivia walked over, Kevin in a brown leather jacket and Olivia wearing a peach sweater and jeans.

"Hi, Luiz," Olivia called out. "You and Emily still producing miracles in the lab."

"Not since we got kicked out of prison," Emily said, walking over and wearing her trademark denim jacket, T-shirt, and jeans. She held Sparky, who, always happy to see everybody, barked.

They all laughed.

"He's going to wag that tail right off of him," Breanna said, rubbing his head.

"When will the new building be ready, Jon?"

"It's already up. We only need to populate it with equipment,"

Emily looked at Olivia. "When did you get those boots?"

"Yesterday. Kevin suggested that I wear them all day today to break them in."

"How's that working for ya?" Luiz asked.

"I'm going to make him put 'em on and walk back home from here."

They all broke up laughing.

Jon watched them all. Last year, this team was new to him, unknown to each other, uncertain of their mission, and doubtful of the outcome.

It was just like his first team—Wild Bill, Dale, Breanna, Robbie, and then Rayiko.

Rayiko, Jon shook his head.

After the vaccine project, they all went their own ways, journeymen and women looking for something new.

And now just as that team was dissolved, their successors were fragmenting, and he realized that, once again, he was presiding over the death of the thing that he loved.

He shook his head in rapid-fire movement. "Hey, everybody," he called, "unless you want to burn to a crisp in this morning Arizona heat that's coming, let's talk it up for a bit, then skedaddle."

They all walked without being told to the one spot that they all knew and loved and had avoided for weeks.

"This is where our Cassie died," Jon said. "Brimming with pain and self-loathing, she didn't know that she was emblematic of us all, broken, begging to be healed, only to find that her healers were next to her, just needing to be asked.

"And there we stood and helped her, and each other. I'm told that CiliCold is a private corporation." He shrugged. "Maybe so but I know that it's nothing but people, us. It is our hopes and fears, pain, work, and ambition.

"We've built CiliCold twice and we will build it again."

He turned to Breanna. "Make up your mind where you're headed yet?"

Jon watched her smile through her tears. "My kiddos and I are headed to Philadelphia. Family's there."

"Okay. Let us hear from you." He wasn't going to mention her, but he had to. "Rayiko?" he said, coughing her name out.

"I only know that she left two days ago," Emily said in a low voice. "Apartment being leased."

"Family probably moved to LA," Kevin added, wiping his nose. "I hear that her husband has quite a career out there."

"We'll miss her," Luiz said.

Jon, close to tears, simply nodded and dropped his head.

"Olivia?" he said, at last, exhaling hard. "You're headed to the DC area?"

"Yes. Some business, both new and unfinished."

"You going to leave this guy with us?" Luiz asked, pointing to Kevin.

"You can keep him," she said, hugging Kevin's left arm and leaning on his shoulder. "But just until I get back." Her voice choked.

"Well, Kevin," Jon said, smiling now, clapping his friend on the back, "as the new president of CiliCold, launch this ship."

"I'd love to, but," he said, smiling, "I, uh, don't know what we're going to do."

"What?"

"Really?"

"Take him with you, Olivia."

"I mean," Kevin said when the laughter died down, "we don't know. We're not vaccine producers. There is a world of manufacturing that has taken that on, right? So really, what do we do now?"

Jon saw him look his way and opened his mouth. "We—"

"We will do what we always do. What they say that we can't, and what we know that we can."

"Signed, Emily." Luiz finished.

"Let's get outta here," Breanna said.

They broke up ten minutes later. Jon saw that they were all in tears.

●

He stopped for gas just a mile down on state highway 60, walking inside the small junk food/grocery store. There, Jon worked his way over to the ICEE dispenser and poured a large watermelon freeze into the plastic cup.

Something pushed against his leg.

He jumped, spilling the drink in front of him.

Looking down, there was the back of a person, a woman.

"Listen," he said, leaning over to help her to her feet.

Maybe a worker here cleaning up, but what do I know? "I am so sorry for running into you. Here," He gave her a wrinkled and clean handkerchief from his jean pocket.

She wiped her hands and stood tall facing him, saying nothing, saying everything with no words and silent.

After a few seconds, she broke the gaze.

Jon watched her, shoulders a little uneven as she returned to the floor, now cleaning his mess. He turned and after pouring and paying for his drink, walked to his car, clueless.

That night, he dreamed of Rayiko.

CHAOS OF THE UNIVERSE

" **I**'ll miss showering with you, Kev."

Olivia jumped out in front of Kevin who had just stepped onto the bath mat, reaching for a towel.

"You bet you will," he said, leaning forward and smacking her pale-ass cheeks.

Olivia dried off, wrapped the towel around herself, and fell back on the bed. Her gray tresses fell around her face. Kevin lay next to her, putting his arm around her waist.

"Are you going to look for another house?" she asked, brushing the end of his wide nose back and forth with her finger.

"Hadn't thought of it. How long do you think you'll be in Washington?"

He watched her ponder. *She is the delight of—*

"I don't know. It may be just a week. On the other hand, maybe a few months."

He smiled and worked his hand under her bath towel. "I guess it depends on whether you want to stay for just the writing or the actual passage of your bill."

"I'm sure we can write it and get it to the committee. Unless the American people are riled up, there is just no chance that it will pass."

The sixty-two-year-old jiggled on the plush bed. Kevin leaned over her.

"You can always go fallow with it, you know," he said, admiring her trim legs. He knew he could not persuade her to stay. Ever since that terrible day in the high country, she had been seeking her purpose.

Now that she'd latched on to it, he couldn't, wouldn't get between them.

"Fallow?"

"Sure. It requires a tight-knit group to do the actual writing," he said, sneaking his hand between her thighs. "Once done, let it sit. When the time is right, you release it to the right members of Congress and, uh senators. This allows them to move forward while the iron's hot."

"If you're a senator, you're a member of Congress, silly."

"I uh, must have gotten myself distracted by these soft thighs,"

"Hmmm."

"But the key must be to keep it on the down low. No matter how tempting, you must say nothing to congressmen and women." He sat up on the bed.

"That protects you from having one of them shoot their mouth off, warning your enemies about its presence."

He sighed, "Olivia, when they find out, they'll murder you."

She nodded. "Doesn't matter. These people have done despicable things of which the public knows nothing."

"Don't be so sure. The public may know and just not care."

He saw her stiffen.

"Kevin, you don't believe that."

He exhaled. "I want to believe it's not true, but you don't know Americans. Many hide their real feelings because they know they'll be criticized for voicing them. Others don't mind the callous, company behavior. They see that as part of progress—"

"Regardless of who gets hurt?"

"We are a selfish people. How are you going to manage the FDA?"

He watched her lips twist into a sneer. "Well, Big Pharma and the agency are mobbed up. But the FDA should support our goals."

Kevin kissed her on the cheek, his lips just brushing her skin. "Olivia, you of all people know the FDA. They have a public health-modeled credo, but in the end, they're an established institution populated with bureaucrats who want to keep their jobs. Plus, they're paid by the pharmaceutical industry."

He watched her drop her head, gray tresses falling around the smooth skin of her face. "I guess I don't know how the agency will react."

"They will position themselves with Big Pharma."

"That's twisted."

"But where their best interests reside."

"And the country loses, 'Jesus wept.'"

"He didn't save countries, sweetheart. He saved people." He lay down next to her, stroking her bare back. "What do you want to do?"

She was silent, staring straight ahead.

"Taking your time to write the bill on the *down low* is a great start, " he said, more to break the silence. "Then study congressional members to see who would be most helpful. Do all of the preparation that you can and then wait."

"For what, Kevin?"

"For America to move to you."

●

Olivia agreed to go to Scottsdale to eat. After spending a few minutes walking in and out of several of the shops in Old Town in the orange early light sunset, they strolled arm in arm to Tony V's for an early dinner. Olivia was delighted with Kevin's conversation. The death of his wife led to their hooking up. The Triple-S takeover of their company and the depths of its descent.

I never wanted babies until Kevin. Kind of late—

"You know Meredith Doucette, don't you?" he asked as their entrees arrived

"Oh, yes," she said, looking across the small table at him. "We're not friends, but we are, well, we're starting to think the same way."

"Thinking about talking to her?"

"Yes."

"You'll need to be careful. She's still CEO from what I've heard."

"I spoke to her once or twice before the blast."

"I didn't know that," he said. "Good for you."

"She'll be on our side."

"I hope so," Kevin said, wiping his mouth with a napkin. "But her situation is different. Talking with her when she was trying to get Triple-S under control before the attack was one thing. But now she's responsible for the wounded company. Motivations change."

"Yes," Olivia said, holding the fork of chocolate pie midway between the table and her mouth. "She can help me as I've helped her."

She hoped.

"Let's get the check."

●

"I know you're committed," Kevin said, entering 101 South a few minutes later, "and nobody works harder than you, but you're entering an arena in which you have never played."

"A pilgrim in an unholy land," she whispered.

"And you were a strong and well-recognized drug regulatory affairs director, but to succeed, you'll need new skills."

"Such as?"

"You'll have to manage the mess you'll have created. Expect the bill to pass and consider the consequences. Expect it to fail and consider the consequences. Expect treason on your team. Expect loyalty. Expect political triumphs and political failures. Incompetence. Technical glitches. Terrible communication."

He turned to her as they approached SR 60 west.

"The way to beat the chaos of the universe is to expect it all, at once."

"Nobody can do that, Kevin,"

He glanced at her. "Decide to be that woman, Olivia. Don't try to be. Don't want to be. Don't be afraid to be. Just be."

Why am I leaving him for so long?

"Take me home so I can be who you need me to be."

●

Later that night, legs wrapped around his back, aroused and full of him, the retired regulatory director cried out for his baby. The older, childless man delivered strong and hard. When done, they laughed, cried, laughed, and did it again.

HER SONG

"Jon? Jon."

"Uh, yeah. Hi, uh, Kevin"

"I just dropped Olivia off at Sky Harbor," he said, stepping out of his car. "Glad to be here at the new DeLeon Institute." He wiped his brow. "In the hot July sun."

"You know," he said with a smile, "Olivia couldn't believe you gave it your name."

"What?"

*He's unfocused, Ke*vin thought. The scientist's head hung, and the new bags under his eyes broadcast to the world that he hadn't slept for at least a night.

It had to be Rayiko.

He didn't know everything about the two, but one thing was sure. Jon thrived on their closeness that had been building for years. Her sudden departure weeks ago had hit him hard, and he was confused and uncertain, her song still playing loud in his head.

All ladies had their secrets, Kevin thought, but Rayiko had been a difficult read.

Like the mountains, she seemed near but always far away.

"Welcome to your new corporate headquarters," Jon said, a little too loud.

Kevin closed the car door and looked up. "Goodness. This must be one hundred thousand cubic feet."

"Bigger than the Florence prison," he said with a smile, "but you don't command all of it."

"I hope not. Show me."

"Sure, first let me tell you where we are," the scientist said, running both hands over his tangled hair. "We're on McQueen Street, between

Queen Creek and Ocatillio Roads. Not far from the 202 and easy to find."

Kevin listened as Jon described the surroundings. It was tightly zoned, pretty much residential in this section of McQueen with an occasional commercial block. This is here, over here is that.

This was not like Jon, Kevin thought. Yammering about inconsequential things, running his hand through his hair over and over.

"Hey," Kevin said, resting a hand on his shoulder. "Let's go to my office, wherever that is."

"Sure thing, Jon said, pointing. "We got a lot of yardage over here."

He walked, Kevin following down the hall to a large open space surrounded on three sides by huge offices.

"All on the first floor," the scientist said.

"Great, I won't have to carry the groceries upstairs."

They both laughed. "Or the lab equipment and computers," Jon added, scratching his chest through his blue shirt, sleeves rolled up to the elbows. "Emily will have her computers here and just around the corner, will be a large cell lab for Luiz and space for the rest of the team." He pointed, running his hand through his hair.

"The corner spot is nice. Lots of light through those windows," the new CEO said.

"Heat in the summer I bet but still the light is . . . is . . . the light is good. I insisted on the northeast side so we won't get the brunt of the sun. Look." He pointed to his right. "Here are six contiguous offices. Yours is in the center."

"In the thick of things."

"Just the way you'd want it."

"Furnishings?"

"The lab equipment and Em's computers are slated to arrive later today. You can choose your office furnishings that will arrive within a day after you order them."

Kevin looked around. Jon was sounding like a tour guide.

"Sweet. I like this Jon," He looked back at the scientist. "When do you think we'll be operational?"

"August 1, I hope. I still have a nanotechnologist and uh, measuring, I mean measure theory expert to recruit."

He watched Jon shove his hands into his jeans pockets as he sat down on the carpeted floor of his empty office.

"Please," he said with a smile, "be seated."

Sitting, they both stretched their legs out, backs against the cool wall. After a moment, Kevin asked, "Operational to do what?"

Kevin watched Jon purse his lips as new life flowed through him. The old Jon was connected to himself, at peace with his science once more.

"I want to ask a question no one has thought to ask."

LEARN THEIR LANGUAGE

Kevin sat up, focused on Jon.

"Okay, fire away."

"Did you ever want to ask your body a question?"

This was Jon, he thought, smiling.

"No."

"No?" Jon sat up. "What? Why not?"

"Because I'd be too afraid of the answer."

They both laughed.

"No joke, Jon. I'm a thoughtful guy, but I don't think I ever considered that."

"I guess most people don't, but I think about this a lot. I mean about how the body communicates with itself."

"Certainly our bodies communicate with us," Kevin said, shrugging. "Hunger is one such message. Also, with fever and chills, it communicates illness. And nobody can say that they miss the message of a toothache."

"Right, Kevin. But I think the body communicates on a deeper level with itself."

"Without us knowing?"

"Exactly. On the quiet side." Jon leaned his head back on the wall.

"It makes sense. I guess the adage 'The right hand needs to know what the left hand is doing' comes to mind. Kevin looked at both of his. "Most times."

"Yes, but on a deeper level. For example, the brain senses that an increased metabolic rate is in order, and it commands the thyroid gland to increase production of thyroid hormone."

Kevin scratched his neck. "Nothing new. I guess I remember that from a high school or college course somewhere. When will the HVAC kick in?"

"Yep, but, Kevin, how did the brain know that more thyroid hormone was needed? Thermostat is just above you."

Kevin thought for a moment while getting up to adjust the temperature. "It must have gotten a signal."

"Right, but not a verbal signal, or a radio signal. A chemical one."

"The body communicated to the brain, and the brain responded," Kevin said sitting down.

"Just like there must be a signal to the brain that says 'Thanks, that's enough hormone. You can turn it down now.'"

Jon leaned forward. "Our cells contain life as individual cells, by themselves, but they live together. And living together means communication."

"And they communicate using hormones?"

"Most times no," Jon said, shaking his head. "I think they communicate using short strings of amino acids strung together— peptides and proteins."

Kevin inhaled.

"People are studying cell signaling. The cells communicate, uh *speak* to each other by sending out proteins, and they *hear* each other by absorbing the protein of other cells."

"I would say they are talking and listening to each other, every minute of every day."

"I bet you would," Kevin said, smiling. "And of course, a cell communicates with itself."

"That's kind of a corollary, isn't it?"

Jon stopped and turned to his CEO. "I aim to learn their language."

•

"Hey, wait a minute," Kevin said, sitting straighter against the wall. "How many cells are in the adult human body?"

"About 38 trill—"

"Okay. Thirty-eight trillion cells. Each is always *talking and listening* to use your metaphor. And cells don't sleep, right?"

Jon leaned against the wall. "That's the fact."

"So assume they speak ten times a second. So in an hour that's . . . 1.4 sextillion messages whipping around your body. Not only is that more messages than stars in the Milky Way, it's more than the number of stars in a . . . billion Milky Ways. And that's just in a single hour. Not considering electrical messages, right?"

"I'm not saying it's the easiest thing we've ever done, bu—"

"Well, you'll never do it."

He watched the scientist stiffen.

Kevin gestured. "Come here, sit down, and let's you and me talk like the friends we are."

Jon walked over and sat just in front of Kevin, crossing his knees.

●

"You'll never get there, Jon, not like this."

The scientist shook his head. "It's just a question of technology. We're going to hire—"

"Not what I mean. You'll never get there as long as the best of your emotions and intellectual energy are wrapped around Rayiko."

He felt his friend freeze up.

Kevin took a breath. He respected his imaginative colleague, who had made game-changing advances in building vaccines. Even admired him, but for the sake of his friend, he continued, "It takes too much out of you, Jon. Your drive, your imagination, your innovation, all of that is trying to fire you up. I see that. But you're always pouring energy into trying to figure out what happened with Rayiko. That's the water that keeps dousing the flame."

"Yeah."

"Look at me. Look . . . at . . . me." He was surprised to see tears flowing from the scientist's eyes.

"You are smart, Jon, but it is you that should command your mind, not the reverse. You don't have to be driven in the direction it chooses."

"What?"

"You are more than your mind, just like you're more than your biceps or your liver. They are part of you, but you're more than them.

"So you don't need to think what your mind wants you to think. You need it for sure, but right now, it's caught in a *Rayiko loop* that pulls your emotions. Step out from that.

"The only way to win this thought game is not to play it."

●

Jon got home well before sunset, having run himself into the ground setting the institute up. In bed by seven thirty, he practiced what his friend had told him. In ten minutes, he was asleep, and for the first time in a week, the scientist slept through the long and blessed night.

SEE YOU IN HELL

As Meredith stepped off the elevator on the fifteenth floor in midsummer 2017, the fear corkscrewed down her neck.

Yet here I am, she thought. *If you're strengthening my character, God, please take a break from building me up.*

Stop it.

She was three months post infections. Three months post two near-death experiences. A month after her latest hospitalization, the eight in ninety days, that is if you kept track of them as they went by.

And let's not forget the left hand, she remembered as she began her walk down the bright corridor, severed and reattached twelve weeks ago and still acting like it wanted to die.

I'm not dying, she thought*, so you'll not die, seaman. We're not quitters.*

No way, she thought, taking one step after the other down the wide corridor. She had kept every one of her sepsis and post-surgery appointments. When she couldn't take a company car for the twenty-mile trip to the medical center, she Ubered or taxied, and when that failed, she bussed it.

She never missed an antibiotic dose, even agreeing to treat herself with intravenous piperacillin every six hours without fail for two weeks, bending her left hand to her will as she managed fluid pouches, plastic tubing, and injections.

Almost there now.

She had gone to see physicians that she didn't know and whose language she didn't understand and had taken their advice.

Because if one thing mattered, it was that she was going to beat this thing. And if she could beat the disaster's effects, then she could damn well beat Jasper.

She stopped at apartment 1507P

The apartment door was ajar.

•

She reached for the door with her right hand, heart pounding. Her left hand was numb, really numb. The surgeon explained that re- plantations were over 85 percent successful, but the thick clumsiness of her reattached fingers hadn't even begun to go away.

"Hello?" she called out, recoiling from the urine stench.

"Get the hell out of here," Jasper said.

Her pulse jumped at the grating voice that scratched her nerves raw. "It's Meredith and I'm coming in."

She walked in, holding her breath.

Jasper lay on a sofa in his underwear, facing away from her and toward the window. His right leg, looking swollen and tight, was exposed up to the mid-thigh. It was pale with multiple red and purple blotches.

The left leg was gone from the hip down.

Pills lay spilled on and over his chest, falling down into the sofa crease on one side and the floor to the other.

He popped one.

"I'd ask you how you feel," she said, "but I think I know."

"You don't know anything," he said, lifting up and farting, "except how to remain as CEO."

She towered above him. "Did you have anything to do with the bombing?"

Jasper sat up.

He's lost so much weight. She shivered.

"What," he yelled, sitting up, spilling more pills. "How can you ask me that? I was motivated to demolish your career, not the whole damn floor. I wanted to rule SSS from up there."

He closed his red-rimmed eyes. "I was poised to strip you of the CEO title. The executive committee was with me. And," he said, lifting up to her, grinning, "I would have succeeded but for the blast."

He collapsed back into the couch, breathing heavily.

"Yes," she said, turning from him and walking to the chair four feet away. "But I think that you know who did it."

"Why would you say that?"

"A young man was seen coming in and out of your office just a few days before. Some say it was Stennis's son. Apparently the young man spent hours alone in there."

Jasper smiled. "Maybe he was studying for his law degree."

She sat on the upholstered chair and shrugged. "Maybe. Anyway, I told the police,"

"You did what?"

"And they tracked him to an eastern shore seditious group."

"Jesus."

"Jesus has nothing to do with this. It's only a matter of time for you."

"One way or another." He belched so loud she thought it echoed.

"How's your hand?" he asked.

She lifted it, allowing it to glisten in the pale late October afternoon sun. "A little better than useless. The skin color's coming back, but it's still weak, and I can't feel much. They tell me my feeling will return, but slowly."

"An inch a month."

"What?" She looked down at him.

"That's how slow the regenerating nerves grow. One inch each month."

"Then I need to be more patient."

Jasper grunted and then took another pill." Lucky you. I feel too much. One leg's gone, but both hurt."

"Not seeing a doctor?"

He glared at her. "I got my pills, Meredith, and if there's nothing else, you can leave my apartment."

Flushing, Meredith stood, putting all of her weight on her right hand as she balanced on the chair arm, heart pounding. She hated him yet ached for the wreck of his life.

"Jasper, when I started at Triple-S, you were the best corporate lawyer money could buy. Sure you were ambitious, but that's no flaw of people in this industry. When Cassie arrived, she was happy to work under you, to learn from you."

"I've always been just my own client," he said, shrugging, voice softer.

She looked away from his hideous attempt at a smile, shaking her head.

"I know that you detest me, but that could not have been the entire reason for this . . . abomination, this ruination of us."

She pointed to her weak left hand and then to the stump of his left leg. "Look at the pain you have caused me and you. Plus—"

"If I lost my leg because of you, then it was worth it."

"The other deaths and injuries. The loss of your friend Stennis. Nita is now blind. Why all of this senseless agony? What drove you to this?"

"Because I'd rather be in eternal hellfire than serve you," he said, thick spit flying from his mouth. "I hate your righteousness. Every good you do, I will labor with my last breath to destroy."

She walked over to him. "I don't think we'll see each other again."

"You're wrong," he said, belching. "See you in hell, bitch."

●

After she closed the door behind her, he popped another pill

Stennis's son screwed the pooch on this one. Hitting the twenty-ninth floor instead of CiliCold, it was such fucking betrayal. What did he expect though? It was Stennis's son. The fucking apple doesn't fall far from the fucking—what was that?

It was not a pain, more like something just lodged up in his chest somewhere.

And all at once, he felt like he wasn't breathing.

But he was.

He saw his chest expand and collapse with each of his breaths. *What the hell's going on?*

Seconds went by as he moved more and more air through his lungs. Air was getting in, but he felt air-starved.

His right leg howled in pain, but all he could think to do was breathe.

Yet moving more and more air in and out still felt like it wasn't enough, like he wasn't breathing at all.

Now his chest hurt.

He tried sitting up but collapsed in agony.

He moved his arms as if that could help with the breathing.

Lightheadedness, where did that come from? He couldn't breathe any faster.

No dice, Jasper, he thought, sweat pouring off him. *Your fat ass is dy—*

He rolled off the couch, breathing no more.

A-E-I-O-U

"What a waste this despicable man had become," Meredith said to herself, head pounding from the encounter with Jasper. Yet as she walked back out of the lobby and into the drizzle, she was consumed by confusion. What sign had she missed? Had his weakness been hiding in plain sight all along?

Meredith, don't be so Catholic.

Her limo driver pulled around into the brick circular driveway.

"Don't bother getting out, Rico," she called over the top of the car when she saw his head. "I'll manage."

"Back to headquarters, ma'am?" the tall driver with the handlebar mustache said when they were both in the car.

"Hopefully the drive won't take too long."

"No, ma'am," Rico said, turning back around to the steering wheel. "This rain will slow us up some, but we should be there in twenty."

She collapsed back in the plush leather seat, her left hand throbbing. She hoped that was a good sign but didn't trust her read of anything anymore.

•

Twenty-five minutes later, Meredith was out of the car and was picking her way around the construction crews outside. It was raining harder now, and the men and women were wiping the water from their eyes as they cleaned up the debris, awaiting the arrival of the next shipment of concrete and rebar, plaster, and steel. A burning sensation just below her sternum started, but she ignored the temptation to reach under her blue blouse to scratch skin that she knew wasn't really itching.

Four months later and the first floor was still a mess, she thought, getting off the elevator onto the second floor to pick up a turkey and ham sandwich. She waved back into place the well-wishers who moved aside to let her approach the cashier desk faster.

"Where do you think you're going?" she said to a thin young woman in dark slacks and a white skirt. "Don't you work here for a living too?" They laughed.

Minutes later, holding her cold sandwich tightly in her numb left hand, Meredith entered an elevator.

"How do you like floor ten, ma'am?" someone from the back of the elevator called out.

The elevator chuckle was contagious. Everyone knew that the reconstruction of the ruined twenty-ninth floor forced a move of senior administration to part of the tenth floor. Meredith insisted that her people take as little space as possible on the already occupied floor, doubling up in offices if necessary.

"A little cramped, but I have a good office mate," the CEO said smiling as she exited. She then turned left to follow a short man who almost tripped over himself carrying a chair.

She entered her office. There waiting was Nita.

●

"Nita, my heart soars." Meredith let the maintenance man leave and then placed her lunch on the table, turned, and walked to her CFO.

"It was so good to talk to you on the phone when I was hospitalized, but so much better to see you."

All of a sudden, Meredith wasn't sure what to expect,

Nita, in new sunglasses, extended her arms. "Hi, boss."

They hugged for a few seconds, and Nita began to cry. The CEO held her. "It's not okay, but know this. If you let it, it will get better."

"You mean my eyes."

"No, I mean you. And who is this?" Meredith asked, stepping back, smiling but careful not to play with the well-harnessed guardian dog.

"That is Sinsa," Nita said. "The best guardian around."

"So you went with the German shepherd?"

"I owned two shepherds years ago," she said, raising a hand to adjust her glasses. "So it seemed like a natural choice."

"She's gorgeous," Meredith leaned on one knee, then suddenly fell down on her side.

"It took a while for us to get to know each other, but it's working now. We both had a little trouble, negotiating our way into the building just because it was new to us. I need to tell you about Monica's firing—Meredith, are you okay?"

Meredith was on the floor flat on her back. *Breathing okay,* she thought. No chest pressure, no jaw angle pain, and her left arm felt fine. Still, she remembered that heart attacks could be different in women than in men.

Her stomach knotted. "I wish I could throw up, Nita," she said.

Nita felt for and touched her friend's forehead.

"You're burning up."

The CEO vomited on the office floor, but she saw it was just liquid, nothing solid. Nothing stunk. It was clear.

"Nine one one, we have an emergency on the tenth floor of the SSS building," Nita said into her phone.

She then called building security. Meredith was now laying on her right side, bending then straightening, kicking her legs

"My chest, my stomach. Jesus Lord, what's going on with me?"

●

"Pressure's 190 over 115," the first guard said, removing the blood pressure cuff from the CEO's arm. "Goodness."

"Jesus," the second guard said. "A-E-I-O-U"

"What's that?"

"Acidosis, epilepsy, infection, opiates, uremia. The main causes of loss of consciousness."

"She's not diabetic and to my knowledge does not have epilepsy," Nita said.

"Drug use?"

"She's the CEO," Nita shouted, regretting it at once, as Sinsa jumped.

"So what?" the security guard said, shrugging. "Anybody can use."

Nita felt a soft hand on her knee. "Look, I'm not trying to fight with you," the guard said. "It's just that the more we can learn, the more we can help the EMTs—"

"Who have just arrived," the first guard called out.

"Did anybody see what happened?"

Nita explained what she heard and felt.

"Please give her some pain medicine," Nita said.

"When she wakes up, she's going to need it," the burly security guard added.

He placed a hand on her forehead.

"Yipes. She's on fire."

"Is she going to die?" Nita asked, heart pounding.

"I don't think so," one of the EMTs said, helping to place the prostrate CEO on the gurney, "but she may feel like it until we get her to the hospital."

MAKE FRIENDS

Start with what you do know, Meredith thought.

She didn't know how she felt. Things were so disconnected.

She picked her head up, saw nothing.

Maybe open my eyes?

Light flooded in.

She snapped them closed and then opened them as slowly as she thought that she could.

Okay, light is coming in, so I can see. Looks like a hospital bed. I hear sounds but don't recognize them.

Maybe I can try some movement, she thought.

Left hand is not doing anything.

That figures.

Right hand back and forth. Okay.

Feet move back and forth as well.

I can move my head and neck as well. That feels good.

She strained some.

Don't have to use the restroom. Good.

She strained again, trying to listen to her body.

Not hungry. Okay, I guess.

She waited for a moment, no pain at all, actually.

Okay with that. She sighed.

She turned her head to the left.

Cabinet, hand mirror.

She rolled over with a grunt and a lot of work, using her hand to reach for and then grab the mirror. Then not bothering to sit up, she looked into the mirror.

There was a stranger with blotchy skin and swelling.

Her eyes now seemed so small, almost sucked into her face by the thick encroachment of the puffy tissue, hideous.

She gasped.

Her heart tried to pound but gave up after a few seconds.

'I can't stand it." She let her arm with the mirror collapse onto the bed.

"That's called periorbital edema," a female voice said.

"I don't care what you call it, dear. Just don't call it mine."

She heard the doctor laugh. "Well, hopefully it won't be yours for long. We have the kidney problems under control, at least for the time being. You haven't been able to talk until now. Would you like to?"

Meredith opened her mouth, then closed it. "I think that I'd . . . I'd just like to listen."

"Can I sit you up in bed?"

"Sure . . . I think."

The doctor walked over and then grabbed Meredith under her armpits, lifting her to a sitting position.

"Why don't I feel like myself?"

"Well, ordinarily I would say that we'll get to that, but I'm told that you like plain answers to plain questions, so here it is."

Meredith, taking deep breaths, looked at her.

"Sepsis," the doctor said.

Meredith tried to shake her head, but couldn't move it much. *Strange.* "What's that?"

"Fatal for many people and," she continued, looking down for a moment, "very costly for survivors."

●

"I am Dr. Vazquez." She moved her jet-black hair out of her face. "I've been your hospitalist for some time now."

"My what?"

"Think of me like your main doctor in this place. I call on many other doctors to take care of you. Months ago, when I first met you, I brought in intensive care experts. Then, I contacted a surgeon for your hand," she said, pointing to Meredith's left hand.

"I remember."

"How's that going?"

"Can I give it back?"

She saw the doctor look at it.

"No, you get to keep it. Do you know that you have been in the hospital under my care for two months? Following your first series of hospitalizations after the bombing."

"So it's October 2018."

"Two thousand seventeen."

Meredith was puzzled. Of course it was 2018. The Sovereign building explosion was in 2017 so that would make it sixteen months ago.

Right? Wait a minute.

"What is today's date?"

"October 13, 2017."

Meredith sighed. "I didn't think so."

"Sepsis is an internal infection where organs typically not exposed to bacteria, are, well, laid open to these organisms and their toxins."

"How did I get it?"

"We can't be sure, but you had a piece of metal enter your abdomen during the blast. At first, we thought it did not penetrate into your bowel, but it did. From there, the Clostridia—"

"The who?"

"*Clostridia septicum* is the name of the bacterium that caused you all of this trouble."

"Sounds like a disease caught by the queen's mace," Meredith said, trying to smile.

"Very good. We initiated antibiotics, but the bacteria had a head start on us. It affected both the small and large bowel and also the liver. It then spread to your kidneys, lungs, heart, and brain. Left untreated, it can generate gas gangrene."

Meredith hung her head. Then she straightened up. "Yet, Dr. Vasquez, here I am."

"Yes. Your kidneys shut down and we had to place you on dialysis. We gave you medications to keep your heart pumping effectively. Ultimately we controlled the clostridia, but its toxin had far-reaching effects."

"Like what?"

"What is 22 + 12?"

"Why that's . . ." She could add the 2+2 from the ones column. Nothing to carry. Then the tens column was 2 + 1.

But what was in the *ones* column again?

She shook her head. Started again, 2 + 2 and then 2 + 1.

Over and over.

"I can't put it together."

"An effect of the toxin on your brain cells. Your brain can still control the ordinary things that you need it to, breathing, heart, muscle movement, hormone control, but the tentorial functions—memory and cognition—have to be rewired. How are your dreams?"

"Pretty strange. I don't recognize them, like they belong to someone else."

"For a while, you'll not recognize much. Bowel function will be different. You'll have some weird thoughts."

"Like killing my doctor?"

Dr. Vasquez smiled. "Well, not that weird."

"Sorry, my sense of humor's not sensing much humor."

"Try not to overreact. This is your body trying to recover. Let it move at its own pace. Make friends with it."

Meredith sat still for a few moments.

"When can I go home?"

She watched the doctor look down at the chart, hair falling over her face.

"Well, your cultures have been negative for two weeks now. Plus the white cell count's down." She flipped electronic pages with her index finger. "Kidney and heart functions are good. Electrolytes are fine. No more blood pressure excursions."

She looked up. "Are you willing to have homecare? Nurses visiting you. Helping with grooming, medications, fixing food."

"I'm hardly in a position to say no."

"Well, it will take me some time to get your discharge papers in order. How about tomorrow?"

WATER BALLOON

"No . . . no . . . God . . . no."

Meredith had just arrived home. And Francine, after seeing that her new charge could navigate her own one-story home, had gone out to buy some groceries.

Meredith went into the bathroom to prepare for a shower. But after removing her clothes, the sixty-three-year-old CEO was wasted and zapped.

Turning to go back to the bed to sit for a few minutes, she couldn't resist first looking into the full-length mirror.

Staring back at her was a swollen, unkempt, and ugly woman. From the neck down, she was a bloated milky-white water balloon with nipples.

There was nothing to delineate the chest from the abdomen. There was no muscle mass anywhere to be seen. Her breasts had been absorbed back into her chest wall, It was Elmer's Glue skin, and hideous.

Meredith leaned forward on the sink shunning the image facing her. After a few moments, she sighed and staggered back to the bedroom, falling facedown on the bed.

For just a second, she saw the image of her mother.

Yes, sitting in the wooden chair across from the bed, reaching her arms out to her daughter.

The CEO broke down, the loss of everything breaking through on her.

Ruined, she thought, openly and freely weeping. She mourned it all, her colleagues and adversaries at Triple-S, the momentum to change the company, Nita's blindness, and the firing of Monica.

And well, just look at me, she thought. Left with a distorted and bloated body and half a mind, *I can't even do arithmetic, for God's sake. Memory in tatters, all I have is a nurse who could do little but feed me, groom me, and put me to bed. I should have stayed in the hospital. I should have died.*

"Why, God," she called, "do you demolish me when I'm doing all I can to bring Your life and Your principles and Your ideas, Your concept, and Your charity into my company? Am I not Your agent in that plan? What else do I have to do to serve You now? Is my life and energy so deficient that You would do this to me?

"This may be some crazy cosmic game to You," she cried out, "but it is all that You have given me and all that I can do."

Exhausted, she fell asleep, waking just when she heard the nurse walk into the room.

And she had a simple choice, living or dying.

Here it was, all on her.

"Who are you, Meredith?" she asked herself.

She sat up.

"Someone who is living,"

She inhaled like it was her first breath. All things must pass.

Something would kill me to death.

But it would not be this sepsis, this damn septicum thing.

And if she was to be judged, it would not be based on this disgusting disease with its ugly effects.

After all, He had left His son to hang on a cross for nine hours. *Who am I to complain?*

She yearned to see life on the other side of this illness. And she'd fight for that chance.

"Francine," she called, "let's get this showering done and get some food in me."

PLAYLISTS

"**D**idn't they used to call the airport Weir Cooke?"

Dr. Jubal Laws, the new PhD in mathematical statistics, walked down the aisle of the packed Southwest Airlines plane heading to Indianapolis International Airport and turned in the direction of the unfamiliar voice.

"Uh, yes. For an Indiana World War 1 aviator I think."

"Yes. Of course. You know, I liked the original name better. Why don't you take the window seat, and I'll take the middle?"

"Good enough for me." The twenty-nine-year-old mathematician scooched, stumbled, and then fell into the window seat.

"I guess that you're going to Bloomington?"

"That's right." Jubal blushed. "How did you know?"

"You look like an academic. It was either West Lafayette or Bloomington, and you didn't look like the Purdue type."

"What do I look like?" *Who is this guy?* Jubal wondered, not that he minded the chit-chat. The DCA-IND flight always seemed longer than it actually was, and he was anxious for release from his thought-plagued mind.

Jubal watched the stranger study him. Then the man said, "Like someone who doesn't run to class. Like someone who's in mathematics for the love of it, and can't stay away from the leaves in the fall."

Jubal nodded. "Indiana is gorgeous this time of year. But in December, watch out. Looks like World War 3 was fought there."

The two laughed.

"Time to buckle up, gentlemen," the attendant said.

"We're on it."

Jubal noticed the attendant study the stranger for a moment. "Do I know you, sir?" she said, leaning closer.

"I would remember if I knew you. Those blue eyes are unforgettable."

"Get outta town," she said, laughing and turning to walk away.

Jubal watched the stranger turn to him.

"So how's academic life panning out for you?"

"Not so well." Jubal cleared his throat.

The stranger ran his hand through his curled hair. "What was your PhD in?"

"I focused on measure theory for my dissertation. Uh, do you know what that is?" *Come to think of it, this guy does look familiar.*

"Why don't you tell me."

"Well, do you remember all of that set stuff you learned in grade school?"

"Sure," the stranger said, shrugging. "Intersections, unions, complements, my parents hated it."

"Well, I trained in measuring the value of those sets."

"Value? What kind of value?"

"Well," Jubal said, squinting as he pushed a thick shock of black hair out of his eyes. "Let's say you have a collection of music tracks. A wide range of artists, genre, years, and what not. Let's call that collection the universe of your songs.

"Now let's say you want to hear all songs from the 1970s."

"Which I do, sometimes. Okay."

"Then we call that smaller group of tracks a subset. Each track in the subset is part of the original track set."

The stranger squinted. "Then, there are all kinds of subsets, right?"

"Sure," Jubal said, "for example, All tracks by Peter Buffett, or all tracks that contain jazz as their genre, or all tracks that are shorter than four minutes long."

"Playlists?"

"Right. Playlists are an example of the implementation of set theory."

"You should work for Apple."

He saw the stranger smile at him. For reasons Jubal didn't understand, he was feeling better.

"And you measure these, these playlists?"

"Sure. One way to measure might be simply the sum of the playing time in the tracklist. Another would be there must be at least one song by Roberta Flack."

"Why would you choose these as measures?"

"There are many different measures you can choose. But not every metric that you can think of is a measure. There are certain rules that they have to follow. The trick is to choose one that is really of value. One that teaches you something about the univ—"

Jubal stopped at the commotion in the aisle.

"Why are the pilot and all of the attendants coming back here?" he asked.

"No idea," the stranger said, shrugging.

The captain stopped her purposeful walk at their aisle.

Jubal stared, not breathing.

REMEMBER THIS DAY

"Dr. DeLeon," the officer said. "I am Capt. Elisa Seris. Thank you for your vaccine work. It saved the lives of so many, including my mother."

She extended her hand.

Dr. DeLeon? Jubal thought.

The stranger stood up, reached to hold her hand, and gently pulled her forward. She leaned over and they embraced.

When they released, he said to her, "Any woman who gave birth to someone as special as you deserves my best."

Jubal saw the man turn his head to him. "Wouldn't you agree, Dr. Laws?"

What! Dr. DeLeon knows me? What's going on here?

"Uh, yes yes, Dr. DeLeon," Jubal said, looking at the passenger next to him.

Keeping his eyes on the pilot's, Jon asked, "What's today's date?"

"November 5,"

"Well, I will remember this day. You honor me by sharing as you have."

"The honor is mine, Doctor." She turned and with a hand over her mouth, hurried back up the long aisle to the cockpit as people in the surrounding rows clapped.

Jubal watched Dr. DeLeon take a deep breath, then turn to him with a smile. "I have a job for you. Do you want to talk, or just stare?

"Are you kidding? I want to stare."

ROI

"How do you know me?' Jubal asked.

"Well, I read your dissertation, and thought you might be interested in my project."

"You've been following me?"

He watched Jon shrug. "I arranged to be on this flight. It would give us a couple of hours to talk some things through."

"But the world's been following you. You are uber-famous. Giving us all something of value for free was so . . . so genuine. Plus, it had power. It's an act that everyone appreciates. It moves through all cultures. We all get it and love you for it. How do you manage all of that attention?

"By the way, since you've been stalking me, I've earned the right to call you Jon."

He watched Jon sit back in his seat. "In the 1920s, Albert Einstein was caught up in a frenzy of fame after his general relativity theory had been proven. He was invited to the home of Charlie Chan, a world-famous actor. At some point in the evening, Einstein asked his host what did all the adulation mean.

"Chan replied, 'It means absolutely nothing.'"

Jubal was silent.

"I try to remember that when there are too many episodes like the one that you just witnessed," Jon said. "I enjoy my team. Sometimes I enjoy people. But I really enjoy my solitude."

Jubal sighed.

"I don't socialize very well, Jon. People really weren't sure what to do with me and my ideas in graduate school."

"What was your idea?" Jon asked, eyes closed.

"That simple functions would be of value in people's lives, and not just exist in the cloistered recesses of pure math folks."

"Do you have an example?"

"Sure. Consider a winding river. There is a concern that the banks of the river and beyond are toxic. Now, there are instruments so refined that they can estimate the presence of many toxins in a cubic millimeter of soil. So you run this assay on each cubic millimeter, and from that you get a string of zeros and ones, reflecting the presence or absence of each toxin in each millimeter. I call that a spectrum."

"So you can look at the spectrum and know the presence or absence of each toxin in that cubic millimeter."

Jubal leaned forward, talking faster. "Now to help keep our sets mutually exclusive, we need to construct *donut sets*."

"What did you say?"

"Uh, donut sets."

"We keep talking like this, my favorite pilot will throw us off the plane."

Jubal took a deep breath. "Got it. But my point is that, uh, these ideas were not accepted, I guess. Thing is though," Jubal said, heart pounding as he scratched his head, "I wasn't bothered by the ostracism. I really did want to be alone. But maybe that's not such a good idea for me right now, I just don't know."

"Well, I think our team will help you with that, Jubal. In the meantime, welcome."

Welcome to what? "How did you choose me?"

"It was easy. You were the best measure theoretic probabilist among the graduate students in your cohort. Fortunately, you graduated just when we needed you."

"Well, I don't mind telling you that I was floundering some."

"Of course you were. Many people with your ability go into either theoretical mathematics, which can be fun if you have the head for it but doesn't pay well. You're learning that now."

"Right."

"Or they go into investment banking, which pays a lot of money but doesn't give heart ROI."

"Uh, what do you—"

"Return on investment. Doesn't make you feel good from the inside out."

"Right. No soul satisfaction."

He saw Jon smile.

"That's it, Jubal. I thought you were interested in that part of things from your take on what simple function analysis could do for communities."

"So," Jubal asked, heart suddenly pounding, "what do you have in mind for me?"

"I want your functions to teach us a language."

"I don't know if . . . what is it?"

"It has no name, and it's very old."

"How old is that?"

"Over three billion years."

THROWN FROM THE SADDLE

Jubal's mouth flew open.

"Did you say three billion years?"

"I am assembling a group of scientists who want to learn how the body communicates with itself."

Jubal scratched his was through his hair. "Isn't that at best just signal processing? I mean rather than audio, its chemical, or electrical, or something, right?"

"But it's language nevertheless."

Jubal's pulse pounded as Jon explained his ideas about the notion of cells communicating using short peptides as language.

"I think I followed that, Jon. Each of these proteins produced by a cell is a letter, right?"

Jon shook his head. "Close, I believe each of these proteins is the message. That message could be from a neighboring cell that says 'increase acid production' or 'I am dying'."

"It's a fascinating idea. I mean the richness of it would be overwhelming. Really exciting. What's my role in this?"

"We have to translate."

"Who on your team does that?"

"You do, Jubal," Jon said with a smile

"Oh. Well," Jubal thought for a moment. "How long is the message?"

"You have a sequence of, say thirty amino acids. You have to figure out what message they are conveying to the cell that absorbs them. That means translate the amino acid sequence into, well, English so we can understand."

"But the translation's going to be simple, right? I mean, it's not like we're translating Shakespeare over here."

Jon laughed.

"Well, we have to build the language up from the information in the amino acids. I'm thinking something like your simple functions would be useful.

"Who would have thought that Henri Lebesgue, in a 1919 dissertation that he finished, then walked away from, would lay the seeds for this kind of work." Jon shook his head.

"Of course," Jubal said, "we're going to need to develop a message in response, right? I mean, to the message conveyed by the original protein. That's going to involve some protein construction. Who'll do that?"

"Robots."

"What?" Jubal felt like he'd been thrown from the saddle yet one more time on this flight.

"First, though, we need to get you to Arizona. How soon can you get the–"

"Give me a week."

'Good, we'll have to go somewhere special."

"Where?"

"High school."

Jubal laughed, shaking his head. "I didn't do so well then."

"This is your second chance."

SWIMMING IN THE SAME LAKE

It was 9:30 AM Monday, a week later when Jon walked with Emily and Jubal to his car and spied Luiz walking in.

"Luiz, where do you think you're going?" Jon called.

"Well, Emily and I have some work to do setting up our new equipment. I'm just bringing some calibration units in."

"Well, put them down and come with us."

"Where we going?" Luiz said joining the three of them.

"School."

●

"It was quite a surprised when Dr. DeLeon agreed to speak to our high school," Principal Sidwell said, bending over to speak into the mike. "His background in vaccine production is a legend. While he won't tell you, I will say that for several months last spring, he was the most famous person in the world, not just for his revolutionary approach to antibody construction but his open-hearted attitude to simply give the technology away.

"While he communicates with scientists worldwide to improve the process that he discovered, the impact of generosity has resonated around our planet. Some inexplicably call his team 'socialist' because they give their work away. I call them 'heroes' and 'heroines' because of their charitable spirit."

"I give you Dr. DeLeon."

The applause was thunderous. Jon had been told to expect a large audience because parents would want to show up as well to see him. But he didn't expect the hundreds of people jammed into the auditorium.

"Before I start," Jon said to the audience of Grand Castle High School. "I want to introduce three of my colleagues on whom I rely totally and completely.

"None of us is a billionaires. I don't think the world is waiting for the next billionaire. The world is waiting for the person who can cure malaria. Or rid us of viral pandemics. Or help patients with relapsing polio. Those are the individuals the world is waiting for.

"One of them is Luiz Sandoval. He is an expert molecular and cell biologist. That means that he knows the chemistry that makes cells work. Much of what I tell you today I learned from him. Luiz," he said, pointing to his friend behind him, "please stand."

The entire audience stood and clapped. Jon saw that Luiz, embarrassed, stiffly bowed and sat back down.

"Emily Nuson is our expert computationalist. She uses computers to understand how molecules combine in ways that allow us to live. And our newest member, Jubal Laws, just got his PhD. He's an expert in advanced mathematics."

When the clapping subsided, he continued.

"I need this team and others to pursue a radical notion. You have to be patient with me. We are going to end up today talking about something magnificent. But first, before we get there, we have to talk about the small.

"Let's also agree, that for the next hour, there are no stupid questions. You can ask anything you want about what we're talking about. Don't be embarrassed. Don't be humiliated. The best way to learn hard things is to first learn simple things. And you can't learn simple things unless you ask simple questions.

"So can somebody tell me what a cell is?"

"Yes," a student in the front row said, hand raised. "A cell is the smallest living part of the human body."

"That's not bad." He held his arms out. "Anybody have an idea how many cells that I have. I'll start the bidding at a hundred."

"Tens of thousands," someone said.

"Millions and millions," said another.

Jon raised his hands. "Does anybody know how big a trillion is?"

"More than a billion?" someone asked.

Yes, it's a thousand billion. A huge number. The sun is 93 million miles away from the Earth. Thirty-eight trillion miles is about 409,000 times as far.

"So I have thirty-eight trillion cells. Now how many miles of blood vessels do I have? I'll just tell you. Sixty thousand miles. That sounds like more than we need, doesn't it?

"But in fact, no matter how small these blood vessels get, from large arteries to smaller arteries called arterioles to the smallest vessels called capillaries, there will not be enough vessels to give each of our thirty-eight trillion cells its own blood vessel.

"So how does this work? Well, nature was very ingenious. What she did was not supply a blood vessel per cell. Instead, she surrounds our cells with fluid that leak from blood vessels. Like rivers that flow through communities, the capillaries go around and by cells like streams. All of our cells swim in the same lake.

"That way cells get what they need from the leaked blood vessel. Now what are some of those nutrients?"

"Sugar," someone said.

"Great. Next? Anybody else?"

"Oxygen."

"Also necessary."

"Salts?"

"Proteins."

"Yes, both small and large. So these capillaries which are themselves only one cell thick, leak these substances into this lake, which them make their way to the cells. And waste products that come out of the cell go back into this fluid, which is absorbed into the capillary.

"It's not unlike having the trash man come to your house to pick up the garbage. They don't come in your house to get the garbage, right? Garbage goes out in the street where it gets picked up. Some of you put it out there, right?"

"For money," a student shouted.

The room erupted with laughter.

"And nutrients. Just as some of you have food delivered to your homes, the capillaries are delivering nutrient-rich fluid to the cells.

"This fluid that surrounds the cells is called, listen carefully, 'Interstitial fluid'."

"Can you all say that?"

"Interstitial fluid," the audience said.

"Right. We will call it 'ICF', because it's so easy to say 'ICF'. So this ICF is busy moving nutrients like oxygen and sugar and proteins into the cell and is busy moving waste products that the cell releases back into the fluid, and the fluid takes waste back to the blood vessel.

"Now, it's easy to think of a cell like you see it in a book. Flat. And you might think of this intercellular fluid washing up on the cell like water washes up on to a beach house, but it's far prettier and more elegant than that.

"Look at your bodies. There you go. Three-dimensional bodies, right? Height, width, thickness. Now think of the atmosphere that surrounds you. The atmosphere doesn't just touch your head or touch your arms, or touch your back. It completely surrounds you. Envelopes you. That's what the intercellular fluid is like to a cell. It completely surrounds it. The cell bathes in it.

"Why doesn't it get in? Because the cell has a membrane. Now, the membrane is not a wall, Think of the membrane as a thick froth on a beer. It's sudsy, always shifting, moving, and changing.

"Now, that froth is very particular about what it lets into the cell. It lets in nutrients. It lets in protein and sugar. But it also moves waste products out. When a virus attacks a cell, it works its way through that frothy membrane into the cell contents.

Jon paused and took a deep breath. "Okay. So much for the buildup."

You have thirty-eight trillion cells. Have you ever heard of a cell fighting a cell?

Silence.

"The one real example that might occur is in cancer when cancerous cells get so strange and so deranged that they begin to fight other cells. But cells by themselves, healthy cells, are friendly and, more than that, they communicate with each other.

"How? Now one thing they don't use is 'cell' phones, right?"

Somebody laughed.

"Ok, I'm no comedian. Cells communicate chemically. They send proteins from one cell to another cell. Now this should not be new to you.

"There are cells that make insulin. Anybody know where that's made?"

"Pancreas,"

"Right you are. And then insulin goes to all the other cells by first getting in the blood stream until it gets to a capillary, leaks out, then rides in the ICF to a cell to help that cell convert sugar to energy."

"But it's more exhilarating than that. We think the communication is far more intricate. Cells need to understand what other cells are doing around them,

"Suppose we could absorb five hundred messages a second, every second of every day of our lives. Phone calls, texts, email, notes, books, blogs, streaming, radio, social media, semaphore, what have you. And we could understand, and respond to each. And still eat, make energy, grow and defend ourselves. Think of how richer, more intricate our lives would be?

"This is what I believe cells do. They communicate with each other using small proteins, every second of every minute of every hour of every day. And what do they use as their conduit? Their river."

"The ICF?"

Jon pointed to the girl in glasses. "Bingo. One way, I like to think about this though, is not as coordination, but as language. A very special language. It's not a language of words. It is a language of chemistry. But it serves the same purposes words do. Communication. And it's a very old language. About three and a half billion years in the making. And my friends here and I are devoting ourselves to trying to learn this language."

The roar was deafening. Jon invited the team up with him.

"Oh no," Jubal moaned.

"You don't expect only me to sign autographs, do you?" Jon said, smiling.

OPEN CARRY

"Hey, Emily, you got a sec?" Jon said, several weeks later. He stooped over and then sat on the office floor to pet Sparky.

"He's always been delighted to see me."

"He's delighted to see everybody here. So am I. What's up?"

Jon put the dog down which started walking to Emily. She picked him up.

She was as she was when he hired her last year, short cropped blonde hair, svelte in boots and jeans, and wearing a long-sleeved T-shirt. But he noticed something different around her waist.

"Em, I didn't know you'd gone 'open carry'?"

"About a month ago. Kind of keeps the crazies away from me."

"Keeps some sane people away too, I expect."

"Only if I go *snake eyes.*"

They laughed, and Jon stood, leaning back against the table holding the two servers. "I just wanted to let you know what my plans were, Em."

"Okay." She grabbed the diet coke on the table and sat down. "Shoot," she said with a smile.

"Can't do that without a gun." *She's so much more confident,* he thought. Eight months ago, she would have already asked if she was going to be fired. His heart swelled with the trust that she had in him.

"I don't think we'll need so much of your computing power as much as we'll need your . . . your intellectual imagination"

"What a thing to say to a girl."

"I aim to figure out what cells say."

"I know."

He watched her study the floor. "Anybody else looking at this problem?" she asked.

"You know I never let myself be concerned about what other people do in their research," he said.

"Well, that's certainly the truth. We caught the world napping on our vaccine work this year."

"Your work, Emily. Yours and Luiz's. Anyway, we're going to bring in an expert in nanotechnology."

He paused and then drew in a deep breath. "I'm thinking about bringing a linguistics person in, but I don't think I have to because I believe you're it."

She looked at him. "Seriously? I just speak English, and I really don't do that well."

He shook his head. "Doesn't matter, Em. You have the capability to be open to what words that you don't understand and yet you learn to use them. That's really the secret behind coding, isn't it?"

"Hadn't thought of that."

"Anyway. We need you."

"Bad guys around?"

"Of course."

"We going to do the same thing with the product as before?"

Hands in his pockets, he shrugged.

She looked at Jon. "The fact is that after our vaccine work, a lot of companies and groups wanted a piece of me, but they are strangers. I really got nowhere to go."

"Well here we are late 2017, and we need you more than ever."

"I'm here."

"I always knew you were my open-carry kinda girl."

"I'm nobody's girl, but I'll do everything for you."

The two scientists hugged.

"Get outta here before I shoot you," she said with a laugh.

TAKE THEM DOWN

Olivia jumped out of the Uber, hurrying into the Holiday Inn, Chevy Chase, Maryland.

Freezing, she thought. On this frigid DC, late December day, she longed for Arizona's afternoon warmth and Kevin.

It had been six weeks since she had seen him, a glorious and solitary Queen Creek Thanksgiving.

It was all too short, and as she walked over to the large check-in desk, her heart ached to be home.

She got directions for the conference room suites and walked forward and out of the lobby. She passed the small dining area and took a left turn right into Audrey.

The two new friends laughed and then hugged.

"I'm so sorry," Olivia said. "I must be more nervous than I thought." The two walked forward together, Olivia following Audrey's lead and letting her friend pull her arm gently through the ex-lobbyist's.

"Well, you should be," Audrey said, stopping, turning, and fixing her friend's collar. "You have quite a selling job in there."

"I'm so glad Kevin introduced us four months ago to show me the ropes of this bill-passing business."

"I'm just a lobbyist who fell out of love with her job," the older woman said, laughing as she brushed her own red and white curls away from her face. "I've enjoyed our time together. But first, we have to write the thing before we pass it."

"I'm lucky you never represented Triple-S"

"They could never afford me."

Olivia stopped at a closed door

"Are our authors inside?"

"Young and waiting," Audrey said, pointing to the hotel conference room with the doors closed. "They're energetic with good ideas."

"But not getting paid," Olivia said, placing her hand on Audrey's sleeve. "How many of them are there?"

"Four, and we need to talk about their compensation," Audrey said. "I have some funds but they're restricted. Plus, when my firm's accountant *forensics* me, I'll have some *splainin'* to do."

"You've been so much help so far," Olivia said, placing her hand on Audrey's left arm. "I'll pay them from my stash."

"Oh?"

"Well, they may be motivated, but they're young and likely poor. I want to pay them for their trouble. When do I get to meet with them?"

"Right now," Audrey said, pushing the conference doors open.

•

Olivia, holding her breath, walked into the small conference room, populated by a table with six chairs, four of them occupied.

Each was young, and the three women and one man were each well groomed, dressed in casual business attire, and hungry.

How eager will they be when I'm done with them, she wondered. Hot sweat rolled down her back.

The ex-regulator sat at one end of the table, Audrey at the other.

"Hello, everyone," Olivia began, her Georgia accent a river of honey. "I have a project that I will need some help in the short term from you."

"And what's that?"

"What's your name?"

"Julie," the young woman in a dark blue business dress said. "What's yours?"

"Well, Julie," the ex-regulator said, swallowing. "I'm Olivia Steadman and I want to take Big Pharma down."

AHEAD OF YOU

Expecting anger, even hot hostility, Olivia braced herself. What she heard was laughter.

"Fat chance."

"A fool's errand."

"Good luck, Don Quixote."

"It would be easier to go after the Pentagon."

"You have no idea what you're up against."

"I think I do," Olivia said, taking a step toward them.

"Listen," the young man in the room said, bulging out of his gray jacket. "Big Pharma is a multibillion-dollar industry."

"Over a trillion dollars worldwide actually," Olivia said with a smile. "Who are you, by the way?"

"Angelo," he said, pushing his black hair back off of his forehead, "and thanks for making my argument for me."

She watched him lean forward over the table. "Listen, almost half of Americans used a Big Pharma product in the last thirty days."

"That doesn't mean that they like the industry," a young woman with long black hair said.

"No, Sharra," Angelo said looking across the table. "It does mean that Americans are not afraid of it. They're comfortable using the industry's output. You cut them off from those products. You arouse the ire of much of, if not most of America."

"Even the idiot politicians who get nailed for talking about killing Medicare will laugh at you for going after Big Pharma," the lady in white said, shaking her head.

"And you are?" Olivia asked.

"Rashida." She smiled.

"Thanks, Rashida. Plus," Angelo continued, "drug companies are the vanguards of new medications. Turn your TV on tonight, Olivia. What do you see? New medications for bipolar disorder, depression, thyroid, eye disease, or tardive dyskinesia, whatever that is. Advanced stages of lung cancer, breast cancer, colon cancer, they even advertise on Amazon for goodness sake."

"Angelo's right," Julie added, tapping the yellow pad in front of her with her fingers. "Plus, new medications for cholesterol reduction and diabetes."

"What about the prices they charge?" Olivia said, sitting down now.

"Well, the medications don't come from nowhere," Rashida said, adjusting the sleeve of her turquoise blouse. "Someone had to develop the molecule, right? Then do all of the testings? Why should they not get paid for it?"

"Well, maybe because they got them for free," Julie rested her hands on the table. "A third of the molecules that they discover," she said, miming quotes in the air, "are in fact, not discovered by them at all. They were discovered by researchers at the National Institute of Health, taxpayer funded. The pharmaceutical companies leech from them and develop these molecules and act like they're their own."

"And also," Rashida added, "don't forget the tax breaks they get from the federal government. Paid? They are already paid. Any other money that they make is sauce for the goose."

Olivia watched her turn toward her.

"If you had cancer Ms.—"

"Just call me Olivia."

"What would you pay for the medicine that had been shown could and would cure you?"

"More than its worth," Olivia said, "and they know that. It would be a lot less if they used the lobbying money to offset my cost. Audrey, how much is that?"

"Over a quarter of a billion dollars."

"Jeez."

"Didn't know."

"That's a ton," Alonzo said, shaking his head. "But people rely on these companies."

"Because they're told to," Julie said, looking straight at him. "We're told every day of the good they do for us all. New medications, new treatments. Therapies that we can take and then look forward with a spirit of bold curiosity to the future. And we're supposed to believe that?"

"Well, there's oversight, right?"

"Paid for by Big Pharma," Sharra added.

"Way wrong answer," Rashida said with a wave of her hand.

"No, it's not. The pharmaceutical company pays for much of their own oversight."

"Sharra is right," Audrey said. "Estimates are almost a billion."

"What?" Rashida said.

"How do you know that?"

"Don't underestimate we ex-lobbyists."

Everyone laughed.

"Paid to the FDA by Big Pharma to oversee Big Pharma."

"That's a ton," Angelo said, "but isn't that how the FDA modernizes its equipment and keeps its personnel?"

"Who jump ship to Big Pharma for more money as soon as they can," Rashida added.

"Okay," Alonzo said, hands up. "I don't know where this convoluted system came from, and I concede that it needs attention but not a death sentence."

"There's an understatement," Sharra said, smiling, "but I'll take any *Angelo concession* when they come."

Olivia watched the two smile at each other.

"People rarely talk about the profitability of the companies," Julie said.

"They talk about it all the time on the web," Alonzo said, shaking his head.

"Anybody know what the net price increase in drug costs has been recently?"

"Just from $149 to $353 in Medicare Part D and from $147 to $218 in Medicaid," Audrey said. "That's over about ten years."

Rashida shrugged. "Doesn't sound like much."

"Multiply that by the millions of people who are enrolled in these programs."

"But keep in mind that 90 percent of those prescriptions were comprised of generic drugs, available at substantially lower costs. Sounds like at least that part of the system is working," Alonso said, leaning back, arms wrapped behind his head. "Drugs are expensive, so people wait until generic drugs come out on the market,"

"How would you feel," Julie asked, "if your loved one had to decide between eating or buying their medication that was not yet generic?"

"But don't you get the generic right away?"

"It's available when it comes off patent. Everybody knows that." Angelo leaned back in his chair.

"You're clueless. Drug companies patent all new molecules and processes using intellectual property rules and sue the hell out of any drug company that comes even close to infringement." Sharra jabbed a hard finger at the table. "Bottom line is that it takes years, not minutes to get the generics available to the public after the original goes off patent."

"And is that illegal?" Angelo said, smiling.

"No, and not even immoral but for the sick people eating cat food, waiting for the drug to be affordable." Sharra put both hands out. "Sorry, just making a point."

"I think," Rashida said with a sigh, standing and stretching, "that it comes down to whether you think medications are a right or a privilege. If they are right, then you demand the best drug all the time. If a privilege, then you wait for your generics and thank God you can get them when you can."

"Well," Olivia asked, "why can't Big Pharma reduce the drug cost burden? Where do they get their money?"

"Investments."

"Drug costs."

"That's capitalism for you," Alonso pitched in, all smiles. "Why shouldn't people pay for what they buy?"

"Because without buying it, they may die," Sharra said.

"That's capitalism too."

"No, Alonzo," Rashida said, "that's cruelty. We talk about equity in this country but not giving an Appalachian child a chance to beat lead poisoning because his parents can't afford to buy the medications is—"

Olivia watched Rashida search for the word, "Shameful."

"No. Its capitalism. Even Darwinism."

"And you're missing the point," Julie said. "Capitalism is not an end to itself. It's a means to a philosophical end."

"Then what is the end?" Angelo asked.

"The simple, basic belief that people have value regardless of their demographic or financial standing. Do you deny that?" she said, raising a hand to Alonzo.

"I think that a forty-seven-year-old PhD engineer in chip manufacturing has more value than a fifties-plus illegal, illiterate Nicaraguan migrant sick with TB," he said.

"They don't have more innate value. The engineer is just more productive, at least for right now."

"What's the diff?"

"Productivity is being active, working, and contributing. Value is yours simply by being.

"And, Alonzo, if you don't exalt value, then you've thrown us back over five thousand years. All of the pain and suffering our species has endured producing the Ten Commandments, the Koran, Hammurabi's Code—"

"Hold on. hold on,"

"Jesus and the New Testament, the Magna Carta, the Rights of Man, the Declaration of Independence.

"Remember 'We hold these truths to be self-evident. All men are created equal,' Alonzo? Through the Constitution and its amendments, the Emancipation Proclamation, and the UN Charter, all painful steps to affirm that human innate value is the characteristic that binds us together. If you don't accept that, then you don't accept Western Civilization."

"So? Maybe we've come as far as we can with the *value* thing. What happens without it?"

"Go to a dog pound. That's what we become."

"No. I don't buy that," Alonzo said, waving the thought away with his hand.

"No? Ask the Huguenots, the Armenians, the Jews, the Laotians, and the Bosnian Serbs. The Tutsi," Sharra said. "And who knows what ghastly horror is on its way."

"Who are the Huguenots again?" Sharra asked.

"French Protestants killed by Louis XIV's forces in France. Up to thirty thousand were butchered."

"Jesus."

"The problem with perceived diminished value is that it equates to annihilation."

"Genocide," Julie said. "We slaughter each other."

"Let's take a break," Audrey said.

●

"They are engaged," Olivia said, a half hour later, taking a bite out of a roast beef sandwich.

"I'll say," Audrey said, picking up her tuna wrap. "For a couple of minutes, I thought they were going to jump across the table at each other,"

Olivia smiled. "They're passionate, not violent. But how've you been?"

She watched Audrey relax in the stiff plastic chair. "Better since you brought me into this plan of yours. I—"

"What, dear?"

Audrey shook her head. "You are so determined, Olivia, and I want to be more optimistic for you than I am. You did a great job arousing those four MBA/legal types in there to be involved—"

"Where did you find them anyway?"

"Around. Julie is a lawyer. Alonzo is a lobbyist wannabe. The other two just finished their MBAs. I think Rashida just received a master's in FDA Regulations."

A master's in regs? Olivia shook her head.

Audrey finished her drink. "Brave new world and all of that. But that's one thing. Actually passing national legislation against Big Pharma." She shook her head. "Impossible."

"Yes, if it's just us doing the pushing."

"What do you—"

"We'll be fine." Olivia smiled. She knew that you could always count on Big Pharma to fumble the ball.

This time though, there will be somebody else there to catch it.

●

That afternoon, as the group tore into financing, stock buy-backs, the role of investors, and morality versus risk, Olivia lost herself in thought.

It was time to choose.

How far did she want to take this? Were they going to just "pitch the corners" or would she try for an existential change, evolution, or revolution?

Revolution was difficult, she knew, but evolution, slow steady progress? She shook her head. *It would all de—*

"Hello? Earth to Olivia."

It was Alonso.

"What are we going to do?"

Olivia took a deep breath, straightening up in the chair. "I know what I will do. I will pay each of you $20,000 for a month's work. In thirty days, I want a bill that takes corrective action against Big Pharma."

"What?"

"Twenty K?"

"Why are you surprised?" Olivia said, lips straight and face set. "Aren't you tired of being disrespected, being shouted at by someone with half your IQ while you work for peanuts?"

Olivia looked around the table. Audrey stared at her, mouth agape.

"Quiet is the mouth, sharp is the eye, and quick is the pen," Olivia continued. "Now, who is with me?"

"We're not," Rashida said, standing up.

Olivia stared.

They all now stood, facing her.

"We're ahead of you. When do we start?"

"Tonight. You've got rooms here for thirty days. Tell your parents and lovers you won't see them for a while."

"Thank God," Alonso whispered.

GOOD WOMEN MUST BE ANIMALS

"It was great talking to you, ma'am."

"You too," Olivia said, exiting the Uber. "Thanks for making the one extra stop."

"No problem. Sure smells good."

Olivia stepped out of the SUV and hurried up the walkway to 2317 Odem Place. As she reached for the gleaming doorknob of the well-finished wooden door, it jerked open.

"Olivia. Finally."

"Meredith, hello, and Happy 2018. And I am stunned. You look fantastic."

She had great stature and magnificent silver hair framing sparkling blue eyes but so thin.

"I thought I would bring us dinner rather than find a place to eat."

She watched Meredith smile.

"That depends. What did you get?"

"Chinese."

Meredith laughed. "You must have spoken to Nita. Come on in."

Olivia walked through the airy entryway, following Meredith through the well-lit living room into the dining room. Each was awash in the yellow light of a waning January sun.

She put a sheaf of papers down and then followed her host.

"I didn't get anything to drink," Olivia said, putting the food down.

"I have just the thing if your heart's not set on alcohol."

"What's that?"

"You'll see. Any problem finding me?"

Olivia leaned back, laughing, "I don't know Delaware but Uber to the rescue."

"Outstanding," Meredith responded, putting some plates on the dining room table. "Umm. Smells wonderful. What flavor would you like, grapefruit, grape, fruit punch, or pineapple coconut?"

"I love coconut."

"Then pineapple coconut it is."

In a moment, Meredith reemerged from the kitchen with two iced pineapple coconut drinks.

Olivia served each of them chow mein as Meredith poured the drinks over cracked ice.

Olivia took a drink, opening her eyes in reaction to the sensation. "Carbonated and what a taste. Wow."

"Some of these carbonated fruit drinks are heavy on the sparkling water and too light on the flavor. These though." She took a drink. "They work for me."

After some small talk, the two women ate in silence. Olivia was at ease with this damaged, strong woman.

"Meredith," she said after twenty-five minutes, "I've been working on a new initiative I wanted to share with you, but first I have to ask, how are you doing? You look fabulous, not like the grim stories I've heard."

The CEO nodded. "It's been a roller coaster. I actually did ok for a few weeks after the explosion. I went through the hand reattachment surgery several days after the event and then attended every funeral."

Olivia caught herself looking at Meredith's left hand. "So shocking."

"It's the sad way of things." She sighed and put her fork down. "I didn't believe that I could absorb so much pain." Olivia watched her exhale. "Anyway, to continue answering your question, unbeknownst to me and the doctors, an abdominal infection was developing. One day, it just exploded."

"Like a toothache," Olivia said, nodding. "On Thursday you notice a nothing-twinge, but by Saturday, you can't sit still in the dentist's chair."

"Exactly. Anyway, I developed more sepsis, and it knocked me out for months."

"You were in the hospital that long?"

"Let's see," the CEO said, putting her fork down. "October through most of November. I came home just before Thanksgiving and was a mess."

"How did you get better?"

"I did two things. Here let's start cleaning up. I still turn into a zombie around seven."

The two moved into the kitchen. "First I wanted to get better."

Olivia felt the strum of a distant but familiar chord. "'Get busy living or get busy dying.'"

Meredith turned off the water and looked at her. "Exactly. Who was that?"

"Stephen King."

"Well, I don't read his books, but you make me think that I should. I couldn't take living for granted. I chose to fight for it."

"I had a similar thing."

"Oh?"

Olivia explained what had happened to her and Kevin with Officer Siphod. "I always believed that I was a good woman, but—"

Olivia felt Meredith's hand on hers. "Sometimes in this world, good women must be animals."

The ex-regulator nodded. "Yes. It wasn't as though I was changed, but—"

"You changed yourself."

"Never to be the same again. And the second?"

"The second?" Olivia watched Meredith's eyes glaze over for a moment. "Yes," she said, "yes, the second was that fundamentally, my organs were sound. They had been through a new, terrible shock, but once the bacteria were beaten back, they recovered well on their own."

"Kudos to healthy living."

"But, Olivia, I had absolutely no muscle strength. I could walk a short distance but could not climb a single step."

She watched the CEO point to a shelf at eye level.

"I couldn't lift a can of soup to this cupboard. And when I fell, I really could not pick myself back up."

Olivia watched her friend's head shake. "I don't laugh at those commercials anymore."

The CEO leaned down to put a plate in the dishwasher. "So I got a good PT specialist and we worked. One daily session to wake these muscles up and let them know who is in charge, later turning into two sessions each day to build strength."

"Are you driving?"

"Just some, but I was never fond of night driving, and these days, I absolutely avoid it."

"Now," Meredith said, putting the last of the dishes in the dishwasher, "let's go to the living room and have the conversation you came all this way to have with me."

EVERY WAY, ANYWAY YOU CAN

Meredith followed Olivia into the living room, turning on the light. *The sun abandons us early this time of year,* she thought.

Motioning Olivia to sit on the sofa, Meredith sat in the leather chair just to her left, facing her. Looking at her visitor sitting comfortably with a face now set on her mission, the CEO said, "Ask me what you want to know."

Studying Olivia's face, she thought, *No reluctance in those eyes.*

With a full, committed voice, the ex-regulator spoke, "Months ago, I sent you information from a disgruntled safety officer of Tanner Pharmaceuticals, a company Triple-S acquired."

"I received two deliveries from separate authors."

The CEO sighed. "One died in the presence of Cassie. And Cassie herself died, haunted."

"And you and I had some short, surreptitious conversations. Now though, with my intentions now clear in my own mind, I want to 'spill my beans' to you."

"I want to destroy, then rebuild Big Pharma oversight."

Meredith sat back, eyes riveted on her friends. "Olivia, I am the CEO of a major pharmaceutical company. With what I think you'll tell me, I could break you. After sharing your intentions with the industry, the lobbyists and their goons would come at you hard. Your bill would be DOA, your reputation would be ruined, and they would see to it you would never work for or consult with Big Pharma again."

Meredith watched Olivia lean toward her. "I am committed to this," the ex-regulator said, "and I don't believe I was wrong about your conviction. Your attempts to change the direction of Triple-S have not gone unnoticed."

Olivia leaned back. "You actually may be pleased to find out that there is more support for you than you know."

Meredith nodded. "I haven't yet used the information that you gave me." She sighed. "I don't know what I'm going to do with it."

"I will leave that to you. What I'm going to lay out for you I believe is in the best interest of the American people but not in the best interest of your company."

Meredith leaned forward. "Let's get to it, then."

"My team is writing a congressional bill that provides additional regulation for drug companies—"

"What will it in—"

"Entailing several things. I'm working with a small group to hopefully keep this bill very short. It's in its very early stages. We worked out the key points last night. I wanted you to hear it first. I trust you,"

Meredith studied the ex-regulator. "Pray, do continue."

"The first is that review of any drug company's clinical studies will no longer be under the purview of the FDA."

"Who would take over?"

"A financially fortified National Science Foundation."

Meredith exhaled. "What about the FDA?"

"The FDA will help the DOJ set a metric to govern corporate behavior."

Olivia laid out the steps she had in mind, and Meredith listened carefully. *Wonderful ideas,* she thought.

"What about the agency?"

"Essentially, the FDA would be an enforcement agency and be moved into an arm of the Department of Justice."

"My god, Olivia, the FDA will never stand for that."

"They are essentially an arm of Big Pharma now. They can't correct their own course. It has to be corrected for them."

They talked some about the budgetary effects of this on the agency.

"What if a company breaches the behavior *redline*?"

"Then the Department of Justice will direct the FDA to seize control of the company, stopping the operational segment that they find in dereliction. All other activities will proceed. The FDA will make any changes in the personnel structure and operation of the company to correct the egregious conduct."

"And Triple-S?"

"I think that you know what this will mean for your company."

Olivia leaned forward.

"I am concerned about you, Meredith. Triple-S has some of the worst behavior in the industry. I know that and you know that. How are you going to be able to stay there?"

"I am fighting to wrestle it to the ground. Perhaps I can housebreak it."

"You're talking like it's a wild animal."

The CEO paused. "Maybe I am." She shook her head. "Still, the stock owners are not going to sit still for your changes."

"Then, don't give them a vote."

Meredith just stared. She saw Olivia clench her fists in her lap.

"I will be honest with you, Meredith. I think the shareholders are part of the problem. They buy stock in Big Pharma companies and really don't care how the company makes its money."

"They trust the company's judgment and the regulatory oversight."

"Come on now," Olivia said, sitting back on the couch. "Shareholders have no interest in the ethics or morality of the company. They simply want the dividends. I know that's how the system is set up, but you know there are some organizations that serve public health, like drug companies, whose absence of moral oversight can't be tolerated."

"I understand how you feel about shareholders. But taking on shareholders is taking on Wall Street. That's a much bigger dog."

"Our bill," Olivia continued, "will make the shareholders pay for the operation that the Department of Justice through the FDA undertakes to correct the company's malfeasance actions."

Meredith sat back. "The response of the shareholders will be dramatic and profound." She began to sweat, thinking through some of the implications.

"You know, investors won't invest in a company with that kind of restriction."

"I know, and expect that some of them—"

"They will abandon the industry."

"But do you really want investors at any cost? How about if an investor offers you millions for SSS to make a genetic weapon? Where do you draw the line? Must it be an all-investors-all-the-time argument? Can we not do better than that?"

"You draw the line with the Executive Committee."

"Oh really. Last I checked, SSS's exec com was pushing hard against you and your commitment to improving its . . . its corporate conscience."

Meredith raised her hands, smiling. "You got me on that one. They sure want me the hell out of there."

They both laughed.

"Seriously though, Olivia, you know the capitalist model is amoral. It was designed that way. It's our economic foundation."

"How lazy and convenient. *Amoral* in practice translates to immoral in the real world."

Olivia stretched her hand out shifting on the couch. "I don't get it. You act like trying to change capitalism is trying to . . . to change the mass of the earth. Capitalism is not a principle of the universe, like time or gravity. Capitalism is man-made, not God-given.'

The ex-regulator shook her head. "I won't debate history with you, my friend. Maybe unadulterated capitalism made sense in some . . . some epoch, but time changes as do the needs of society. We invented capitalism and we can break it, change it, alter it to our needs. It takes just moral perseverance and courage."

Meredith inhaled deeply. "And my concerns for you still remain. I know that you'll surround yourself with people who are fully educated in this matter. But I don't have to tell you that this is an industry with tremendous firepower. They're going to come after you."

"I know they're going to try to hurt me."

"No, Olivia," Meredith said, sitting forward and pointing a finger toward her. "They won't try. They are going to hurt you. If I were you, I wouldn't read my mail for the months that you're planning to put this into operation. By the way, when is this going to start?"

"No clue," the ex-regulator said, shifting on the couch. "Right now, the American people would toss me out of the room if I were to talk about this."

They both laughed.

"But there will come a time when there'll be a cataclysm so terrible that the American people will cry out for fundamental change. I'll keep my powder dry until then."

"You may not have to wait very long."

FIGHT IT OUT, ANYWAY YOU CAN

"What do you mean?"

Meredith got up and walked over to the table on the other side of the living room that held a black briefcase. Holding it open with her weak left hand, she reached into it with her right, pulling out a piece of paper then walked back, giving it to her friend.

She watched Olivia study it.

"This is an FDA expedited approval request," her friend said. But I . . . I don't know this drug."

"You will soon. It's a medication that prevents autism."

Meredith explained the side effects.

"You really expect approval?"

"Olivia, I am not even supposed to know of it."

"What?"

"They used my medical leave to name my exec VP as acting CEO."

Meredith watched Olivia stand, feeling the fury in her friend's eyes.

"This went in over your signature with full knowledge that you would be back in the office and disapprove of this action?"

Meredith looked up. "I hope that I am wrong. But should this play out the way I anticipate, then there will be anger that I would never imagine would be possible among Americans."

Olivia nodded, apparently lost in thought. "Now this makes sense."

"You have to let this play out."

"Sooner than you think." Olivia reached for the papers she dropped off in the living room. "Here," she said, handing them over.

Meredith unfolded the top sheet and read.

I knew it. I knew it. I knew it, she thought holding her breath.

"How . . . how did you get this?"

"Old friends at the agency who don't feel differently than you about this drug," Olivia said in hushed tones.

Meredith felt the emotional blow slam into her gut. She bent over, all but in tears.

"This is an approvable letter. The agency approved this drug?"

She felt Olivia's gentle touch and rubs on her back.

"We will have to move fast."

"What . . . what should I do?" Meredith was breathing rapidly.

"What you have known, what you have always known to do, Meredith, fight it out every way, any way that you can."

Meredith looked up, wiping her eyes.

"We'll be ready."

They both stood.

"We should stay in closer touch."

"Count on it."

Olivia sighed. "I wasn't going to bring this up, but, Meredith, you and I have another point of intersection."

"Yes," Meredith said, "Cassie. I miss her very much."

Olivia dropped her head. "I was such a bitch to her when she first showed up in Florence."

"I knew what she did, loved her, and then abandoned her," Meredith said.

"And I hated her for what she did, rebuked her, and then gave her every chance I could. I think we were both right."

"How is Jon?" the ex-CEO asked.

"Struggling with another loss, I'm afraid."

Meredith shook her head. "A brilliant but crippled mind."

"Gauging by what the rest of us normals do, maybe they were and are our best chance."

As Meredith watched Olivia leave, her heart swelled with admiration for this woman. Closing the door behind her, Meredith walked over to her purse and opened the compartment where she had put the phone number that Olivia had given her a year before.

Not yet, she thought. But like the sunrise, the time was coming.

ASCENSION

Just one thing left to do, the CEO thought the next day as she walked into the tenth-floor cubbyhole that she and Nita shared at SSS headquarters.

The excitement that had powered her, that had fueled her plan to return vanished, vaporized by last night's conversation with Olivia. Her planes that had once filled the sky had all crashed around her.

"What do you think you're doing, Nita?" the CEO said, working hard to drive some levity into her voice. "Security will help you with these things."

The chief of financial operations put down a small box she had been holding.

"Hi, Ms. Doucette," she said, pushing the tangerine-covered hajab back from her face. "Packing up is harder than I thought. I'm doing the same thing that I know you will."

"Let's sit for a moment," Meredith said, guiding Nita and Sinsa over to a chair by the door.

"What happened with Monica?"

"Fired because she would not sign off on the SNW17012—"

"Don't they have a name for this drug?"

"Safety package. They have more than just a name for the drug. Advertising has an entire marketing campaign laid out and ready to go. The distribution plan is the most audacious we have ever set up. Once we've—"

"Well then, what's the name of the drug?"

"Ascension," Nita said.

"Of course," Meredith tapped the numb fingers of her left hand on the plastic table next to her. "Short and right to the point. It gives parents the opportunity to *ascend* to a better feeling about what they are doing for their child while their child ascends to a healthier state, free from the fear of ASD," the ex-CEO said, restraining her nature to play with the guard dog.

"Once Monica was replaced, there was no question but that they were closing in on me. My antipathy to this drug is on the record."

"And you're an easy target because you're blind," Meredith said, reaching over to stroke her friend's hand.

"Your feelings against this drug are well-known around here, ma'am," Nita said, taking a deep breath, "and I think at the FDA as well. So after the attack, the surviving members of the executive committee decided to band together and push forward with the drug.

"They ended the *clinical hold* on the trial, converting the decision to conclusively end the study prematurely."

"On what grounds?"

"Clinical efficacy, ma'am."

"How dare they convert a hold for a safety review into a conclusion of effectiveness, disregarding the safety signal that led to the hold in the first place." Meredith swallowed back the bile that had just filled her throat.

"They submitted the entire package to the FDA in June, and well less than six months later, the agency approved it."

"So," Meredith said, teeth clenched, fighting to control her voice, "let me guess. This drug is going to be rolled out with great fanfare. Parents who fear having an autistic child will fight to get their hands on this drug. How could they not?'

Nita nodded.

"Meanwhile," the CEO continued, "the FDA and SSS will walk forward together, all smiles, demonstrating that the drug design, testing, and approval process are a well-oiled productive machine, removing yet one more public health scourge.

"And all that would be fine if the drug is safe. What's the treatment plan?"

"One pill a week for six weeks."

"Cost?"

"Total cost $120,000 per treatment plan. Just one treatment plan per patient is sufficient."

"Medicare is not involved because these are children. Cost to SSS to provide this pill?"

"Twelve thou per patient."

"So a huge profit margin and the targeted population?"

"Well, one in every forty-four eight-year-olds have ASD."

"Yes, but this is pre-disease treatment, right?" Meredith pursed her lips. "That's the pernicious beauty of this drug. A parent will work to get Asension not because their child has ASD but because they fear the child will get it."

She closed her eyes. "And what parent isn't afraid their child will be afflicted with the disease? There are twenty million children aged five years or less. Hmmm. That's more than two trillion dollars in revenue that parents will be happy to pay. Plus there are more children entering the cohort each month."

"That's how they see this working," Nita said.

Both were quiet for a second.

"Well," Meredith said, shaking her head, "I hope that they're right. I hope that this drug is not just effective but safe. I just haven't seen any data suggesting that it's safe."

"The data that you and I saw submitted was the data that you used to put the drug on clinical hold. Then they submitted a second data set."

Meredith looked up. "Another clinical data package from where?"

She watched the ex-CFO shrug. "I don't know and can't find anyone who does."

"And the FDA was that excited about it that they moved on with approval? My god."

Meredith's blood boiled again. She'd been warned against this kind of emotional energy. It would wreak havoc with her blood pressure, throw her blood sugar off, and even slow the healing process.

"Nothing we can do here to reverse this course?"

"The ship is already sailed, Captain."

"Well, this is not a ship I command," the ex-sailor said. "May I have some stationary please?"

Meredith's head pounded. She hadn't been this angry at the people who destroyed the World Trade Center. Who dismembered and killed her entire family.

She wasn't as angry at the terrorist who shattered the upper floors of this building, costing her a hand and costing Nita her vision.

But now, as she scribbled, hands lost in gross tremors, head pounding, hot blood flooding her, and for the first time in her life, Meredith Doucette hated and she reveled in it.

NOT DEAD YET

M eredith read the note back.

Date: January 19, 2018

To: Vannesa Seymour: Executive VP and Acting CEO, Triple-S Pharmaceuticals

From Meredith Doucette: CEO, Triple-S Pharmaceuticals

I hereby tender my resignation as of this moment, on this date, as chief executive officer of Triple-S Pharmaceuticals.

"Not sending this by email?" Nita said.

"No, this one gets delivered personally. Where's Vannesa's temporary office?"

"Actually, right next door."

•

"Hello, Vannesa, may I come in?"

Meredith watched the acting CEO turn from her computer and look up at her, surprise filling her brown eyes.

"Hello, Meredith, how are you feeling?"

"Good, Vannesa, until I got this note about the expedited approval."

"Of Ascension, I presume," the acting CEO said, eyes now filled with studied neutrality.

"Why else would I be here?"

"Please sit down, Meredith."

The ex-CEO, for all the world, did not want to sit. She felt her face flush as she faced the adversary that had been behind the Ascension approval process all along.

"I want to know your assessment of the safety of this."

"Meredith, I don't think—"

The ex-CEO put her hand up. "Perhaps I've not made my feelings plain? I understand the effectiveness argument here. That data that I saw earlier was clear. The drug can prevent autism. What I want to know is how safe you think the drug is."

The acting CEO shrugged. "Well, the FDA approved the drug, so they thought it was safe. I'm more than happy to go along with that."

"That's what I thought, Vannesa. And actually, I hope that you're right. But if you're wrong, then you're exposing the American families to the neuroleptic disorder that we all experienced the horror of watching last spring."

"That's your point of view. The company and the FDA feel differently. You know," the acting CEO said, trying to sit back in the plastic chair, "I never understood why you don't trust the FDA. They look at a lot more safety data from different studies than we do."

"You gave them some additional data I hear."

"Just what the clinical team developed."

Meredith stepped forward. "Before or after they all died."

"Just leadership died in the blast. We put the rest of the team on it."

"Real or simulated data?"

Vannesa paused for a moment. "What does it matter? It's what the agency wanted."

"Well, Vannesa," Meredith said, handing over the letter, "I'm not part of the company anymore."

Vannesa looked at the brief handwritten note.

"Your final decision?"

"There could be no other."

Vannesa dropped the letter on her keyboard. "I would tell you that we're going to miss you, Meredith. But frankly, these past two years, nobody's really understood you. You have a company that was fighting to be stable.

"And now, just when we have a drug that will lift us out of our misery as a pharmaceutical mediocrity, that will allow us to recoup all the money that we put into drugs that were losers, that will allow us to have balance sheets we can be proud of and will permit us to reward our shareholders and gain new ones, you turn your back on us."

Looking into the face of a new and terrible evil, the new ex-CEO said, "Vannesa, all of those concerns that you just raised pale in significance when compared to the millions of children that you're putting at risk in this country alone. Of course, you know that Europe's going to follow suit."

"Yes, the European Working Group has already asked us to submit our application. Can you believe it?" She laughed. "They actually asked us. We didn't have to go begging."

"Well," Meredith said, standing, voice rising, "you enjoy that feeling of triumph because I fear that it's not going to last long."

"You're wrong. It will last. You, however, will not."

●

After saying goodbye to Nita. Meredith arrived home. She dropped her coat onto the couch and went to the dining room, sitting at the table, her back to the hall mirror,

She didn't cry. She didn't slam the walls. She didn't fix a big dinner.

All these things she had done when her family died during the 9/11 attack but not this time. This time she allowed herself to be embraced by her anger. This time there would be no outburst. There would be nothing but grim determination.

She sat and thought, *How could she get the word out to people about what was really going on? Would being interviewed on TV make a difference, 60 Minutes? Writing editorials for newspapers? A web presence? Maybe speaking at FDA or even drug company meetings?*

Somehow that just didn't seem quite enough.

Her lips twisted.

She was hurt and thwarted despite her best intentions to turn a despicable company around to become one of the best.

But she was not dead yet, and she would strike back.

If not from within SSS, then from without.

NEW YORK CHRONICLE

Blockbuster drug by SSS now FDA approved. CEO resigns in protest, declaring the drug a potential public health hazard.

January 19, 2018. Triple-S Pharmaceuticals announced during a hurriedly called press conference that the drug, now known as Ascension, had cleared all FDA hurdles and was ready for marketing and purchasing.

This first-of-its-kind drug, which protects children from autism, is expected to be a blockbuster.

Vannesa Seymour, the new CEO of Triple-S Pharmaceuticals announced that "our drug produced phenomenal findings in its ability to reduce the risk of autism. So many parents have spent so much time helping but failing to protect their children from this complicated syndrome. Doctors have been frustrated for generations. We now have a drug that will prevent this terrible scourge."

Yet the announcement was marred by the sudden departure of Meredith Doucette, CEO of SSS. The now ex-CEO was not available for comment. However, early this morning, she released a brief statement, saying, "I was opposed to this drug during its development and remain opposed to it after its hasty approval. It may not be safe."

Nita Laghari, the chief financial officer who was blinded in the terrorist attack on the company headquarters last spring, also resigned due to health reasons.

Monica Stephens head of safety was fired.

When the FDA was approached, the agency said that this drug had met all of their requirements for approval and that bringing effective drugs to market was what the rapid review process was designed to accomplish.

On SSS's recent spate of resignations and firings, the FDA spokesman said, "As a policy, this Agency does not comment on the internal personnel issues of its colleagues in the industry."

The drug, which is a pill that is taken once a week by children at risk for autism showed phenomenal results in early studies. There were rumors of concerns about possible side effects, including muscle weakness. But the number of cases was small, and the drug and Triple-S along with the FDA decided that the benefits of this drug were worth the risk.

Autism, also known as ASD, affects 3.3 million people in the US, and 77.5 million people worldwide. Its cause or causes have eluded physicians and research scientists for decades. Some say . . .

"Olivia," Jon said, while scanning the rest of the article on his phone, "I had no idea this was going on."

"I just met with her a few days ago," Olivia said over the phone.

"She gave me a hint that there was going to be a problem with the approval of this drug and I told her that the FDA had already approved it. She was stunned, even hurt that this compound was pushed so fast by the FDA, given the safety concerns. Just before the explosion at SSS headquarters last May, she was in a desperate fight with the executive committee of Triple-S to follow her lead and support the removal of the drug for approval consideration."

"She doesn't think it will work?" Jon asked.

"She just doesn't think there's enough information for us to be convinced of its safety."

Jon heard Olivia take a deep breath.

"Jon, she feels strongly about keeping people safe from harm. She wasn't always that way, but that's who she is now."

"I spoke to her a few times." Jon looked out of his office window. "I felt the tension in her."

"Plus her comments in the article concern me. They're not the kind of comments a CEO would make even if they were leaving."

Jon held the phone closer. "I don't follow you."

"A CEO who is departing doesn't damn the company before they leave. They try to make sure that workers and shareholders still have confidence in the company, even though they themselves will be gone. But, Meredith—"

"Speaks her mind. Yes, I remember. Do you know what her options are?"

"There are a few actions she can take outside the company that would raise public awareness about these problems, but she knows very little about these avenues, and I'm afraid that her anger and her hatred are going to lead her to do something radical."

Jon shook his head. "I can't see Ms. Doucette breaking the law, Olivia."

"I don't mean break the law, but she may do something that will ruin her reputation and do no tangible good for the community of patients served by Big Pharma."

Meredith was a woman of courage. Jon felt his heart move. "Ms. Doucette and I have had a couple of conversations. One about CiliCold. The other concerned Cassie. She didn't have to reach out to me, but she did. Where is she now?"

"Delaware."

"Well, I have a meeting with FDA scientists two mornings from now. Maybe we can arrange to have lunch?"

"I think that's exactly what she needs. She has a lot of respect for you. I don't want to see her ruin herself. Even though she feels deeply about it, she wants to make those deep feelings count."

"Okay," Jon said, "and here's somebody who wants to talk to you,"

Olivia laughed. "Put my man on."

Jon handed the android over to Kevin.

●

"So what do you think?" Jon asked, walking back into his office after Kevin put the cell down. "Olivia sure sounds good."

"Sure does. Sounds far away from here."

Silent time passed between them.

"Meredith's in a bad way."

"What are you going to do?" Kevin crossed his arms.

79

Jon stared at his friend. "I'm headed to DC this week. I think I'll try to meet with her. She's a powerful woman, moved by the deepest of motivations, but she's swimming in new and hazardous waters."

"I know you're savage about this but not helpless." Kevin put his hand on the scientist's shoulder. "So am I. But what else can I do?"

"I'll have the words."

MELLIFLUENT INEPTITUDE

Sebastian Jenkins, deputy director of the Federal Food and Drug Center for Drug and Evaluation Research (CDER) stood triumphant in Building 21's lobby, shaking hands with all of his colleagues who were closing in.

He turned to his assistant deputy director.

"We approve a major drug that will have a profound impact on autism, Sam, and we did it without any public fights with the company or the media."

"What do you think of the people's reaction to the SSS discord?" Sam Morrison asked, as well-wishers walked over, hands extended.

"The American people just need to know that there is a new drug out there that is safe and effective for the prevention of autism."

Sam shrugged. "You're the star of the show, having put this Ascension approval together, boss."

"Plus," he added, jabbing a pointed finger into his subordinate's chest, "I arranged to have a guest speaker who is just finishing up his sessions with some of our FDA scientists."

"That was you?"

"You bet," Jenkins was almost shouting. "In fact I want to hire—"

The cell rang.

Sebastian picked up.

"That's him calling now. He must be done. Will you excuse me?" He turned around to look at the crowd. "Take a bow for me, will you?"

He walked off before his subordinate could speak.

"Hey, Jon. How are you? Thanks for the call and damn, thanks for being here."

"Sebastian, unfortunately, I'm going to ruin your week."

"Something that we did, Jon?"

"No, something that I want you to stop. I need fifteen."

"I'll get us a room."

●

"We have this space for ten minutes, Jon. What gives?" Sebastian said in a small secluded conference room.

Jon explained.

"You have to be kidding me," the deputy director said, raising his voice. "There is absolutely no way that I can reverse a decision about Ascension. We've already gone through all of the reviews, and everyone has signed off on this, clinical people, epidemiologists such as yourself, biostatisticians, the works. We're issuing a public statement supporting it and Triple-S. You need a much bigger monkey wrench that you've got to throw off the Ascension machinery here, my friend."

"Why was there no public advisory committee meeting? You usually have that for first-of-its-kind drugs."

Sebastian waved his hands. "Because we didn't need an external panel of experts who themselves are very busy to come in and read our watches for us. We understand the data. We saw very little controversy with it. And the public support for the drug was overwhelming, like nothing I've ever seen."

"I promise you that the acclaim that you have heard is nothing like the public criticism you'll get if this drug fails," Jon said, sitting back in the old wooden chair. "And there are clear warning signs. Doesn't it bother you that the company has thrown itself into confusion about this drug? When was the last time you ever saw that happen?"

Sebastian sat. "I have to say, Jon," he said in a quiet voice, "I've never seen that before. But again, the disease is an impactful one. And we have to move forward with any good treatment we have."

He watched DeLeon close his eyes. "You don't know it's good. You believe that it's good. You hope it's good. But you don't know. Why not wait to find out?"

"How convinced are you that you know the truth here, Jon? And what's your interest? You don't do autism research. You don't work for SSS. And I know you don't have children. What's pushing you about this?"

Jon leaned forward in his seat. "What's pushing me is that there are eminent scientists in the company who disagreed with the use of this drug and for the first time in US history, an entire population of children is threatened. That's a pretty big push."

Got him. "Then you should know and be comforted that we got data, new data, from these Triple-S scientists."

"I know," Jon said, nodding. "Think about it, Sebastian. The data that you received was not data from the top SSS clinical trial experts. They all died in the blast. The data that you received was much later and from junior people. Maybe even simulated."

Sebastian shook his head. "You don't know. And junior scientists are not bad scientists. You yourself should know better. Or have you forgotten your earlier, university days?"

Jon shook his head. "Junior scientists can be overly influenced by new job pressures. And no, this is not personal."

So naïve. "Everything is personal."

"And maybe that's the problem. This approval is a boost for you. But, Sebastian," he said, crossing his arms, "you're convinced that there was no pressure to push forward results to your agency that perhaps shouldn't have been provided."

"Yes?"

"Why not?

"Because it's not my job. My job is to oversee scientific teams that review the data, not puzzle through what disgruntled scientists there may be at this or any company."

"Your job," Jon said, leaning forward, "is to approve drugs that are safe and effective. What is it with you people? Why do you roll over for these companies? You're like a woman being pursued by rapists, yet every time we stop defending you and turn around, we catch you showing them some thigh."

Sebastian rubbed his hands together hard in his lap. *It's time.*

"You know I was pushing to hire you as a top consultant for us. Serious coin. But I have to say—"

"Sebastian, the government hasn't printed enough money for me to take that position or any spot with the Agency. It's gone too far."

Sebastian just stared.

"I'll not be absorbed, managed, or manipulated by the mellifluent ineptitude that you have here," Jon said.

"I—"

"But let's move on."

Sebastian saw Jon pause for a second. "Doesn't it bother you that the sponsor CEO put out a statement saying that she believes this drug may be inherently unsafe?"

The deputy director tapped the table with a stiff index finger. "That CEO is not a scientist, goodness. Doucette is simply the widow of the prior CEO, a station keeper."

"Who has had her job for over sixteen years."

"What's your point?"

"That even though she's not a scientist, she understands what the mission of the company is. And that she has gained, through all of the *approvable* and *nonapprovable* letters she has developed a good strategic sense of what makes credible research and what does not."

"Well," Sebastian said, blowing his nose, "the CEO did sign off on the drug."

"You mean her replacement signed off on it. And how about the firing of the SSS head safety leader? Did you know she was fired like the CEO—"

"Ex-CEO"

"For not signing off on Ascension."

"Again, not my wheelhouse."

"No, of course not. Look, I know that I'm out of time. I'm—"

Damn right

"Asking you directly and specifically to reconsider the approval of this drug."

"That's impossible."

"No, it's not. Apparently, what's impossible is for you to be willing to withstand the heavy criticism that you'll receive when you reverse course even though your reversal can save the lives of thousands of children."

"And also perhaps damn children to autism."

"This is the biggest mistake of your career."

That's it.

"Dr. DeLeon, are you threatening me?"

The CDER deputy director watched Jon walk up to him face-to-face. Sebastian swallowed.

"I'm not threatening you. Bad decisions threaten. then they destroy. Then they haunt and torment. That's your future."

"So nice to have seen you again, Jon."

The deputy director turned on his heel and stormed out.

•

Sebastian arrived late at his next meeting to hear about more agency cutbacks.

This time, review personnel were being axed.

The budget just couldn't sustain the current administrative as well as scientific review approaches, which were resource intensive.

The administration had to grow. There was no doubt about that.

His boss had told him so.

And as for Jon, what did he know about administrating science or approving products?

Jon had made fantastic strides, but in the end, he was a small-time owner of a six-member organization working on God knows what.

He looked down at his cell.

There was an email from DeLeon.

The deputy director deleted it.

Mellifluent ineptitude? Sebastian almost spat.

Fuck him.

UNLOCKED

That afternoon, Jon walked into the Cheesecake Factory, checking his smart watch.

It had taken awhile to find the Christiana Mall in the sleet, but here he was wet and shivering.

It was definitely not an Arizona welcoming.

Settle down, he told himself. At least he arrived early for the one thirty lunch. Maybe he would have time to scope out a table for two in a quiet spot of the restaurant where they could talk. He would appreciate the change of pace after the hard-edged morning conversation with the FDA.

"Dr. DeLeon?"

He whirled. "Yes?"

"Ms. Doucette is waiting for you. This way, please."

Jon followed the waiter, making one left turn and then one right turn along a long row of tables that stretched along a window, now covered with ice.

At the end of that row sat a solitary, slender woman in a white turtleneck and velvet jacket. Her hair was white. Closer now, he noticed the curls at the end.

She was sitting still, lost in thought.

But the well-applied makeup could not disguise a face taken over by anguish.

She stood up. They shook hands.

"Ms. Doucette, it is my honor to finally meet you."

"Thank you for asking to see me, Jon. I can't believe you have taken the time from your crushing schedule to spend time with me."

"A common friend of ours told me that I might help."

Jon saw her tired eyes brighten. "Olivia."

"Let's not say anything about what has occurred in the past forty-eight hours. How are you after that terrible attack in the spring?"

"I was more fortunate than most. My left hand is slowly getting better." She lifted it up, twisting it while moving her fingers. "I couldn't do that a month ago. I am now almost over all of the sepsis side effects. I sleep well at night now. That is to say until recently." She put her hand down on the table.

The waiter came to get their orders. When she left, Jon asked, "How much time do you have?"

"Not much at all, I'm afraid. I'm going to a Big Pharma convocation here in Dover. I would like to give them my perspective on this."

Jon sat back in his chair. "What is your perspective?"

"That Triple-S and the FDA have betrayed America," she said, through tight lips, a hard edge taking over her voice.

Jon was astonished at the tough statement. But more than that, the steel and her voice and the fierce determination in her eyes shouted her anger.

"Are you here to talk me out of this?" she said as their lunch arrived.

"If you got my email, you know what my morning was like."

He watched her lift her phone out of her purse, studying it.

"You get it too," she said in low tones.

He smiled. "Actually I did have a little speech prepared. I was going to say that this meeting is a big step for you and that you're facing a complex problem, that I think that you're right, in that these companies do cause a lot of difficulties. It's not all difficulty that they cause, and that difficulty can be fixed, but with radical surgery.

"And I would tell you to think carefully about how you go forward. We don't want to be so adaptable that the problem is never solved, but we want to be forceful in the right way to compel a solution.

"But," Jon said, finishing his ginger ale, "rather than say all that to you, I think I'll tell you a story."

"A what?" She sat back in her chair.

"Let's eat for a bit first. So this is the largest mall in the state?"

"In five states," she replied. "Somebody should teach you some Delaware."

The two laughed and then ate in silence for a few minutes.

Jon looked up. "Ready? It goes back to Germany in the late 1920s. There was a young, married couple in a small community where maybe less than two hundred people lived. The couple gave birth to a healthy boy.

"They rejoiced and treated him well in infancy. However, when their son turned five, the father became increasingly coarse and rough with him. He would scold the child unnecessarily. And he beat the child severely.

"These beatings took place throughout his childhood with increasing frequency and savagery. His mother would try to intercede for the child. And well, she would catch a beating too."

"Despicable."

"This man devoted himself to breaking his son physically, intellectually, emotionally, and spiritually.

"When the boy reached sixteen years of age, he had taken all that he could stand. So he left the community, leaving his parents behind.

"He settled into a larger town, about one hundred fifty miles away."

"Now this was the late 1920s in Germany, and it was very difficult to grow a business in the economically unstable times. Nevertheless, he cobbled together the money for a very small printing company, and when he reached his early twenties, he was actually turning a profit.

"Then one morning, he received a telegraph that said that his mother had died.

"Well, the dutiful son took the train back to the community of his birth, arriving just in time for the funeral. While his father was not there, the young man noted that many in the community were attending.

"So he sat through the service, and all who were there noticed that while many of the attendants were crying at the death of this good woman, her son did not grieve.

"He didn't shed a tear. He sat there stiff and wooden. The town's people were amazed because they had lived near where his abuse took place. They knew how the father had beaten him. They knew that his mother tried to help and oftentimes was hurt in the process. They were astonished that he showed no emotion. When the ceremony was over, he left and went back to his town and his business where he got back to work at once.

"Three years later, he heard that his father had died. Again, he received the telegram. Again, he took the train to his hometown for the funeral.

"However, this time, he arrived at the service early, and sitting in a pew, he cried like a baby.

"He cried completely and utterly, all during the service.

"Again, the townspeople were amazed. They had never seen a man break down so completely and at what? The death of the man who abused him?"

"Go on," she said.

Jon looked at her, "That's the end of it."

She put her fork down. "What? How can that be?"

He watched her lean forward in her chair. He leaned toward her, taking her left hand in his.

"It's a warning," he said.

"A warning?"

"To you."

She stared at him, eyes large, questioning.

"Meredith, you, like this young man, have an object of hatred. This man devoted himself to demonstrating to the world that his father was wrong, that he could be productive, that he could run a business, that he could be moral, and educatable, that he could have adult friends who would respect him and whom he would respect.

"So when his father died, he did not mourn the death of the man. He mourned the death of what had become his reason for living."

Meredith said nothing. "Then . . ." She stopped.

He reached over and touched her hand smiling.

"I'm just telling you a story. Please don't destroy the woman that we have come to love and respect. Find a way to get what you want and spare yourself a life of suffering through hatred."

He checked his watch. "How much time do we have?"

She glanced at her watch and jumped. "Oh. I should have left five minutes ago."

They stood, saying nothing. He stepped out from the table, walked around to her, and hugged her.

They stood that way, him holding her, her arms limp by her side. The wrung-out ex-CEO was simply standing.

"Thank—thank you, Jon. I needed to be, well, unlocked."

"Just a storyteller here."

They gazed at each other.

"We'll meet again," they both said at once and then parted.

DOUBLE PLAY

"Dr. Sivova?" Kevin called out in the El Paso airport.

He didn't have to yell. The energetic short lady, all smiles, was working with a baggage handler to move a pile of bags out for the passenger's arrival.

It had to be her.

It was a good thing he rented an SUV. He'd need a derrick to load the baggage

"Welcome to West Texas in February," he said.

He saw her rush over to him, thinking she was going for a hug.

"Yeah, yeah, yeah. You must be Dr. DeLeon."

"No," he said, keeping her hand in his. "I'm Kevin Wells, CEO of CiliCold. I work with Jon."

She threw her head back, laughing. Kevin smiled having no clue what was so funny.

"Yeah, yeah. So you are the support structure on which our genius rests," she said.

"No, I just make the easy decisions, Dr. Sivova. I—"

She said, holding her hand up to him, "Yeah, yeah, Ava please. The people who call me Dr. Sivova are journal editors or the police."

Kevin smiled. "Ava it is in then. Should we get your gear loaded?"

"Yeah, yeah, yeah, Sure, I'll help."

Before Kevin said anything, she had bounded to the SUV, had its back gate and all the doors open, and was throwing suitcases in. Five minutes later, they were heading out on Airport Blvd south to I-10 West.

●

Kevin watched her stare out of the window like she was trying to memorize all that she saw.

"Yeah, yeah, I didn't know what to expect. I thought you were Dr. DeLeon. He goes by Jon. Is that right?"

"Yes. He's in DC now and has a cold, so is working from his hotel room—"

"Yeah, he should be resting, not working all of that good energy out of himself."

"Well," Kevin said looking over at her, "he asked me to come and get you. I am honored to do it, Ava."

"Yeah, yeah. I like you, Kevin. I am sure I will like the entire team."

Kevin saw her shiver and turned the heat up.

"Yeah, it's cold here," she said. "Is that unusual?"

"I don't know. I've just been out here a year myself."

"Yeah, yeah. Well, it's cold."

"I understand that you're from Poland?"

"Yeah, yeah, yeah. I am and have been in this country for ten months, Wisconsin."

"So," he said over the howling wind, "I thought you'd be used to the cold."

"Yeah, yeah. I'm used to hating it."

He laughed as the wind buffeted the car. "So do I."

"Yeah, how long a drive do we have to Phoenix?"

"How about five hours."

They were silent for a minute as they crossed into New Mexico.

Actually, we won't be in New Mexico long before we get to Arizona."

"Yeah, yeah. Billy the Kid country."

He laughed. "So you've done some homework."

"Yeah, yeah, yeah," she said, turning back to the window. "I just love Westerns."

Kevin was silent for a few minutes, focusing on driving. The wind was like an iron bar, shoving the car right and into the emergency lane as they headed west to the Arizona border. He looked over at Ava who was now silent and had both hands clasped in her lap.

"What can you tell me about your background, Ava? You work in nanotechnology?"

She smiled. "Yeah. I used to make these clunky microscopic robots, like bite-sized primos. But at least in biology, that's pretty old thinking now. We are using molecular machines."

"I don't think I know what that means," Kevin said.

"Yeah, yeah. It means that just as we have mechanical machines that haul dirt, metal sheets, and you know, do construction, we now have molecular machines. Ever hear of kinesans, Kevin?"

"Sounds like a UK soccer team."

Ava laughed. "Yeah, yeah. Fair enough. It's a molecule that can carry a bigger molecule along a path called a microtubule."

"So the microtubule is like a—"

"Molecular road."

"And this kinesan drags the bigger particle along it."

"Yeah, yeah, yeah. The kinesan doesn't drag. It carries the particle and actually walks the path. Have you ever seen a tiny ant carry a grain of rice? That's what we're talking about here."

Kevin shook his head. "Does it have earbuds?"

Ava clapped her hand with delight." Yeah, yeah. Not yet. But they already respond to pH and light. Why not Madonna?"

They both laughed.

"Yeah, yeah, yeah, so you can have a kinesan walk a particle from one chamber of a giant molecule to the next," Ava said, pulling her coat tighter. "In that chamber, you can do a simple chemical assay that may say, slice the carried molecule into two. Then you can have two kinesans take the two fragments out on different microtubules to different destinations."

She sighed and looked forward. "They just need instructions."

"So you can—one moment"—he had both hands on the wheel now working to keep the big SUV in the lane—"operate on a molecule within the cell."

"Operate? Kevin, yeah, yeah, we have molecular tweezers, balances, molecular motors and propellers, switches, and shuttles. We even have molecular logic machines that insist on a combination of molecular conditions before they operate. And we can now use these in sequence."

She sat back in her seat. "Yeah. Give me a month, and I'll have these molecules turning double plays. Can you crank up the heat a little more?"

"Sure. We need to get some gas. You stay in the car."

He pulled into the gas station and opened the door. At once, the wind tried to snatch the open door out of his hands. He held on until he could get out and slam it closed. Then, walking around the back of the SUV, he began to gas up the vehicle.

As he stood there, he saw two young boys playing around the gas pump island in tee-shirts and shorts, the wind and snow whipping around them.

Not knowing how to think about that, he finished and walking carefully, got back to the driver's seat. He cracked the door open, slid in, and closed it with fingers that were red from frostbite.

"Yeah, yeah. Tell me, Kevin, is buying gas always an adventure?"

"Never like that." He looked west at the blue-black clouds approaching. Turning the engine over, he said, "Finish telling me about your work."

"What I've been working on is molecular communication."

"Communication with who?"

"Yeah. With us of course. I mean, after all, they already communicate with each other, right."

"So intercellular wireless."

"Yeah, yeah, yeah. We are working with a combination of heavy elements that look more like they can mimic the infrastructure of Bluetooth."

"I don't think T-Mobile is offering that plan here just yet."

She shrugged. "Yeah. 'Coming to a store near you soon.' In fifteen years, it will be on your wristwatch."

"Well, this is all phenomenal. I'm just trying to figure out how this enters into what it is that Jon has in mind to do."

"Yeah, yeah. Well, I'm going to rely on you for that, Kevin, because I'm not sure what it is he wants to do either."

"Well, he's interested in understanding the chemical language the body speaks to itself."

He watched Ava think for just a few moments. "Yeah, yeah, you know, I never thought about things that way, but"—she shrugged—"it's a good way to consider it."

"Well then," she continued, "we build a molecular machine to discern the message of the protein and radio it back to headquarters."

Kevin said nothing, in awe of her ability to size up the conversation.

"Yeah, yeah. I'm in. Yeah. Welcome to Arizona. Look."

Ava strained to see. "That looks like—"

"Tumbleweed."

Ava clapped her hands. "Yeah. What's this?"

Driving slowly in the snow, they both looked right at a hill, sloping down from the highway.

"Yeah, Kevin, what are they?"

"Men with guns."

NO BETTER CHANCE

"Yeah. Where are they going?" Ava said, turning at once to him. Kevin placed his hand on her arm. He saw five men slipping and sliding down the icy embankment.

"They are walking to that long car. See it? Looks like it belongs on a train, but it's hauled by a truck. It must have slipped off the highway and tumbled down the mountainside. Cattle in it are dead or maimed. They're going to put the animals out of their misery."

"Jesus, yeah, yeah, yeah. I know guns are popular in the US. I don't do well with guns," she said, holding her hands to her chest.

"They won't hurt you or me, Ava," Kevin said, smiling at the ease with which she showed her honesty. As they crawled by the desperate scene along I-10. Kevin estimated that they were thirty miles southeast of Tucson's warmer temperatures.

"Yeah, your turn Kevin. Tell me about Jon. Of course, he is world famous now with his work on the rapid development and deployment of vaccines."

"Although he doesn't say very much."

"Yeah. when I spoke to him, he promised me that I would be able to work without any want for the equipment that I need. Is that true?"

"Yes, that's true. And actually, that's my job, one of my jobs."

"Yeah, yeah, yeah. Maybe what you can do is start with this list," she said, pulling a sheet of paper from a notebook that to Kevin appeared out of the blue.

"Well, Ava," he said, putting his right hand up. "If you can hold on to that for me until we get to our offices, then we'll get right to work on it. Jesus."

He swerved right just as a gray F-150 flashed by in the left lane fishtailing

"Yeah? Goodness, we're crawling along in this snow and someone is driving forty miles an hour?"

"Unfortunately, they don't really respect good winter driving skills here."

"Yeah, Kevin, look," she said, pointing to the right. Kevin saw the green SUV blast out of the entrance ramp, racing ahead to merge left. It shot up ahead fifty yards, then its brakes came on. A moment later, it swerved hard right over an embankment.

"Just terrible," Ava said. "Terrible."

"Many of them are still not used to having many people on the road with them."

"Yeah. They are killing themselves. Yeah, yeah," the scientist said as Kevin watched her grind her hands into her lap.

Kevin's heart went out to the scientist, a formidable intellect unnerved by the carnage. "Ava, we'll be out of this very soon now. What did you want to know about Jon?"

"I've seen Jon's presentations on the internet, although I have just spoken to him on the phone. The one thing I get about Jon is that he is—"

"Genuine?"

"Yeah. I was going to say authentic."

Kevin kept his eyes on the road. *This snow really needs to end soon.* "Jon presents who he is without pretenses. It's easy for him to do this, but it doesn't always work to his advantage."

"Yeah," she said. "Yeah, yeah. I understand that he had some difficulty in his early academic training."

"Yes, at the university, he was accused of intellectual dishonesty.

"There was a huge investigation and his entire team was investigated, even deposed. The administrators took all of his computers and they shut him down for six months."

"Yeah, yeah, but he was, oh what's the word, exo, exo—"

"Exonerated. He—"

"Yeah, yeah, yeah. Exonerated. Right."

"Was exonerated, but it scarred him emotionally. He left the university trying to build a career on his own."

She squinted. "Yeah. So in America, sometimes you're not innocent until you're proven guilty? Yeah, yeah."

"In academia, the accusation is essentially the same as guilt."

"Anything else I should know? What is that?"

She leaned over to Kevin, craning her neck to see outside.

"A semi just slid into the ravine."

She collapsed back into her seat.

"Outside temp is creeping up, Ava. It won't be long now." He reached over and gave her hand a squeeze.

"Yeah, yeah, yeah."

"Jon is a blue-jeans kind of guy, work and let others work. But he does take it hard when someone leaves. He picks his team carefully, and to him, no one is expendable. It's a personal failure when they do walk away."

"Yeah. Never had a boss like that."

"Neither have I."

"What's the temperature outside?"

"Thirty degrees. But it's supposed to be warmer when we get to Tucson. The one demand that Jon makes is that you understand what your role in the project is and that you fulfill that role. But you must also be willing to help. Assist when somebody else is having difficulty."

"Yeah. How many people are in the group?"

"Emily and Luiz were part of the vaccine project and are still here. And then we have a math specialist. Then there's Olivia and me.

"And Olivia is?"

"Our regulatory expert and she's also my girlfriend."

"Kevin, you go. Yeah, yeah, yeah." Ava smacked him playfully on the arm.

"We have a history before we got to CiliCold."

"Yeah. Life is experiences. Have as many good ones as you can."

"Jon also does not enjoy working through money issues.

"Yeah. Who does?"

"Well, I don't, but it's my job now to help to manage CiliCold financing. It's much easier with the donations that we get."

"Yeah, yeah. So he keeps his projects big, even majestic, and only works them one at a time. And so you're able to allow for a small number of individuals to be well funded and make good progress."

"I don't think Jon would have said it that way, but that's a good description of how this group works."

"Yeah. Rumor has it that he doesn't have many friends in the pharmaceutical industry."

"They've banged heads."

"Yeah, yeah. Do you think Jon can pull this off?"

"I think most scientists had never even thought about doing something like this. Whether Jon can pull it off, well," Kevin said, "with the right team, nobody has a better chance than he does."

"Yeah. Ah look, the temperature is up to thirty-three degrees, Kevin. We have a chance to make it."

"We'll get there."

The two headed down the mountains through the blowing sand and slush to Tucson and then on north to Phoenix.

SALTINESS

"This is someplace," Angelo said, now walking through the spacious living area. "Are we working in here?"

"No," Olivia said, walking beyond the kitchen, "let's work around the conference table. But please, by all means, drop your coats on the living room furniture. Oh hi, Audrey."

"I like this," the ex-lobbyist said, closing the door behind her and entering the foyer. "Did you decorate it?"

"Absolutely not," Olivia said, laughing. "I'm just renting from a friend. Let's all go in."

As the bill-writing team formed around the rectangular conference table, choosing chairs bathed in golden light from the overhanging chandelier, Olivia checked her watch, 7:00 PM.

It was February 15, two days away from her deadline.

"Can we not work at the table?" Julie asked. "I feel like all I've been doing is stressing my ischial tuberosities."

"Damn," Alonso said, covering his eyes, "even I don't want to see those, whatever they are."

"The pelvic bones that bear your weight when you sit down. My dad's a doc. He says that all the time."

"Then may heaven help your mom."

They all laughed.

'Okay, let's take it to the sitting room," Olivia said shepherding them all to the right.

Olivia loved this room. Three overstuffed leather chairs plus one black leather sofa that could easily sit five.

Olivia let the four authors sit first, and then she took the remaining leather chair and saw Audrey take a corner seat on the couch.

"I've seen what you have written so far," Olivia said, picking up the thick document.

"And?" Sharra said.

"It's magnificent," Olivia responded.

"We didn't know the final format."

"Don't trouble yourselves about that," Audrey said, "The final preparatory work will be carried out by the Office of Legislative Counsel."

"Who are they?" asked Sharra, sitting back in her chair. She had kicked her shoes off.

"Nonpartisan attorneys whose job it is to turn our concept into the proper legislative language. They insert the standard language that you couldn't know we need. Nothing you have to worry about."

"The removal of the FDA's clinical trials arm and its insertion into the National Science Foundation seemed smooth," Audrey said, looking at the documents in her lap.

"At least on paper," Julie said, leaning forward on the couch.

"NSF doesn't have the staff though."

"Maybe take them from the FDA?" Rashida offered.

Angelo through his hands up. "Please."

"We've been over that," Sharra said, turning to face him. "Those FDA employees blew it. They had their chance to apply state-of-the-art metrics to clinical trial review procedures. Instead, they reduced the required quality of the studies. For this change to succeed, they now must be completely extracted."

"I just thought of something?"

They turned to Angelo.

"For NSF to take over, shouldn't they generate their own metrics for clinical trial success?"

"Why not use the FDA's?"

"Because," Sharra said, "the FDA *salt* has lost its saltiness. We need new rules, and new teams of reviewers."

"I love your debates," Olivia said, flipping the pages back and forth. She could hear the wind howling outside. *How could they have missed this,* she thought. "But something's left out."

WHIPLASH

"We know."

"This bill," Olivia said, standing, "says nothing at all about what befalls a company it if violates federal code. What happens if they misrepresent results or deliberately misbrand the drug? The FDA will be involved in the investigation. But what happens to the company?"

"The FDA would be under the Department of Justice. It would give up its clinical trial oversight role as you just said, but it would take on the role of reactive law enforcement," Rashida said.

"Julie," Olivia said, watching the incessant drumming of her fingers on her cord slacks, "what's on your mind?"

"The soft underbelly of any of these drug companies is the shareholders," she said, looking up. "The shareholders are the ones who contribute their money to the company in order to receive dividends. We need to include language that defines and attributes shareholder culpability."

"There you go," Angelo said, Olivia could feel the edge in his voice. "All shareholders do is give money to the company, not legal expertise but dockets. Wampum. Yet you want to penalize them if the company breaks the law?"

"Aren't shareholders responsible for what the company does with their money?" Sharra asked.

Olivia jumped at the chorus of yeses and nos that filled the room.

"Sharra," Rashida said, "companies, in particular their boards of directors, are responsible to the shareholders for what happens to shareholder money.

"Plus," she continued, stretching in the soft leather chair, "that's better. Plus it's not as though the shareholders can do anything to affect

101

the company's behavior. The shareholders aren't specialists in molecular biology, clinical trial design, or safety reporting."

"Still," Julie said, "if we are going to penalize shareholders if the company willfully violates federal law, shouldn't these shareholders exert moral authority?"

Angelo shook his head, leaning over to Julie sitting next to him on the couch. "I would agree that shareholders can influence the directors as the directors determine the direction of the company, b—"

"How would they do that?" Sharra asked.

"By replacing directors with new directors who would be consistent with the views of the dominant block of shareholders," Angelo said through a cough.

"The problem with that," Sharra said, scratching her neck, "is that the viewpoints of shareholders are transient. Shareholders may feel strongly about the environment one year, then three years later feel equally strong about divesting from China, then change their focus again to the medically underserved in this country."

"The company would get whiplashes from these direction shifts," Rashida said, nodding.

"Right," Angelo said, "remember, these companies are not speedboats. They're more like oil tankers. They can't jig wildly every three to four years based on every wild hair that the shareholders have. Look, folks,' he said, leaning forward, "we can't deny the logic of shareholder primacy."

"And," Julie asked, "what exactly is that?"

"It's the proposition that the one real responsibility that a company has is to increase profits for its shareholders," Angelo said.

"Just the kind of vapid and amoral principle you'd expect from a capitalist worshipper," Rashida said. "Damn the people. Full speed ahead toward profit paradise."

Sharra placed her hand on Rashida's arm. "So a company should not feel any moral obligation? By that reasoning, it would be perfectly acceptable for companies to make poison milk, especially for immigrant babies. Because, hey, after all, it's profitable. I know the metaphor is bad—"

"I'll say."

"Ugh"

"But you get the point. Makes me want to spit."

"Keep in mind that companies have to follow the law of the land," Angelo said, grimacing.

"Well, that's not worked very well so far for drug companies has it?" Julie added. "Withholding adverse event reports, downgrading the reports of serious side effects, and overpricing their drugs makes them more money, so they do it. They break FDA rules. Hell, they break US civil code. And their actions appear justified because they make more money. My goodness, companies can anticipate the financial penalties that they incur and build them into the cost of the drug."

"A self-sustaining, immoral colossus," Sharra said.

"Getting back to the shareholder point, shareholder culpability requires that they know what the company is up to," Sharra said.

"And?"

"Not only do shareholders not know the subtle effects of the board of directors' decisions, they don't even know what companies they are invested in."

"Hell no,"

"What do you mean?"

"Shareholders get statements every month or every quarter, but those statements don't say what companies hold their investment. Here."

She took out a sheaf of folded color pages.

"This is my parents' quarterly statement."

They all got up and came around the back of her chair.

"See? It looks at the investments from an entirely different set of dimensions in terms of low risk, medium, and high risk. Companies can move from low risk to medium risk back to low risk or up to high risk. The report is focused on risk, not company practice.

"In fact, the investment group that the shareholder works with may completely divest the shareholder from a drug company, and the shareholder wouldn't know."

"Obviously, the current reporting system is not going to work," Audrey said.

"And let's keep in mind that we are not trying to cripple the drug company industry by saying that we don't want investors to invest in them."

"Well," Julie said, returning to her seat, "the point of this is to give the shareholder a responsibility for the direction of the company."

She rubbed her forehead. "But maybe our problem is that we are treating all companies equally when they're not."

"How so," Angelo said.

"I can understand how shareholder primacy can make more sense in some corporations. But we are focused on companies that produce drugs and medical devices, not slinkies. The US population has little to no choice but to rely on these companies."

"Society relies on carburetor production too. Do you want to cripple them as well?"

"Well," Julie said, turning to Angelo, "when that glorious day comes when carburetors increase cardiac output or renal function, then we can ink them in, but today is not that day."

"Okay, so what are you saying?"

"Drug companies need to be compelled to operate with a moral as well as a profit metric."

"If we can't rely on shareholders, then who?" Rashida said.

"How about through eminent domain?"

"What do you mean?" asked Sharra.

"Well, the government, either local, state, or federal, can take homeowner property under eminent domain if it's deemed to be in the public interest."

"Can they take businesses as well?"

"No. They can swipe business property but not the business itself," Angelo said.

"And you know that? How?"

"Parents are deep into real estate." He shrugged.

"The government can buy shares in a company then control it though," Sharra said.

"Yes. But in order for that to work, the company, I mean the government would have to already own shares in the company to help to govern this action. That means not knowing what companies are going to fail in the future, the government has to buy shares in all of these drug companies.

"Plus, it allows the company to make a profit. This needs to be something that is so punitive that companies will have a vested interest in following the requirements that they produce drugs that are safe and effective."

"How about a hostile takeover?" Audrey suggested.

"That also involves the government owning a controlling share of a company's stock."

"And besides, the government already does that. It's called the federal inheritance tax."

Sharra shook her head. "Very funny, Angelo."

"Well," Rashida said, "why don't we just nationalize the miscreant drug company?"

NATIONALIZE

O livia watched everyone turn to Rashida.

"Well sure, la conquistadora, if this was Ecuador," Angelo offered.

"Very funny," Rashida said, smiling. "Ecuadorans nationalize companies that are owned by non-Ecuadorans. Here were talking about nationalizing companies that are run and by and large, owned in the United States."

"You're saying there are no foreign investors in drug companies?" Sharra stretched.

"No, I'm saying the principal investors in drug companies are within the United States."

"Wait a second," Olivia asked. "What does nationalization mean?"

"Well, it's the process of taking privately controlled companies, even entire industries, and putting them under the control of the government," Sharra said.

"In this case, it means that the government completely takes over the drug company."

Everyone was quiet.

"Has this ever been done before?" Audrey asked.

"Yes," Angelo stated. "The government has nationalized telephone and telegraph industries as well as . . ." He paused. "Yeah, as well as industries that make war materials and railroads. Sorry. I didn't study my Marxism before I came up here." He looked at Julie.

"Don't you worry about him, girl," Rashida said. "You just have to utter the S word before he goes hiding under the bed. Such a capitalist coward."

"S word? "Olivia asked.

"Socialism."

"So," Olivia said, sitting back, "anytime the imminent failure or incompetence of an industry threatens the national security interest of the United States, the government can nationalize them?"

"Yes, but typically the company is in trouble and there is a stock buy-in by the government."

"Not for Amtrak or the airlines' security industry either after 9/11," Rashida said.

"Right." Angelo turned to face her. "So we are talking about a full government takeover mandated by federal law."

"And the rationalization would be?" Sharra asked, leaning forward.

"To protect the health of its citizens."

"Sweden nationalized its pharmacies," Julie said looking up from her iPhone.

"Really?"

"Sure did."

"This ain't Sweden," Angelo said.

"Damn right. We're way worse."

Sharra twisted in her seat. "But the takeover should be just temporary, right?"

"The effects could be long-lasting," Angelo said, leaning toward her.

"So what if they are?" Julie said, glaring at Angelo. "It's the industry's fault."

"Wait a second," Olivia said, putting both hands out. "We're not trying to nationalize an industry. We're focused on a single company due to their inability or unwillingness to follow federal law."

"Hey, you're not suggesting that federal workers march in and be inserted on the bottling assembly line, or immediately take over vaccine design, are you?" Rashida asked.

"No," Julie said, shaking her head. "I'm suggesting that we decorticate the company."

"What does that even mean?" Angelo asked.

"Let me write that down," Sharra said, pretending to take out a make-believe pen.

"Strip out its management."

"You mean fire them?" Rashida looked incredulously at Olivia.

"Either this has teeth or it doesn't." Julie brought her knees under her. "You strip out the management, and you allow federal experts in drugs to take over the strategic operation of the company in order to root out the problem. Let middle management stay in to oversee drug development and production as long as there are no manufacturing issues.

"Once that happens," Rashida continued, yawning, "the nationalization period ends, and the drug company gets out on the open market to be purchased."

"By the same people who drove the company down?" Olivia asked.

"Sure, when they're released from jail," Rashida said.

"Good Lord," Angelo rolled his eyes.

"And what happens to shareholders in that determination?" Julie asked.

"The money that's required to manage the company would come from their dividends," Julie said,

Olivia watched Angelo ball his hands into a fist.

"So," Olivia said, "it doesn't cost the government any money to take these companies over for the months it would take to straighten the company out."

"But shareholders would get hurt."

"So what?" Julie looked at him.

"The end result is that our bill would require a moral obligation on the part of the shareholder to ensure that the drug companies are, in fact, following the rule of the laws of the land."

"And how would they do that?" Sharra asked.

"Shareholders will stay away from companies that they fear are going to be nationalized."

"I think that drug companies would do almost anything to protect themselves from nationalization consequences," Rashida said. "Not a bad outcome."

"Even follow the law?"

Everybody looked at Olivia.

"It's late," she said. "Go back to the hotel, then write it up tomorrow."

TWO MASTERS

"Here's your car coming up now, Audrey?" Olivia said as the sleek Porsche SUV navigated the drive circle.

"Yes. This was a great session," the ex-lobbyist said, opening the back car door.

"How long a drive to your condo?" Olivia shivered in the face of the hard north wind.

"About twenty minutes. Oh. It's really cold."

"Well, if you don't mind some company, how about if I tag along?"

Olivia saw Audrey look at her, a puzzled smile emerging. "Well—"

"I think we have one other issue that you and I need to talk over."

"Of course. Ned," she called to the driver, "you have two passengers tonight."

Olivia walked around to the driver's side and slipped in the back.

"You hearing from Kevin much?"

"Yes. Every other night we talk for a little bit."

"For weeks, right?"

"Yes, we have," Olivia shifted in her seat. "I'd like to get back to him. But I'm busy now."

"You know, there are options other than the telephone. Video communication is available now."

"Hmmm. Sounds complicated. And really, I have enough electronics in my life without adding to my . . . my tech overhead."

"Well then, the one option is to see him."

Olivia thought for a second. She'd been away longer than she anticipated. And Kevin had been so patient with her, listening to her ideas and giving her kind and good advice. But more important than that, she missed his attention, his gentle voice and strong arms, and the way they were intimate.

"I think I will."

"Good for you. By the way, your team performed magnificently," Audrey said, crossing her legs. "I didn't know what to expect just a month ago."

Olivia smiled, looking over. "I had forgotten the power of youth that brings new and fresh ideas to the table. Were we that energetic and knowledgeable years ago?"

"Yes, but years brought wisdom."

"'Experience is a great teacher, but she sends terrific bills'."

"That you or someone else?"

"Mina Antrim," Olivia said.

"You should hire her."

They rode in silence for a minute.

"Well, what did you have in mind?"

"The bill doesn't say anything about safety reporting,"

She watched Audrey turn to face forward, eyebrows furrowed. "You're right about that. It's a complicated topic, though."

"I think the solution is easy. Just let the NSF take it from the company."

"Oh. How will the industry respond to that?"

"They won't say it, but they'll love it," Olivia said. "Think about it. Each company has its own safety reporting system."

"Do they ever." Audrey shook her head. "Each more antiquated than the next."

"Yes. Almost all of them are in a state of disrepair. They use the oldest machines, running the oldest code. Electronically decrepit. I don't know of a single one that takes advantage of modern capabilities."

Audrey nodded. "I know some that go back to the 1970s relying on 1960s Fortran code."

"Prelegacy."

"And they have to try to put reports together that reflect both past and present drug experiences. That's difficult to do if not all of the safety experience resides in the same database."

"Plus," Audrey said, "these systems have to be able to collect side effect reports from patient phone calls, from physicians seeing patients, from investigators running clinical trials, from iPads, for heaven's sake.

"In addition, the reporting requirements are imposing but clear. Some adverse events have to be reported to the FDA as soon as the drug company learns about them. Other ones can take weeks or months to report as required. And to do this all with aging systems is asking too much."

"So, dear, why don't they modernize? Ned," she called to the front, "there's a Starbucks. Can you be a dear and please get us our usual."

Olivia said, "Because their hearts aren't in it."

"What?"

"Pharmaceutical companies love efficacy, but they hate safety. Safety is rarely anything that helps propel a drug forward, but it's frequently a finding that will keep what they think is a good drug back. It's a ball and chain for them.

"These companies want to make money on efficacy. They put their time into efficacy because it makes them money. If they needed an expensive computing structure to run hypermodern code to give them state-of-the-art efficacy reports, then they'd buy two."

"But safety?"

"They let the FDA choke on the company's outmoded safety reports," Olivia said, looking out of the window.

"Why put good money into processes and procedures and teams that in the end may sink their new molecule? Thanks, Ned." Audrey said, taking the steamy brews and handing one to Olivia.

"The National Science Foundation should contract. and bring in in-people specialized in writing modern databases. And these modern databases should be deployed to monitor all adverse events across the country for all drug companies."

Audrey shook her head. "Why can't NSF just use a private service and have the private service do it for them?"

"Because private services are . . . I don't know . . . it's late . . . gettable," Olivia yarned. "You can bet Big Pharma will fight to be part of the code development and deployment process. The private developers will be inundated by calls from drug companies to 'help in the implementation.'"

Olivia snorted. "Please. Private industry can't manage because they are too undisciplined."

"You mean focused on money."

"Precisely. They apparently can't serve both the integrity and money masters."

"It may be the one thing about this bill that Big Pharma likes. Oh, we're here now."

Audrey placed her hand on Olivia's. "Would you like to come in, dear?"

Olivia closed her eyes, squeezing her friend's hand. "I have a lot of work to do tonight. Just have Ned take me back."

RAVEN

S he had no body language. She conveyed nothing. She was all on the inside.

CJ Cutter, owner of the Hit It & Quit It and also her boss tried and failed to lean back on the twenty-year-old rocker that refused his biddin'. The small back office of the convenience store that pumped gas out front seemed tight.

He wiped his brow.

March already, and warming up fast.

He leaned forward in the small room, spying on the open door with the sign "Boss Lives Here, or Not Depending on What You Want." *Seen the good and the bad here* he thought, trying to squeeze up a good feeling, knowing he just did that when the bad time was here.

He sighed, looking across the desk at the still, silent woman he was about to fire.

Not my fault, he kept telling himself. It was just no new building development going on in Superior anymore. There were more sellers than buyers these days, especially after the fires over the past few years. They hadn't hit Superior, but they sure pumped fear into the hearts of his neighbors.

All of the real estate action was down in the valley, near Coolidge and Casa Grande. There was nothing much going op here, 'cept highway cars headed up to Globe and Snowflake.

It was not his deal, but he still had to live with it.

"Shit," he said, leaning forward over the scratched-up desk, clasping his sweating hands into pudgy fists.

"I'm sixty years old. Owned this place for fifteen years. I owe you a heads up."

He didn't know, but he'd guess she was just over forty years old. One just couldn't tell about these Indians. Solid black eyes stared back under a cowboy hat that he forced on all of his employees.

She looked at him, saying nothing.

It didn't mean he didn't like her. Raven had a good look alright, clean jet-black hair part ways down her back. She had a good figure back in the day he guessed. But the thick and long dowdy skirts over ill-fitting pants washed any excitement juices down the drain, that and the old scar cutting her right face from eye to lip.

But she was a good worker, quieter than most. That was a blessing, kinda. It took her a bit to learn her job casherin', as well as keepin' up with the stock. But the customers were mostly Superior folks, and they just didn't take to a no-talker in a meet-and-greet kinda job.

He got a new girl who was a looker and chatted people up just fine. But he had to cut this Indian's pay and confined her to stock, clean up, and do occasional gasoline pumping for the old, tanned, and wrinkled biddies who still wanted *full service.*

She never said a word about it, not in over a year now.

But she stayed competent, remaining after hours once to put the store back in shape after the fire sprinklers turned on by mistake, ruining all of the pastries.

But even effort wouldn't cut it in a skin-scraping economy with surrounding raging summer fires burning off small-town life.

"So I'm talking to you because I'm going to have to fire you." Fearing her reaction, he reached his arms out. "I'm not saying I have to do something now, but I'm going to have to let you go by the end of the month.

"Jesus, I put it off for as long as I could, and if you need a recommendation, you let me know, and I'll just call who I need to call to help you get . . . help get you a job. I know that you're struggling. I like you. But we all have the struggles. I wish you luck."

The woman looked back at him unsmiling, saying the first words in weeks of wearing six-day, day-in-day-out work, "Thank you."

"Take the day off."

She stood, then after a moment, held out her hand. CJ stood and shook the hand of one of the members of the Gila River Bend people.

He stood to watch her go to the cold cut section, where she bent over to clean up the latest mess.

When CJ came out of his office three hours later, she was stocking shelves.

"Why are you still here?"

She turned to him. "You didn't fire me today, did you?"

"Well no, not today, but at the end of the month."

"Then I work today."

She pulled several instant soup cans out of the box. "I'll go when I need to go."

As she put the cans on the shelf, he turned, walking back to his office, shaking his head.

Raven was a strange one.

FOG

"She's ready for you, Ms. Doucette."

Meredith, dressed in a gray pantsuit and a blue blouse, stood up, sighed, and walked past the tall male assistant with the slight lisp down the hall and through a foyer filled with air and light.

It seemed full of promise, like this April morning. She turned left into the light and an office that was filled with books everywhere.

There were bookcases that stood twelve feet high filled to overflowing. The desk teemed with them. They were on the window sills.

It was a heavenly library, devilishly disorganized.

Behind all of this sat a woman whose face barely reached over the books. She stood up.

"Good afternoon, Ms. Doucette. I am Leanne Evers. Please, come in."

The ex-CEO followed her guiding hand left to a round wooden table, below a ten-foot window, its bottom third covered by curtains and the remaining upper section spilling over with light.

Meredith sat at one of the two chairs, the attorney sitting in the other across from her. The ex-CEO coughed, then shivered.

"I can actually see a tabletop here," Meredith said with a grin. "You run out of books?"

"I cleared some space for us," Leanne said, waving her hand. "Be careful. I may cover us both with them."

They smiled at each other.

"Well, please tell me what I can do for you,"

Meredith, surprised at her own uncertainty, felt the sweat on her neck. She couldn't remember when she had last. felt this way. *Yes, the Lascom merger, thirteen years ago or so.* "I . . . I need the assistance of an attorney."

"Well, so far, so good," the lawyer said, smiling. "And how can I help?"

"If you had asked me that two months ago, I would have said that I had been the CEO of a major pharmaceutical company—"

"SSS?"

"Yes," she said, nodding. "You heard. Well, they were involved in immoral lapses and inexcusably thoughtless acts. The corporation was and is a danger to the health of US citizens and should be stopped."

Meredith felt the attorney's stare.

"Well, Meredith, if you want to send them to hell, then you'd need a higher power. Are you alright?"

"'Leanne, we had lunch . . . yesterday."

"Nooooo . . . Today is the first day we met," Leanne said, sitting forward.

"We ate yesterday. I know it."

"No. Today is our first meeting."

Jesus, no. Newly impaired memory. Also not articulate . . . whatever, but just can't straighten it out.

She screwed her eyes closed, then opened them.

"Coke. Two Cokes. Please stay me alone ten . . . somethings."

"Minutes?"

Meredith watched the lawyer stretch her brown arm out to her.

"Please."

●

Meredith guzzled down the first Coke, then after a few moments polished off the second, knowing that drinking something cold could decrease the fever and dispel the fog.

Then, realizing that she could not trust her thoughts, she put her head down on the desk and thought nothing. She just pushed them away, one untrustworthy idea after another.

In fifteen minutes, the fog lifted.

HONOR

"Where were we?"

Meredith picked her head up and saw Leanne plus two additional people.

She checked her watch, ten twenty-nine, ten minutes.

"Well, Leanne," Meredith said, sitting up and poised. "Let me explain what just happened."

"Hypoglycemia?"

"No, brain fog."

"Oh." The lawyer sat up in her seat.

"During my treatment with sepsis, I went through several episodes of brain fog. Now, everybody's experience is unique. But for me, well when it descends, I suddenly am disconnected from important parts of me."

"Like what?"

"Knowledge, facts. Recent events and activities. My lifetime fund of knowledge."

"And just as important as all that, I lose the ability to articulate anything."

She watched Leanne tilt her head.

"A word salad?"

"No. The words aren't random. It's more like I can't put a thought together well enough to spit it out."

"Why the Cokes?"

"For me, this fog is directly related to body temperature. That's kind of unique as well. I have a little bit of a cold. So without taking my temperature, I assume my temperature is up. And so I drank two cold drinks and then working on my third one now. I lost the elevated temperature and am normal again."

"Meredith," Leanne said, moving her chair to sit next to the ex-CEO, "how often does this happen?"

"This hasn't happened for about a year now. The further I got from the acute infection, the less frequent and the less time-consuming the brain fogs actually are."

"Sepsis sounds pretty tough."

"It's a bitch, alright." Meredith took a deep breath. "So much better now. So, where were we?"

Leanne took a deep breath. "You were telling me that Triple-S was involved in immoral lapses and inexcusably thoughtless acts and that the company should be stopped."

"To protect both public health and patients."

"Yes. And I told you that you'll need God's intervention to do that."

"That's what I'm learning," Meredith said, her hands wringing themselves on the table. "I visited the Justice Department here, and they referred me to the FDA. I had a meeting with an FDA representative, and she said I should file a Citizen's Petition."

"And did you?"

"Yes, fifty pages chronicling the company's injustices. Thirty-three days later, here came an answer that essentially said that..." Meredith waved her hands above her. "While the FDA could not speak to the motivations of the company, the FDA did review the records in the NDAs of—"

"That's new drug application?"

"Of the drugs in question. Yes. They found no impropriety on the part of the company above and beyond some lapses in safety reporting, and therefore denied my recommendations in full."

"What did you ask them to do?"

Meredith brought her hands down. "Withdraw these drugs from the market, Ms. Evers." She handed over a list to the attorney who accepted it with delicate fingers.

The attorney studied it. "That's a big ask, Meredith. And please call me Leanne."

"I also asked that one drug recently released have its approval rescinded."

Meredith watched as the attorney looked back at her thoughtfully. "Since you have received no relief from these venues, what do you propose to do?"

The ex-CEO leaned forward, breathing fast. "Sue the company."

Watching as Leanne exhaled slowly, she felt a wave of disappointment tower high above, ready to smash down on her.

"Meredith, I'm not sure you understand what it is the courts do here. What do you think they do?"

"They mete out justice." Meredith smacked her hand on the table.

"Well, they try to do that. You would like to reduce the number of deaths caused by this drug?"

"Yes, I would."

"The court's not about that."

"What?" The ex-CEO sat up straight. "They don't care?"

"I wouldn't say they don't care. They care more about the law, sometimes more than about life." Leanne sat back into the plush leather chair. "You know that doctors watch serious adverse events carefully with new drugs. And when serious advents occur, they react. They don't need complicated studies. They don't need odds ratios. They have a new, clear sense that their patients are not doing well, and then they decrease the use of the drug. Ultimately, there will be some studies that show the drug is harmful. But doctors don't wait for that.

"Courts are different. Courts are concerned about determining who is culpable. And in order to decide culpability, one of the things that they need to have is evidence that people have been harmed. And that evidence comes from large studies. Courts rarely react to a drug absent a large study because, without such a study, there just isn't sufficient documentation to survive the evidentiary challenges."

She smiled. "Sorry for the speech."

"I needed to hear that."

"Okay now, you would be the individual bringing the suit?"

"Of course."

"And your argument would be?"

"That this company acted immorally and improperly. And I have some evidence to back that up." She leaned over to pull some papers from her satchel.

"Wait a second, please," the attorney said, raising both hands up to Meredith, "Let's not get to those details. There may be a time for that."

Meredith, bending over, heard the *may* but clamped down on her response.

"Were you personally injured during these immoral and improper actions?"

Meredith cocked her head. "I don't think so."

"Well, either you were or you weren't."

Meredith sat up straight. "No."

"Did you take any of these medications that you now believe are unsafe and should be off the market?"

"No, I never did."

"So you were never exposed to the medications. Is that right?"

"That's correct." *Damn it.*

"So, Meredith," Leanne said, "I'm not sure what your standing is here."

"My standing? I am an outraged ex-leader of Triple—"

"A lawsuit," Leanne said, raising her hand, "to be successful, must successfully jump several hurdles. One is that whoever brings the suit, the plaintiff, must have standing. They must have actual harm done to them. Clearly, you're morally outraged. You have been hurt intellectually, emotionally, and maybe even spiritually. But the company did not actually damage you physically."

Meredith shook her head. "Put that way, no."

"And as we sit here today, the FDA believes that they have received all of the safety information and have reaffirmed their conclusion that the medication is safe, is that correct?"

"It is."

"So, Meredith, I don't see that we could move forward in court driven just by your fervent belief."

Sweet Jesus in heaven, is there nothing I can do? Meredith thought, her pulse rising.

"And even if we found an individual or such individuals who were injured, well, the process would be very difficult for you personally."

"How is that?"

"You know the legal department at Triple-S, right?"

"Yes, I do."

"They are energetic and diligent, yes?"

Meredith nodded.

"They are paid to protect their company. And they are going to do that, right?"

"That's right."

"Also, they will have no compunction about calling in attorneys external to the firm who have a lot more experience in this type of litigation than they do."

The ex-CEO set her jaw. "I can overcome them."

"Overcome them?" Leanne said, rolling her eyes. "Meredith, you don't even know them, Even if we were to bring a case to trial and, you know, I think that's not a good idea, their team will spend hundreds of hours going through your background, perhaps back to college.

"They will unearth anything and everything that suggest that you're not perfect. And they will hurl that at you like rocks at deposition and then in trial."

"Not just defense lawyers. Plaintiff's attorneys as well." Leanne raised both hands. "It's an adversarial game and the rule is to belittle, besmirch, and bedevil the opposing witness."

Leanne leaned forward, shaking her head. "Even for witnesses who are prepared, this is a bruising experience. You run the risk of real public humiliation. And you've never been through anything like this, have you?"

Meredith shook her head.

"It drains most people. And of course, the plaintiff or plaintiffs must identify in great detail when they took the medication in question, how long they took the medicine, and what doses they ingested, followed by a clear depiction of what the side effects were that they experienced.

"We will also then need to have people come in to identify the drug as a cause of their health problem."

Finally.

"Well, I ran the company. I've seen the data. I can testify to that."

"Meredith, are you a physician?"

"No."

"Are you an epidemiologist?"

"No."

"Are you an expert in interpreting detailed statistical analyses?"

"No."

"Do you know what a hazard ratio is? How about the Bradford Hill criteria?"

"No and no."

"Do you know what an odds ratio is? How about a 95 percent confidence interval?"

"No." *Jesus, Mary, and Joseph.*

"Then, you really are not going to be admitted to any court as someone who can opine on the cause-and-effect relationship. That's going to have to be done by scientists. What is your background?"

"I graduated from Goucher College."

"In Maryland?"

"Yes. Towson. I then spent six years in the navy, rose to petty officer, second class.

"In six years? Not bad." She sat back in her seat. "Why join up?"

"Because I wanted to learn how to swim."

She saw Leanne sit up. "What?"

"They'd teach me."

"Goodness, Meredith, so does the *Y.*"

"But I don't have to listen to the instructor at the *Y.* I did have to listen to my basic training instructor in the navy. Anyway, that's why I joined."

"And of course." The attorney smiled. "You learned."

"Yes, deep jump, fifty-yard swim, five-minute float.

"And you left after six years?"

"Yes"

"Honorably or dishonorably?"

What? The ex-CEO looked at her. "Honorably, of course."

"Meredith, I'm sorry, but I have to know the details.

Why did you leave?"

"I married and followed my husband who was a vice president at Triple-S Pharmaceuticals."

"Did he do very well there?"

"Yes. He was CEO until he died on 9/11."

"I didn't know," the attorney said in a low voice. "I'm sorry."

"They told me to do the best I could with the memory," Meredith said, putting her head as far back as she could, looking at the light that streamed into the room. "Familiarize the memory and its hold on me." She looked back at Leanne. "Six thousand and fifteen days later, it's still there, the burning coal that won't go out."

Meredith watch as Leanne sat quietly. Then, in a low voice, she said, "I didn't lose a husband, but I did lose a son."

"No."

"He was a firefighter, one of the first responders. He died when the first tower collapsed." She watched Leanne take a deep breath. "Any memory I have of him, I cloak with honor."

The room was still. Meredith felt a new relief, like a broken bone stopped hurting.

"So, Meredith, how did you become CEO?"

"His death was a shock to the company," she said in low tones. "There was, as there always is at Triple-S, discord at the top, and no agreement was reached as to who should be CEO.

"However, senior leadership agreed that if I could step in as interim CEO, the company would have a familiar name at the top, and I could be managed effectively until they settled on a permanent face with the board of directors.

"But their discord never stopped and in the meantime, I functioned competently. Plus, of course, the company continued to push money to shareholders and—"

"You mean dividends?"

"Yes. And I was allowed to stay."

"Still," Leanne said, shaking her head, "an active CEO's life is very tough."

"Over the years, I learned—"

"No no no. Not your job. You. You were injured as well, right? The company lost a good professional and a colleague, but this same man was your husband and the father of your children. How did you function as CEO?"

Meredith was quiet, shaking her head. "I could stand the pain, but I couldn't take the immobility that it . . . that it encased me in. Staying in that house would not help to release me. So I sold the house and bought another in Dover."

"And work?"

"Much of it was new. However, many people assisted and carried me through the first few months until I was able to get my feet on the ground. I made mistakes. There is no question of that. But slowly, they were fewer and fewer days known for their stumbles. And more and more normal days until most every day was a normal day."

"And your family?"

Meredith looked up. "Always with me even though they can't answer me. Sometimes, though, I can still hear the laugh of my husband or the cough of one of my sons when they had a cold. They had two different types of cough. I can still tell them apart. I hope that always stays with me.

"You know, the hardest thing I had to do was to lead a small memorial service at company headquarters on the fifteenth-year anniversary of 9/11. I wanted to be sincere, to be uplifting, but that required me to open some doors to my own heart that I had closed and locked over the years.

"Reopening those revealed that the memories, the anger, the angst, the twisting, searing pain of having part of me torn away were all there, ready to come back."

Leanne wiped both of her eyes, and with a thick voice said, "Too hard to do."

"No, giving the talk was easy. Closing the door again, that was hard. But I wonder though it that experience ignited the kindling of my own dissatisfaction with Triple-S."

"And, Meredith, what convinced you that the company was so evil?"

"Well, there are specifics that convinced me. My head of safety continually talked about the FDA's dissatisfaction with our safety reports.

"Then there was a new drug that we were bringing to market that the company argued helped to prevent autism."

"Yes," the attorney said, rubbing the skin below her left eye. "That was in the newspapers last year. That was why you resigned, right?

Meredith shook her head. "It was more a sense that the company was misaligned with its mission statement, that it would contribute to communities in positive ways, providing drugs that were safe and effective. There was no . . . no benevolence left. It was all about money."

"Companies are in business to make money, right?"

"No," said the ex-CEO, her index finger stabbing the table. "At least drug companies shouldn't have a *de facto* goal of making all the money that they can. Money should go into the best reporting systems, solid infrastructure, competent—"

"You didn't say shareholders."

Meredith met her gaze. "I know that."

"So you don't fit the company mold anymore."

"We've grown apart."

"Are you religious?"

"Catholic."

Leanne cleared her throat. "Well, you might very well be right. But I think that it would be fruitless for you or for someone else on your behalf to bring a lawsuit at this time."

Meredith reached for her leather satchel.

"Wait a second. I'm not saying that we're done. If you're right, then there will be a circumstance in which the defects of a particular drug made by Triple-S will damage some part of the US population."

"Maybe."

"When that happens, Meredith, you have to be ready if you want to proceed in this matter, to offer your services."

"When will that be?"

"It depends on the drug, Meredith. But if you're right, it may not be very long."

Meredith stood. "I hated to learn to swim, but I learned it, hated my family's death. I endured it. I hated some of my CEO tasks, but I did them as well.

"Sometimes I think that my life story is hating to do things that I must do, then do them. No doubt, I will hate doing part of this, but I will do it."

She closed her eyes. "Because, finally, when you lay down, broken and near the end, the one question you face is 'What else is there to do but to go on?'"

"Always the same question," she repeated in hushed tones, opening her eyes. "What else is there to do?" She stood. Leanne followed.

"Let's stay in touch."

"How could we not? And, Leanne—"

"Yes."

"I will honor your son in my prayers."

The two women hugged, and for the first time in many terrible, turbulent years, Meredith cried.

CONSCIENCE OF THE KING

"Kevin," Olivia said into her cell as she walked out of the secure area in terminal 2.

"Now that's a voice I love to hear."

"Well, I've got something better than that for you."

"What's that, Olivia."

"I'm here at Sky Harbor Airport."

"No."

"That's right."

"Not just to change flights?"

"No, silly," she said, thrilled as his voice filled her head. "Here for a few days."

"Lovely. I need to see you."

"Well, I just walked out of security. "I'm about ready to walk out the door into—"

"Don't do that. You'll broil."

"Well, I'll look for your car."

"Don't do that either."

She stopped walking. "But how am I going to—"

"Turn around."

There he was, comfortable as always, with a smile that pulled her to him. She ran the five steps and fell into his arms.

They kissed, a long, loving luxuriance.

Breathless when they broke, she asked, "What are you doing here?"

"I have my spies."

"Audrey?"

"Yeah, she gave me a call with all the details."

"Thank God for Audrey."

"Let's get out of here." He leaned into her right ear. "I want to have my way with you."

"You nasty man."

They walked through the door.

"I've been looking forward to the Arizona temperatures, but I forgot what Arizona temperatures mean right now."

"The mornings are in the eighties. But it heats up fast. We may get up to one twenty before July is over. How long are you here for?"

"Go back on Monday."

"I don't care." He put his arm around her. "You're here now."

They got in the car and headed to 202 East.

"There's a lot happening, both here at CiliCold, and with you in DC, and I'd love to hear about it all but"—he sighed—"let's not do this now. I just want to enjoy you for a while, be open to you, absorb you again."

She looked at him.

"I never realized how easy it is for me to slip back into the widower mode. You always spring me out of that trap."

"How so?"

"By making me feel like I'm nineteen, lover."

She squeezed his thigh. "Don't be so wicked."

In forty-five minutes, they were back at his house in Queen Creek.

Five minutes later they were in bed.

●

"Are you hungry?" he asked, an hour later.

Olivia stretched out on the bed sheet. "No, not yet."

"Well, I made something for you, a drink."

"Too early for me."

She saw him smile.

"Nonalcoholic, and just for you."

"What is it?"

"You'll have to see."

In a moment he was back, offering her a glass.

'Give it a try. I've made this from my own stash, lemonade."

She held the glass up, smelled it, and then took a swallow.

She puckered her lips, saying, "Ugh, it's terrible."

She let him take the glass from there. He sniffed it. "Damn, I gave you the wrong glass. Take this one."

She took it and swallowed. "Much better."

"Well, there's hope for me yet."

She sat up. "So my head is still full of DC business, so—"

"You look wonderful to me, perfectly naked, sipping my lemonade."

She smiled, leaned, and kissed him. "So dirty. Why don't you tell me what's going on here?"

"We've got momentum now. Jon has put together his team, and we have a very good idea of what it is we're going to do."

"And that is?"

"We are going to learn a language cells use to communicate with each other."

"Oh." She looked at him. "Cells talk?"

"Not like we talk, and they don't listen like we listen." She made room for him and he sat down. "It's all done chemically. Cells produce chemicals and send them on to other cells that absorb these chemicals and respond to them, seriously. So it's communication. But sometimes it's helpful for us to think about it as a language."

"Wow."

"The lemonade?" he said, smiling

"No, silly. The idea."

"Yes, it is. And the next step is going to be to learn to speak the language."

"Oh." She was quiet for a bit. "So by speaking the language, we will be able to get cells to do things that they ordinarily wouldn't do?"

Kevin nodded his head. "Exactly."

"I don't know how to think about the implications of that. I mean—"

"I'm glad you said that. Neither do I. There're some very good things that can come out of this. But we're going to need to walk cautiously through it."

She turned on her stomach, legs bent at the knees. "You know, Kevin, my acceptance of email in the 1990s, seemed like a great idea. I think my first account was something called computer serve—"

"CompuServe. So was mine."

"But nobody told me I would have to spend time sifting through hundreds of junk emails and scams."

"Don't know about you, but I liked my Russian brides," he said, stretching out next to her.

"I bet. But email produced problems that should have been clear upfront. And they were foreseeable. My goodness, we got junk snail mail for years. Why would they think we'd avoid junk email?"

"Because nobody thought about it at all."

"Because the engineers chose not to think about it. It wasn't as much fun as programming new email features that we didn't ask for."

She turned to him. "We're not going to make the same mistake, are we?"

"The implications of this are stupendously good and horrifically bad." Kevin rolled on his back. "That is if we can pull it off. Unfortunately, we have 'Team Technology', focused on what they can do, not on what they should—"

"Or should not—"

"Do. Scientists." She shook her head. "The one group that can get away with not thinking through the consequences of their own actions."

She saw that Kevin was quiet.

"So it looks like you're the conscience of the king here?"

Turning to face her, he said, "I suppose so."

"They couldn't have chosen a better one. What's Jon's position on this?"

"He hasn't said anything about it."

"You all need to talk."

"Now, I'm here to worship my queen."

Time swirled around them as they delighted in each other.

●

On the flight back to Reagan, Olivia thought she was going back to candy land, sweet tasting but artificial.

People were nice but insincere, pretending to be who they knew they were not. And as the desert flew by beneath her, she hungered for the honesty, hope, and raw feeling that she was leaving behind.

MOLMACS

"Well," Jon said looking over his crew, "it's July 13, 2018. Burning up out there in Chandler—"

"Gilbert."

"Chandler."

"The sign says, 'Welcome to Gilbert.'"

"Whatever."

"Well, I'm glad we got all that straightened out," Jon said, smiling as he sat in a chair in the conference room. "Don't want to waste the brain power in this room. Tell me where you think we are with this project."

"Where's Ava?" Emily said, turning around in her chair.

"Yeah, yeah, yeah. I'm right here," Ava said, walking through the door and coming into the conference area where they began to work.

"Ava," Jon said, "I haven't seen you for a while. Where are you living?"

"Yeah, yeah, yeah. Actually, I'm living in Gilbert, which is right across the street from this city, which is Chandler, very interesting."

"Yeah," Luiz said, "we were just talking about that."

"You're renting, right?" Kevin asked.

"Yeah, yeah. I decided to rent initially," the scientist said. "I'm told that I'm going to have to pay attention to housing prices, interest rates, and availability. But it's a nice apartment with lots of room and even a pool. We never had pools in Poland."

"Do you even have a summer in Poland?" Luiz asked with a broad smile.

"Yeah. Your word for it is winter."

Jon saw everyone laughing. It looked like his new team was coming together. But this time he was asking so much of them.

"We actually don't have many in Indiana either,"

Jubal said.

"What?" Kevin asked. "Pools or winter."

"Plenty of winter. I meant pools."

A spasm of worry ran through Jon. He knew that this young scientist believed that he had much to prove.

"Yeah, yeah, yeah, Why don't you just come on over sometime and use it?"

Jon saw Jubal's eyes open wide, like a kid who had just received his most envied toy. "Well, I would appreciate that but you have to teach me some Polish."

Now Jon watched Ava's mouth open.

"Yeah, yeah. Really?"

He shrugged in his sport coat and yellow shirt. "I'll be learning a new language now, and who knows, maybe what you teach me about the Polish language would be very useful for me in my measure theory stuff here."

Ava curtsied.

All were quiet for a second. From anyone else, it would have been a joke. But Jon knew that from this proud Polish scientist, it was a dignified show of respect. He felt his cheeks flush.

"I'd be more than happy to do that for you, Jubal. And whose dog is that? I'm sorry but I know I've been away for a while"

"Ah," Kevin said, "that's Emily's dog, Sparky." Kevin dropped his hand.

Jon watched Sparky come over to Kevin, sniffing the president's fingers and then scooted over to Ava, tail wagging all the way.

"Yeah, yeah, yeah. This dog likes new friends. Like I do. And I love dogs." She leaned over to pet him, and he put his forepaws on her shoulder. She picked him up.

Sparky barked and wagged his tail.

"Don't take it personally, Ava," Em said, running her hand through her short hair. "He loves everyone."

"You know," Jubal said, coming over to pet the mascot. "Maybe we could learn dog language."

Nobody said anything. Then everybody laughed at once.

Kevin lifted his hands. "It's a brave new world."

"Yeah, yeah. I love this area." Ava said, looking at the sofa, chairs, and table lights. "It's a good place to get out of your lab and rest. But of course, molecular machines never rest."

"At least not in your hands," Emily said. "By the way, can we give them a new name? Molecular machines contain too many syllables for my mouth."

Jubal shoved his hands into his pockets. "Molmacs?"

"Yeah, yeah, I like that."

"We have a winner," Luiz said.

"Well," Jon said, sitting on the right arm of the sofa, "let me begin by just asking you all how you're set up. Are there any unmet equipment needs?"

"Yeah, yeah. I'm good. I have my preps ready. I can produce these molmacs to carry out steps in sequence. Carry a molecule to a chamber, reorient it, slice it, and carry fragments to other chambers. But someone will need to help with the sequence."

"I'm a cell biology kind of guy," Luiz said. "But I can help Ava get her molmacs into a cell. Place 'em as close or as far apart from the nucleus as you want."

"And I'm the guy who asks the dumb questions," Kevin said, stretching his long legs out in front of his chair. "How do you keep the immune system from going after these molmacs?"

"Not dumb at all," Luiz said. "You know, the immune system is primed to go after what it perceives as the *foreigner* within us. But the foreign material needs to be of at least a certain size. These molmacs, at least as I understand them, even strung out, are too small to get the immune system's attention."

"Yeah, yeah, Are we ready for ice cream?"

"I know a DQ and a yogurt place nearby. When we're done, I'll drive us there," Jon said.

"Yeah, yeah."

"Em," Jon said, "I think that you and Jubal own some of the most challenging tasks."

"Well, for one thing, we won't need all that code I wrote for the vaccine project."

"The world needs it."

"What we really need to ask is 'What does it mean to provide instructions to molmacs?' Those machines would have to somewhere down the line receive molecular instructions. So we would have to write something like—"

"Molecular software," Jubal said. "Molsoft?"

"That's it," Emily said. "So I'm going to have to learn how to do that, essentially to convert Jubal's translation into a sequence of steps that the molmac can follow."

She leaned back in her chair. "Since Ava has developed molecular logic machines for us, we can string them into a series of instructions that molmacs will understand. That way we convert what we know as binary code into"—she looked at Jubal—"molsoft. But how would we know what we're saying?"

"That's why we need to know the language."

"I wonder," Jubal said, "suppose I wanted to learn Polish by hanging a microphone over Warsaw? What would I learn?"

LET'S MAKE MISTAKES

"Yeah, yeah, yeah. Not too much?" Ava stood on the tips of her sneakers and stretched.

"Converses?" Kevin asked.

"Yeah, yeah. Sneakers of champions."

"I'm envious. Never had them. As a kid, they were $9.99 a pair. Way too rich for me."

Jubal turned to Ava. "Suppose I hung a microphone over Warsaw. What would I learn?"

"Nothing."

"Right," he said, now standing and walking behind his chair. But that's what we're proposing here."

Silence.

"Even though each conversation is meaningful, in the Gestalt, it's a confusing morass."

"Nothing but chemical yammering."

"Well," Kevin said, "you would learn some things. For example, you would learn that there's more conversation during the day than at night. You would learn that there is more talking on weekdays than weekends and that there are some weekdays which are holidays, during which there's not much talk."

"Right," Jubal said, now standing and walking around the room, snapping his fingers. "We can only discern gross patterns, day versus night patterns in our analysis."

"And therein lies one of the complexities, Jon," Emily said. "Our bodies each have thirty-eight trillion cells. That's thirty-eight trillion conversations?"

"And that's assuming a cell just has one conversation at a time."

"How would you pick out anything to respond to?"

135

"No can do."

"Unless they all say the same thing."

"Such as?" Jon asked.

"'Take us to your leader.'"

"That happens," Jubal said, "and I'm out that door running back to Indiana."

They all cracked up.

"Yeah. So what do we do?" Ava scratched her way through her red hair.

"How about just looking at one cell."

They all turned to look at Luiz.

"I can identify one cell and deliver Ava's molmacs to it."

"That cuts the problem down to size."

"Now that message may mean anything. 'Produce this complex carbohydrate', or 'Take me to the mitochondria'."

"Or it may be the mRNA blueprint for a protein."

"Well," Jon said, "nobody said this was going to be easy, but at least working with one cell, we have a fighting chance not to get lost in the background noise."

"Yeah, yeah. They're going to be a lot of mistakes with this, as in learning any language."

"Well," Jon said, looking around, "let's get about to making the mistakes. Kevin can I come by?" he said, heart pounding.

It was time.

"Sure."

CRUSHING

"Let me get this right," Kevin said in his office five minutes later. "You adjourned a productivity meeting to tell me you're crushing on someone?"

"I saw her at a nearby gas station/store the day of our CiliCold goodbyes on the mountain."

"Saw her at a store?"

He watched Jon sigh.

"Was she a customer or does she work there?"

Shrug.

"So without having a conversation, just seeing her for thirty seconds, what, four months ago, you're crushing?"

"You know. 'Just one look.'"

"That song was sung by a teenager. Feel and react. That's what teenagers do. May work for them but not so good for adults."

CiliCold could not stand another Jon emotive spinout, not when the team was just coming together. Kevin grabbed both seat arms tight.

"I would ask you how serious you are about this, my friend, but I think I already know."

Jon nodded his head

"You're the smartest person I know, brilliant, and you feel things deeply. Your heart is an open door. Since it's a kind one, people love to work with you. I think that, next to your science, that experience exhilarates you.

"But most guys enjoy relationships with women. You suffer through them. Why?"

"I set a high bar that neither they nor I can reach."

"Same question, my friend, why?"

Jon was silent.

Kevin knew Jon didn't want his relationships to fail. The pain that he felt from Rayiko's sudden departure was deep and palpable.

"And I know you well enough to know that you'll not be dissuaded from doing it again." Kevin sighed. "Well, if it's not for me to talk you out of it, maybe I can help you through it?"

"How?"

Good question. Kevin thought. "Let's—"

"It's not gotten too bad yet, but I know where it's going and I just . . . can't go there again."

"Let's just talk coping skills. I'm not saying you shouldn't feel what you feel. But there are different ways to react to those feelings.

"But before I say anything else, Jon, you really need to go slow, please. You know nothing about her, what she thinks, who her family is, and who her friends are. My god, what if she's married?"

"I went slow with Rayiko," Jon said, pulling at his hair. "When I hired her, I didn't bring her on because I was in love with her. I hired her because I thought she would be a good manager for CiliCold three years ago. Then as we began to talk, she would say things to me that no one else ever said that were right about my sense of the business. Where I was right and where I jacked things up, she got through to me about—"

"Not magic, Jon. She got through because you wanted her to. You needed to be reached."

"I opened my heart to her. I don't know…"

"But you do know. You were just spun out of a marriage. Still trying to heal from that bad university business. You were—"

"Alone."

"Disconnected as you are now, desperate for a connection."

"Kevin, I'm not looking for sex—"

"Maybe you should ask yourself why not?" Kevin smiled, nudging the scientist. "Anyway, hold your emotions at bay until you learn about her.

"See her in anguish. See her angry. See her laugh. See her in pain. And let her see the same in you. Once you do that, then I think you're on a good path."

"Is that what you did with Olivia?"

I miss my Olivia so much. Kevin felt her pull on him. "Olivia and I just didn't fall in love. We became close as I began to deal with my wife's imminent death. And as time went on, Olivia and I shared more about each other and came to understand each other. We tipped over into a deeper affection. That real connection took time.

"Maybe nature is kinder to you or maybe she's crueler," Kevin said, holding both hands up. "I don't know. You get the blessing of full emotional exultation, but the bill always comes due, doesn't it."

"Well okay, but like you said, I'm crushing on her. What do I do?"

"Why, meet her, of course. Demystify this."

They both laughed.

"Nature may love you, but she loves the unexpected more. Don't be Nature's victim more than you can stand, Jon. Leave your expectations at home."

BURNING BRIGHT

"Yeah. Hi, Jubal." Ava walked into his office, the hard heels of her leather boots *clack, clacking* on the tile floor. "I hadn't seen you all day and . . ."

She stopped talking, letting her eyes be taken in by all of the writing on the wall. "Yeah, yeah, yeah, yeah," *What is all of this?*

The entire writable walls in his office were full of the alpha-i-one-like thingies.

Mathematicians.

"Jubal, you in here? Oh." she felt Jubal bump into her.

"Sorry, Ava," he said, brushing by, "didn't mean to bump you. Are you okay?"

"Yeah, yeah, yeah. I'm fine until I saw all of this."

Jubal looked at it all on the wall. "Well, it's a start. To what, I don't know."

She swallowed. Jubal seemed kinda hangdog. He'd been weird all week, not moping but not saying much.

"Yeah, yeah, well, I came in to tell you that I now have the molecular cars ready on this molecular train. Luiz and I can now take a short protein apart and tell you its constituent parts while still inside the living cell." She stopped there. The more she told him about their progress, she thought, the worse he would feel.

Why did young people see a misstep not as a stumble but a leap into hell?

"So yeah, my molmacs tell you that, and—"

"And I put them in this formula."

"Yeah, yeah, yeah," she said. "But there're just twenty amino acids possible so why do you have almost a hundred terms?"

"Maybe a special sequence of them appears. If it occurs commonly, then I want to pick it up, so—"

"Yeah, yeah. You are trying to extract all the information that's in the short protein, right?"

"Well, I can take amino acids two at a time or three at a time."

"Yeah, yeah. That's a lot of combinations to include?"

"What does that mean about language?" Jubal sat down. "I thought I knew, but I don't know, actually."

Ava sat next to him. Both with their backs to the wall, looking at the formulas. "I think I see where you may be stuck."

He turned to her. "Please tell me 'cause I sure don't see it."

"Forget the math for a few minutes. How do you say my culture in Polish?"

'Wait . . . oh. Mój kultura."

"Yeah, yeah. Right but terrible accent. Sounds like Polish spoken by a Hoosier."

"Well," the young scientist said, now smiling. "Here I am."

"Why don't you find some space and write it on the board."

"Sure thing. He got up, walked across the office, and started writing." When done, he stepped back.

She turned to him. "Yeah. We are both victims of our culture.

"The problem is that you're a mathematician, not a linguist. You and I look at the writing on the page, and we automatically break it down into letters and words. Even if we don't know the language, that's what we do. We also," she continued, waving her hand in front of her, "assume we're going to read in one direction."

"Left to right."

"Okay, but think back three and a half billion years ago, there was no language at all. Communication made no sense because there was nothing, well"—she threw her hands up in the air—"to communicate with. So we have to start with what they started."

"Conformation."

"Yeah, yeah." She clapped her hands. "All these small peptides could do was configure themselves into interesting three-dimensional shapes. And sometimes other molecules reacted to them, fit into them, making more shapes

"Not words. Hieroglyphics."

"And three-dimensional ones to boot. Yeah."

"Chemistry is always three dimensional. Of course its language would match."

"Yeah, yeah. So a three dimensional peptide-receptor fit means communication."

"And your value function, your measure, would be the number of receptors those peptides find."

His eyes opened wide, and his face flushed. She rejoiced as his lights burned bright again.

They both sat on the floor again, watching not the wall, but a new world opens before them.

REDLINES

*B*reathe, Olivia reminded herself, sitting across from Cong. Sydney Pitt in the lobby of the InterContinental Willard Hotel. Pulling his glasses out, the congressman sat them on his bronze, aquiline nose, and in a gravelly voice, read,

> 1- FDA comes under control of United States Department of Justice. Only the Justice Department will issue approvable or non-approvable letters for new prescription drugs and devices.

> 2- Strip FDA of all clinical trial design and review responsibilities. These activities will be conducted by the National Science Foundation. FDA budget to be reduced accordingly with funds going to the NSF. NSF will not hire FDA clinical trial reviewer teams for its work in reviewing clinical trials on behalf of drug companies. In addition, during the review of a clinical trial, there is to be no direct contact between NSF and the sponsor of the drug, all contact going through the Department of Justice.

Olivia studied him, fifty-five-ish, impeccable black suit with a gray tie over a light-blue shirt broadcast his concern for appearance.

The congressman looked up. "My god, Audrey. You—wait one, Leonard?" he called out, turning in his chair.

"Yes, Congressman?"

"Can you please escort my guests and me to a private conference room?"

"The congressman has expressed his approval of the Grant Suite in the past. Would that be suitable?"

"Availability?"

"We had a cancelation for its use this morning. It's actually available now."

They took an elevator to the second floor and then walked down a long hall to a corner.

"Excuse me," the congressman said when they arrived. "Ms. Steadman, have you been here before?" She worked to avoid staring back into his intent eyes.

"Once, many years ago." She tried and failed not to blush.

"When Grant arrived to take control of the Union Armies in late 1863," the Congressman said, "he and his son stayed here. Yet the conference room named for him is one of the smallest if not the smallest in the hotel. I wonder if there is a message in that?"

"They probably named the best room for Meade," Olivia said, smiling.

"Not if Lincoln had a say. He was furious with Gen. George Meade."

"Why? Wasn't it General Meade who won Gettysburg?"

The congressman smiled. "Yes, but Meade didn't push his advantage. He let Lee escape back to Virginia rather than force a day four engagement, crushing Lee's weakened army and ending the war ear— thanks, Leonard. We'll take it from here. Soft drinks?"

"Waiting inside, sir."

"Please ladies be seated," Congressman Pitt said, getting each a drink of their choosing. "Well, Audrey, from what I just read, in two paragraphs, you dismantled an agency that has protected Americans from unsafe drugs."

"Not anymore, Congressman," Olivia said. "The FDA is no longer effective. In fact the agency is in distress and suffering. They are responsible for ensuring the safety of some $2.6 trillion in consumer goods each year but have pitiful few resources to carry that out. And they are slipping."

The congressman crossed his legs. "How so?"

"Too many prescription drugs and medical devices are being approved with too little data on how safe or effective they are, yet marijuana ingredients are blithely sold with little oversight."

"And now, " Olivia continued, putting her Diet Coke down on the cream-colored tablecloth, "they are exposed to political and special interest interference. Plus FDA workers leave the agency and get snapped up by Big Pharma." She shook her head. "It's a shame that they, no, that we let it come to this."

"You're right, of course, Olivia," the congressman said. "Mismanagement of opiates and e-cigarettes is another pair of a black eye that the agency has earned. Essentially, they are now paid by drug companies to do their bidding. Why the no-contact clause?"

"Drug companies meet continuously with FDA during the clinical review process."

"Isn't that good? What if the FDA reviewers have questions?"

"Any questions should be answerable in the drug protocol. These meetings are a procedure to cover sloppy work. The top medical research journals would not permit these meetings, this . . . collusion. Why should the scientists who review these drug applications?"

Audrey put her drink down. "Congressman, it's just one more interface between the FDA and the company where the FDA standards are weakened by permitting a way to bypass them."

"Like so many connections in this field," Olivia said, "what started as a good idea turns into corruption."

He returned to the next points on the pages in his lap.

3- PDUFA ends. Funding for NSF clinical review comes from a direct national pharmaceutical company tax, paid through a new branch of the Internal Revenue service.

"You want to end the Prescription Drug User Fee Act?"

"Yes." Olivia sat back and took a sip from her glass. "It was well-intentioned back in '92, but by paying the FDA, the FDA is beholden to the companies, a tacit quid pro quo."

"Nothing tacit about it," the congressman said, removing his glasses and looking up. "I spoke out against this but didn't get enough of my colleagues to listen. I also like the idea of taxing the companies for money that would go into the review of their own drugs." He returned the page.

4-NSF will be charged with building a *de novo*, a comprehensive adverse event database. All side effects will be reported on prior FDA approved and on newly Justice Department approved drugs. NSF will be responsible for reporting adverse event trends and patterns to the CDC for publication to the general public through all relevant media outlets.

"I'm afraid Ms. Steadman, I don't know much about this one."

"Drug companies have their own proprietary systems. None is state of the art. The FDA's own system is nothing to brag about."

She sighed. "We need adverse event information reported on different but related classes of drugs to be able to cross-correlate, anti-inflammatory agents for example. They are made by different companies and reported using different databases. Yet it's a struggle to understand the totality of information on these drugs across all companies.

"What we need is a comprehensive and flexible national system that collects adverse event information directly from the patients and healthcare providers. This will permit a uniform collecting process that leads to uniform reporting."

"The National Science Foundation can do this?"

"Yes, if appropriately funded."

"Let me guess. The money would come from FDA's current budget?"

"Yes, sir, they won't need it anymore."

"But to work, the database must be used."

"Yes." She pointed to the document. "Please move on."

> 5- Newly approved drugs will be provided to the public at *di minims* charge for one year. All adverse event reports must be made through the NSF safety database. Any pharmacist, healthcare provider, or drug company that does not report side effects of its clients or customers will be punished with fines ranging from $1,000 to $10,000,000 depending on the severity of the infraction to be determined by the US AG's office.

"Free prescription drugs the first year in return for compulsory reporting. I get that, but you're going to have to compensate the companies for that first-year outlay."

"I was wondering that myself," Olivia said. "Why don't we extend the patents that they hold on these drugs for an additional two years? That way, if the drug is successful, then they get complete market exclusivity for this added time."

"I think that I could sell that," the congressman said, putting his Diet Coke down on the table and then reading aloud,

6-The US Department of Justice will set infraction metrics for pharmaceutical companies based on A) misstatement of drug efficacy, B) Notes of Concern and publication retractions, C) drug label infractions in misbranding and mislabeling, D) price gouging, E) inappropriate contact between the company and the NSF using a three strike rule. Three infractions in a two-year period will generate a 'redline' report from the NSF to the Justice Department, triggering an automatic nationalization of the offending drug and or device company.

7- When the redline report is released, the US Attorney General's office will notify the FDA of the nationalization event. The AG's office will terminate senior management of the drug company pending a decision to prosecute and authorize the FDA to conduct a full review of the offenses, placing its people in key, temporary leadership positions.

All costs associated with nationalization will come directly from profits made by non-offending drug company production and shareholder dividends.

The FDA will report in three months to the AG's office. In receipt of this guidance, the Attorney General will determine whether the infractions require company termination. In addition, two nationalizations in ten years generates company asset liquidation, with drug/device production rights auctioned off to the miscreant company's US competitors.

"Good God. This is a ton." After a pause, he said, "A ton, has it really come to this? Nationalizing the industry."

"Congressman Pitt, a few things if I may?"

Olivia thought he looked like a man now questioning the quality of a meal that he just ate.

"First, we are not as you put it, 'nationalizing the industry.' It focuses only on a company that refuses to ensure that its prescription drugs are safe and effective. If the companies accept and comply their survival will not be threatened by the US government.

"Second, in this country, nationalization has come to mean the government will buy a stake in it. There is no such financial link here.

We are taking the company over to help ensure that it one, doesn't violate additional federal government codicils and two, plumb the depths of the infraction for additional concerns. And the takeover is time limited— three months, plus shareholders pay. At its root, it's a shareholder-sponsored investigation and restructuring."

"And why should shareholders pay?"

"Well, Congressman, shareholders have been making money from miscreant companies for decades. There is a price for that."

He shook his head. "May sell on Main Street. But not Wall Street."

So what? Olivia choked back her riposte. "When the time comes, we'd like you to sponsor this bill."

Pitt pulled his glasses down just at the tip of his nose and read again. "You know my record. I have not been a fan of the drug companies and certainly am not a fan of the FDA and its recent decisions. But this is going very far. What do you do again, Olivia?"

"I used to be a chief regulator for Tanner Pharmaceuticals before they were purchased by Triple-S. I, like you, know where many of the bodies are buried. I think it's time for a reformation of the drug industry. And this bill will go a long way to do it."

"I will need to study this in detail. And of course, it's got to go through the legislative writing branch."

"We understand that, Congressman," Audrey said, leaning forward over her cross legs. "I think that there is no hurry with this. We understand it's going to run into difficulty."

"Difficulty?" the congressman said, eyebrows raised looking over the contents of the papers again. "It's going to be dead on arrival. The Republicans are going to have a field day with this. Libertarians, I don't know what they're going to think. Some will say that it's a super regulation, and we're better off leaving things as we are. What do you think's going to happen that's going to change their minds?

"Congressman, one thing that I've learned in the drug industry is you don't have to wait very long before they produce another self-imposed disaster. I fear that's what's coming soon."

He placed the table in front of him. "They're certainly not going to support a bill that looks like this. Plus, how do you know DOJ is going to support this? Or the National Science Foundation, or for that matter, the FDA itself?"

"Well, the Department of Justice is precisely the branch of government that has the teeth we need. The NSF is looking to expand its purview, and they have an impeccable reputation."

"FDA?"

"They don't get a vote."

Pitt sat back. "Nationalization."

"There are many good players in the industry," Olivia said. "But unfortunately, like so many things, the private industry is focused more on money. And year after year, that focus on money increases at the expense of safety.

"We don't threaten to nationalize many industries in this country," Pitt said. "Even when they are highly profitable, for example, the electronics industry."

"But people have a choice as to what computer they can buy," Audrey said. "They choose their own cell phone. They may not have a choice for anticancer drugs.

"Now drug companies compete against each other for money. And when, in fact, they have a winner on their hands, they get the opportunity to make the money that they can from that. But they do not have to skimp on safety."

"Well, I certainly take your point about a national adverse event database reporting system," the congressman said."

"Sir," Olivia said leaning forward, "it is essential to us, and I think you understand this, that our preliminary work on this bill is a closely held secret. The drug companies know the political system and how to manipulate it.

Pitt shook his head. "Resistance, they'll declare war Old Testament style, fire and brimstone, and in an election year."

"But, Congressman, what if, by standing up for this bill you're able to do what your constituency sees is your duty to do? After all, any drug debacle will impact your constituency as well."

The congressman leaned forward, eyes narrowed. "What exactly do you know, Olivia?"

"That the companies and the FDA are manifestly incompetent. With Big Pharma hell-bent on dollars and the agency sucking their kneecaps, the pair won't miss an opportunity to generate a disaster."

The congressman sat back in his chair. "Hmmm. I am sure that I can find some bill cosponsors on my side. What about the Senate though? Anybody in mind to sponsor there?"

"Congressman, we were thinking about Charleston Dukes from Oklahoma."

"What, a Republican?" He shook his head. "Well, that's a thought, and it certainly would be a major advantage to have this bill have bipartisan support."

He was quiet for a moment. "But I just don't think it's possible to bring one senate Republican on board, much less cosponsors, and much less a majority of the Senate that could overcome any veto."

"Sadly, Senator, I think that's going to be the least of our problems."

RECEPTOR SPACE

"Jubal, you're here early," Jon said, walking into the young mathematician's office.

"Hi. Well, breakfast kinda blew up in my face, so I thought I'd nip into work."

Jon studied the theoretician in his trademark jeans, sweatshirt, and bright yellow jacket.

"So assuming for a moment that your breakfast actually didn't explode, what did happen?"

"This girl sat next to me, and we fell into a conversation."

He paused for a moment. "Then I made, uh, I made a mistake."

"What did you do—"

"I told her what I did for a living."

Jon walked closer, squinting. "Which is?"

"I generate language building, measure-theoretic functions in receptor space."

Jon laughed. "She probably thought you were on drugs."

"Maybe I should be."

"I don't know much about women," Jon said, shaking his head, "but I do know that people in general have little patience with mathematics.

"Except," he said, continuing to laugh, "you and my own Indiana legislature a hundred-odd years ago. Didn't they try to change the value of pi?"

"Now wait a minute." Jubal shot his hand out. "I had nothing to do with that . . . that magnificent piece of legislation." He smiled.

Jon put a hand on the young scientist's shoulder. "I've learned that just because you can't figure out what you did wrong doesn't make it right."

"Uh."

"Look. Just explain what you said."

"Is this like a date?"

"Forget it."

They both laughed. "Okay. Ava and I are working on something like this."

Jubal pointed to the board and Jon walked over.

$$\int \Omega(\tau) \int_{\Omega(R)} f(\omega_i) \, d\phi(\omega_j) \, d\tau(\omega_j)$$

"Wow," Jon said, hands in his pockets, "you're capturing the ability of . . . a peptide to make a contribution to . . . the . . . language you're learning.

"So," the chief scientist continues, walking closer to the whiteboard, "translated, this means that your mathematics has built up from measuring the presence of a small peptide to whether it is recognized by the receptor to whether the cell reacts—"

"Making noise"

"To whether it contributes to language. Well shoot, Jubal, why didn't you just tell her that?"

"Because she would have called the police on me."

"Wait up," Jon said. "Maybe you started this whole thing backward."

"Not following you,"

"Why not start your discussion this morning with your formula? When he or she asked what you do, then show them. Don't tell them. Begin with a picture, not words. Mystery, not confusion. If they react with a question, then you can start to explain."

"What?"

"If they ask questions, then start slowly and answer at the level of their question. On the other hand, if they don't ask—"

"Let it go."

"Now go get some breakfast."

"One other thing, Jon," Jubal said, running his hand through thick hair. "I initially thought that small proteins would interact close to where we placed them."

"Which is where?"

"Just inside the cytoplasm, the spot where they were absorbed by the cell. So we wouldn't have to look very far away from the peptides' landing site to see if they combined with a receptor or not. But we saw that our peptides can be destroyed before they have a chance to connect with a receptor.

"How so?"

"Ava calls them lysozymes."

"Yes," Jon said, "small pockets of strong destructive chemicals, like detergent."

"That's what she said. They scoop up and denature the small peptide before it has a chance to react with a receptor. It's like there are walls of lysozymes that these proteins have to fight through in order to find a receptor."

"Like baby turtles on the beach on their first march to the sea, huh?"

"Maybe the lysozymes know something we don't," Jubal said, scratching his head with both hands while staring at his formula.

RUMBLINGS

Laurence "JJ" Swath had just finished lunch with the ex-director of Health and Human Services and reached for his buzzing cell phone as the elevator accelerated down to the first floor.

"JJ, I'm getting rumblings of a new bill."

"From where, Suzy?"

"Private source."

He grunted. "There are rumblings all the time. What's the concern here?"

"Easier if I just get them to you."

"Not email. Can you text them?"

"Yes."

They hung up, and a moment later the phone buzzed once more. He enlarged the attached JPEG file and read the file again and again.

"If somebody's going after Big Pharma, then they're going to get squashed," he said under his breath, heavy wheezing covering his words.

"You getting off, sir?"

"What?"

"First floor."

"No. Back to forty."

A minute later, Swath stepped out onto the fortieth floor and into the Citadel, known for its large offices and breathtaking view of the National Mall.

He yelled, "Cindy."

His receptionist stood. "Yes, sir?"

"Let's convene Alcatraz."

"As you say."

ONE MORE FAN

"Hi, Kevin," Jon called from his android, raising his voice over the background noise of cars sloshing through the car wash.

"Hey, Jon, where are you?"

"I'm here in Santan, trying to get my car washed."

"Satan? Must be a nasty day, you going to hell without dyin'—"

"Santan."

"Oh," Kevin said.

Jon laughed. Kevin was becoming quite the joker with Olivia gone. *Good for him.*

"Jubal is really excited. He wants to talk to you."

"You bet. I heard from Ava earlier and she told me about talking with him, turned him on to an idea."

"Know when you'll be here?"

"Sure, I should be there in about twenty. Bye."

Jon hung up and watched his car being dried. He liked these car washes. Easy to be alone, and easy to talk to strangers.

Paying the attendant, he walked into the convenience store and s—

Couldn't it be the same woman?

Now a customer was in line.

How could this even be possible?

It was her, alright.

It was the same uneven shoulders, the left lower than the right. It was the same black hair and her smell, Light lavender. *Sun heating a wheat field after a rain.*

She paid with cash and stepping to the left, turned around, facing him.

For five, then ten seconds they looked at each other.

His heart raced, but in the rare, sweet world where time slowed. He felt every vibration of every heartbeat.

The determination of her eyes held him, transfixed him.

He relaxed, preparing to stay forever.

She suddenly jerked to the right.

Turning that way, he saw a hand pulling her purse, then pulling her.

He smacked the new dirty arm down and then kicked hard, his heel punching the assailant's soft abdomen.

The man fell back, reaching into a front sweatshirt pocket with his left hand.

Gun, he thought

He fired.

Jon dropped to the ground, clutching his right arm.

The man turned away, and Jon stuck his left leg out, tripping the thief up.

Letting the purse fall, the thief fell.

Jon leaped onto his back, his face in the man's neck, the thief now bucking, screaming.

"You are not going anywhere." Jon put his right knee in the man's low back.

"Somebody give me a damn pen," the scientist called out.

A pen appeared to his right. Taking the pen with his right hand and clicking, he placed the point of the pen hard into the back of the neck, breaking the skin.

"You keep fighting," Jon whispered into the dirty ear, "and I will pith you with what you feel on your neck." Jon pressed the pen harder, blood now flowing freely around it. "You'll never walk again, and the remaining meals of your miserable life you'll eat with a straw."

The struggle ended, and the thief was lying in silence, breathing hard.

●

"That's the story, Officer," Jon said, sitting on a bench outside after he'd about caught his breath.

"What about your arm?" the thin officer standing above him asked.

Jon looked around, catching his breath. "What about the victim?"

"She was unhurt, so after getting her brief statement and contact info, we let her go."

"Thanks." He looked at his arm. "I'll get a tetanus shot."

"Okay with me, but do us all a favor." The officer put a hand on Jon's shoulder. "Let the medics look you over before you go. Just want to be cautious."

"One final question," the burly officer sitting next to him said. "What did you threaten to do to him? Fith him?"

"Pith him."

"What's that?"

Jon saw that the officer had stopped typing on his iPad.

"Take a sharp object and break the skin. Feel for the space between the vertebral processes or spines. Jab down hard to puncture the protective neural sheath. Then move your sharp object violently in and out, up and down, side to side. You'll ruin the neural connections forever to the body below where you stabbed. I'm a doc—"

"We know who you are, Dr. DeLeon. The victim told us."

What?

"Thanks for your help. I hope you don't mind more attention because when the media finds out, they won't let you alone."

He smiled. "Time for another trip."

"Thanks again. Oh," the burly officer said, handing Jon a crumbled sheet, "the victim left this for you. Hope you got room for one more fan, Doc."

●

That night, bone tired, Jon rolled into bed at 6:30 PM. It was already dark outside. He closed his eyes, drifting off.

The note.

He wrestled back and forth for a moment, deciding whether to get out of the warm bed and retrieve the note. But he knew what he was going to do as soon as he thought about it.

Thirty seconds later, he was in the laundry room, fetching his jeans from the dirties bin.

Opening the wrinkled piece of paper. It said,

"Lion, I will find you."

CHASING THE SUN

"Leanne," the ex-CEO said into her cell as she got in the limo heading to Baltimore. "To what do I owe the pleasure?"

"How are you, Meredith? And how have you been?"

"I'm fine."

The usual, reflexive response, she thought for a second. "Actually better than when we first met."

"Meredith, I'm calling to tell you that we have a case involving Ascension."

"Where?"

"Iowa state court. Plaintiff's a three-year-old child. I remember our conversation and wanted to know if you have any interest in being involved."

The ex-CEO held her breath. She had thought about it, the complexities, the work, and the consequences for her career.

"Sure, I've thought about it. Just haven't made up her mind, I'm afraid."

"What do you need t—"

It hit her.

"Give me three days."

"Okay, let me know. This judge wants to move quickly. Discovery will likely end in three months, and we have to get you prepped."

"Okay." Closing the cell she said to her driver, "Let's go back home, Willis."

•

"Good evening, Ms. Doucette," Dillon the pilot said twenty-four hours later. She saluted up at him, then climbed the three steps of the light jet's ladder.

"You're the only navy person who salutes me."

"Make it a smooth one, Dillon," she said with a smile punching him on his shoulder, "or you won't even get that."

"Yes, ma'am."

After she was belted into the six-seater, the two-person crew buttoned up the plane, and then revving the engines, they began a quick taxi to the active runway. One minute later, they were ascending out of the Dover Air Force Base to the Signature Flight Support, FBO in Indianapolis.

I should travel like this more often, she thought. The rest and solitary time restored her. *I should take some notes—*

She was asleep in a moment as the jet continued its climb, chasing the setting sun.

●

"Yes ma'am," the Expert Limousine service driver said the next day, "3405 N. Festomer Drive."

Meredith got out. There was a clear sky but temps just in the sixties. The ranch houses all looked the same, well kept on immaculate bright green lawns, even this house with its For Sale sign.

But no one's home. What did this trip cost me?

"You buying this house, lady?"

A young woman, she guessed maybe nineteen or twenty, riding a bike, had just come around the limo and stopped in front.

'Hi. No. I'm looking for the Sanders family."

"Crisse? Crisse's family?"

"The girl walked the bike over.

"Yes. I am Meredith Cr—"

"Dani. I'm Dani."

"Cristen was going to work for me, but—"

"She died. I know."

"Did she have any family?"

"No. She just talked about her daddy but even that not so much."

"Do you have a minute?"

"Yes."

"You were Crisse's friend? What can you tell me about her?"

The breeze picked up. "Come, Dani, sit with me," the ex-CEO said, gesturing the girl into the limo's back seat.

She watched Dani carefully put the kickstand down and with a gentle touch let the bike rest, then got in.

"Wow, some girls go to prom in this," Dani said.

The ex-CEO watched her look around the limousine's interior.

"Anyway, she worked hard. I saw her a lot except of course for winter. She loved her bike. This is it," she said, pointing to the sparkling bicycle with its glistening wheels. "She gave it to me the last day I saw her."

Dani lowered her voice. "She came to my house that day to give me her bike and left me this note."

Dani got out, stepped over to the bike's small saddleback, then came back with a folded piece of paper.

The ex-CEO read the note.

"A month after you read about me, send this email . . ."

A month. So the suicide wasn't spontaneous, Meredith thought. *It was planned weeks in advance.*

"My daddy could be mean, and he was tough on her. She wasn't mean back, but she squared off on him once without disrespect but wanted to make sure her opinion was heard. I always remember that day. It was the one time I ever saw someone . . . so . . . . so full of—"

"Ang—"

"Bravery."

•

Back in the air that evening, Meredith was lost in thought, the email like a marble following the grooves of her mind.

In a sense, the note was from Cristen to not just Dani but to the future and to people who could pursue multiple drug safety crimes of SSS in which she refused to begin to participate after the merger.

So Cristen did not commit suicide because of some bizarre mental instability. She killed herself because she did not want to join Triple-S and take part in their multiple drug safety crimes.

She would rather die than participate.

Litigation against Triple-S would be time-consuming.

And it would hurt. Leanne all but promised that.

Ten years ago, Meredith would never have considered this, but the denigration and the deaths had occurred on her watch. Now her heart full of grit and determination started its new cadence, its hot war beat.

This had to be corrected, a messy business, to be sure, but at least she could start where Cristen left off.

In the limo heading home after the smooth landing, she picked up her cell.

"Nita? Its Meredith. Where you able to get the records from the Exec meeting"

"Hi Meredith. The last one?"

"Yes"

"I got them."

"Can I have somebody stop by? No, can I stop by tomorrow?"

"Yes, although the afternoon is best."

"I'd love to spend time with your family."

"See you then How are you?"

"The ex-XEO smiled. "Not worried anymore."

●

Kevin and Jon walked outside.

"That was a rough session. You ask great questions."

Jon heard his president sigh.

"You enjoying all of this, Kevin?"

"I don't think there is a more exciting job in the world or a harder one. I feel like my brain is a bike, and I'm riding it hard."

"Don't despair. If this were easy, it would have been cracked alrea—"

A text came. Jon pulled out his cell. There was an image of Santan car wash.

"Hot date?"

"My friend," Jon said, putting his hand on Kevin's arm. "I have no idea."

BOWLING

Jon turned his Cherokee right from Gilbert onto 202 E toward Santan car wash. He had no idea what he was going to say, the sun behind turning everything into autumn gold.

You've been attracted for months. Months.

Yet they had never really spoken, but now she'd sent a text after a note, to what, get to know him?

"Probably wants me to wash her car," he said aloud, laughing.

Have fun, Kevin said, he thought as he turned into the convenience store parking lot. The scientist got out, walked through the store to the back entrance, and opened the door to the drying lot.

"Well, here goes nuthin'," he said to the windshield.

•

There she was, sitting by herself at a round stone table.

"Hey," he said, sitting across the table. She looked up and he saw her face now. He watched her study him unhurriedly.

Her dark eyes were set in light skin under long black hair that swept up and over her head. He tried not to stare at the old scar.

"My name is Jon."

"I know. I am Raven."

She sat tall, maybe five feet ten or eleven inches. Her voice was quiet, steady, and strong.

In command of herself, he thought.

"Raven, I confess I don't know anything about you and don't even know how to begin to describe myself."

He watched her look back at him.

"But what I can do is tell you a story."

"I like stories," she said, smiling.

"Have you ever gone bowling?"

She nodded and as her eyes now locked on his, he breathed easier.

"Well, when I was in college, there was a girl, two years ahead of me, that I liked. Thing is, I didn't know how to get to know her. We didn't have common classes. I thought about asking her to dinner, but I didn't want us sitting across a table, looking at each other with nothing to say.

"So I asked her if she would go bowling with me.

"She agreed. We chose a date, and when the day arrived, I walked to her apartment.

"Now." Jon shrugged. "I'm kind of a shabby bowler. Maybe I bowled 105 or 110 on a good night. Anyway, I helped her put her coat on, and with her purse in one arm, she picked up a canvas bag.

"I asked her, 'What's in the bag?'"

"She said, 'That's my bowling ball.'"

Raven didn't smile, but things felt lighter.

Jon slumped back in his chair. "I know that I rolled my eyes. I mean, seriously. All I'm doing is looking for a simple date, and here she was preparing to bowl me all over that alley.

"Well, we're making small talk on the way to the lanes. When we get there, I ask her what size shoes she wears so I can rent them. I think they were twenty-five cents a pair."

"She says, 'I brought my own.'"

"So you know how this night will go," he continued. "I get up first and threw, knocking down seven. Next throw I miss the standing three.

"I sat down, and she got up. She was really excited, put her own glove on, grabbed her ball, walked her steps to the lane, and threw the ball down the alley. I mean, she hurled that ball. I just sank back in the plastic chair as it flew down, hit the wood, and slammed right into the gutter like a thunderclap.

"Next one. Gutter. Frame after frame.

"Once she knocked down two pins. She was so excited. Then . . . gutter, gutter, gutter, gutter.

"I learned two things that night. First was that you never, ever go by anybody's appearance. How they look, how they comport themselves, how they act, and what they wear. Be guided by performance, then character, not their history or appearance."

"What was the second?"

Jon tried and failed to wipe the smile from his face. "Never laugh at your date."

Raven smiled and then giggled. Then she laughed. And with that laugh, Jon felt the burden of the world was lifted from his shoulders.

When she was done, she looked at him. "So, Lion, want to go bowling?"

•

"How many games did we bowl? I told you I was bad." He said, opening his sourdough burger at the Jack in the Box around the corner when they were done.

"A lot of people are worse," she said. "Fortunately, I am not one of them."

He pointed his finger at her and they both laughed.

"Why couldn't you have this kind of date the first time?"

"What?"

"With the college girl you liked?"

"I don't know," Jon said, putting his burger down on the napkin. "It was so . . . stiff. She was all in with the trappings of the game, but none of the skills. I, on the other hand, was much too eager to laugh at her but you know, didn't laugh at myself. So the date failed."

He shrugged. "Something like that."

"You brought too much to lose," Raven said, wiping her mouth. "Tonight—"

"I had nothing to lose tonight." He paused. "Maybe nothing to hide."

He took a breath. "I'm originally from Indiana. I moved here with my company to get some space to do some work."

"I know."

"You know?" He talked in mid-chew. "How do you know?"

"I found a picture of you on the web. You have done some good things."

"We are committed."

"To what?" She stared at him.

He smiled. "To some of my radical notions."

Jon watched as she sat up straighter. "Why did you help when you saw me the last time?"

He leaned across the small table, eyes narrowing and pulse now hammering. "I could not watch you suffer."

She placed her hand on his arm.

"Tell me about you, Raven."

"Maybe next time. It's time to go now," she said, standing.

He drove them back to where he met her at the car wash.

●

Driving home, he was just as puzzled as he was on the drive to the car wash earlier that evening. Yet there was no anxiety, just a peace he didn't understand.

KIDS THESE DAYS

"Now, Lee, let's just let me do the talking, okay?" Dr. Toliver said as he turned to walk down the hall to the small conference room in his office

The fourth-year medical student's heart pounded. He had chosen a pediatric elective, and here he was in the midst of something.

Lee walked down the hall, sweating as he passed the examination suites, walked into the conference room, and was greeted by a stunner.

He guessed five foot seven. The perfect teeth shown through a smile that itself would melt glaciers. She had gorgeous hazel eyes set in smooth tanned skin and had thick blonde hair down to the neckline. *What's the side view like?* he wondered as she jutted forward to shake their hands,

"Dr. Toliver, so happy to see you again," she said.

"Jasmine, it's been a while. This is Lee Phillips, my pediatric student for the month. Lee, this is Jasmine Edison my Triple-S representative."

"Good morning, Ms. Ed—"

"Any new articles for me, Jasmine?" the senior instructor asked.

Here we go, Lee thought. He didn't worry about the rebuff. Such was the life of a medical student.

"Well, Triple-S tries to keep us all up to date," she said. "And I try to keep you current. The past four or five weeks, there hasn't really been anything. But," she said, peeling the paint off of the wall with her smile, "I understand that you have something for me."

"Yes, I was going to call the FDA hotline, but I wanted to talk with you about it first since you were coming in.

"We have a three-year-old who has sudden difficulty with muscle control after receiving Ascension," Dr. Toliver said.

"Oh," she said, "this is a concern. What else do you know about it?"

She doesn't seem too surprised. Maybe she already knows, Lee thought, watching Dr. Toliver explain.

"Well, he's been admitted to Twin Cities Mercy Hospital. And so far, no one seems to understand what's happening. He was fine until three days ago when his parents noticed he was having difficulty swallowing."

Difficulty swallowing? He was gagging and throwing up.

He watched the leggy blonde sit on the conference table, closer to the doctor. "There was some concern in the drug's initial testing about children with muscle problems," she said. "The FDA looked at that thoroughly, and in the end, they were comfortable. After all, they approved the drug."

She's playing him. Lee's pulse rate kicked up.

"Well, no question of that. But we do have a child on our hands with a disorder that looks remarkably similar to what was described in the original Ascension clinical trial on clinicaltrials.gov."

"Oh, Doctor," she said, crossing her legs and waving her hand at him. "You really can't believe everything that's out there, especially on a federal website."

Way wrong answer, Lee thought. That government website was held in high regard worldwide.

"Oh, I thought they were pretty reliable."

"Trust me, they're not."

"Well, I think it would be wise to contact the FDA."

"Dr. Toliver," she said, leaning over the small conference room, "why don't you let me do that?"

"Why can't I just call them?"

"Well, there are a few reasons. One is, of course, you're no longer the treating physician."

"I'm his pediatrician," he said. Lee watched as Toliver gripped the chart in his hand tight.

"Once this patient was hospitalized, you become disconnected. You don't know the patient's current situation as we sit here now, right?"

Lee saw Dr. Toliver take a long breath. "I suppose that's true."

"You don't know what medications he's on. What's been his progress in the past twenty-four hours? What are the specialists thinking? SSS has relationships with the doctors at the hospital, and we can learn this information in a flash and share it with the FDA. Also—"

"What, Jasmine?"

"I must tell you that some plaintiff attorneys looking for cases search for adverse events reported by physicians. They make the argument that reporting the adverse event makes you complicit in the occurrence of it."

"All I'm doing is reporting it."

"No, sir," she said, staring at him hard. "You gave the medicine that likely caused it. Now, you know I'm not saying that this is all your fault. But in fact, appearances can be very different than what you may think."

Blackmail. Lee was having trouble breathing.

"Certainly. But even if you're not involved, the fact that you filed the adverse event form may bring you into a lawsuit."

"I'm just not following you. Why—"

"By suing a local doctor, it's much easier for plaintiffs to keep the trial in state court and out of federal court where plaintiff attorneys are likely to lose. So they're looking for local defendants.

"And there's no local defendant better than a doctor. Even if they drop you from the suit, don't you have to list on your medical license renewal that you were sued? How about on your request to renew hospital privileges?" She shook her head. "It's all so complicated. Mercy."

Lee'd had it. "It's his right to file. Maybe even his duty," the medical student blurted out. "If you want to file as well, then go ahead, but don't suggest Dr. Toliver shouldn't report this case."

"I love these medical students," she said, winking at the doctor. "So full of zeal, but oh so ignorant about the real world."

She turned to Lee, and smiling, said, "Kids these days.

"Before I go, Dr. Toliver, can you give me the details about this patient? Be more than happy to go ahead and file the adverse event report through Triple-S."

"Thank you," The doctor said, glaring at Lee. "Maybe that would be best."

•

Two weeks later, still in the grip of a hot August, Lee pushed aside his "below average evaluation" by Dr. Toliver and logged into the FDA website.

He didn't see a single case of neurodegenerative disorder from the Twin Cities area listed.

ALCATRAZ

"Olivia?"

She turned, having stepped out into the crisp Chevy Chase air. She saw that it had rained just enough to coat the leaves and bring out their crisp yellows, reds, and oranges.

There was Audrey, one foot out of the back of a limo and on the asphalt.

"Well," Olivia said, laughing, "you stalking me or what?"

"You'd better get in."

Olivia slipped in and closed the door. The driver drove out with the blinker on and made a left turn heading north to Bethesda.

"Something wrong?"

"Everything."

"Are you okay?"

"I'm fine. But word is out about our bill."

Olivia set forward in the seat. "How could that be?"

"We should talk about that. But we are in play. I just heard from Alcatraz."

Olivia's head was spinning. "I don't know what that means?"

"It's a group of action-oriented lobbyists controlled by a super-lobbyist named Swag. His nickname is Super Swag."

"Leaping tall buildings in a single bound?"

"He's a lawyer who's been in the lobbying industry for thirty years," Audrey said, words just tumbling out of her mouth. "He has incredible expertise and gets to talk to anyone. The drug industry has been an important client of his for a long time. And Swag's convening the Alcatraz group about our yet unnamed bill."

"How do you know?"

"Because, dear, I'm a member."

169

FEDERALIST PAPERS

*N*o. Olivia's lunch lurched up and almost out of her mouth. "So, you too—"

"No. I'm just a member in rebellion."

Olivia slumped back in the posh leather. "So we've been discovered."

"Yes. And if we're not careful, there's going to be hell to pay."

Olivia turned to her. "What do you mean?"

"These lobbyists are very good at positive and negative lobbying."

"Translate for me." *This is terrible.* She felt her hand begin to shake.

"Positive lobbying means talking to senators, congressmen, giving them inducements to vote their way. They even gift congressional staff."

"Inducements? You mean money?"

"Principally campaign contributions. But also, there are negative inducements. This group has been known to organize PACs and to *primary* uncooperative members of Congress."

"Should be illegal."

"Tell that to James Madison"

Olivia just stared. "I don't—"

"What do you think the federalist papers were but lobbyist fodder."

"I assume this is all legal then. First Amendment protected free speech and all. And this Alcatraz knows about us."

"No, just that something is in the works. But how?"

"I know," Olivia said. "Take us back to my apartment."

Twenty minutes later, Olivia walked out of her sitting room, phone in hand, to join Audrey.

"Well?" Audrey said, now breathing rapidly. "Who?"

MEN BEING MEN

"Angelo."

"What?" Audrey's hand flew to her chest. "One of us?"

"Not exactly. Angelo's dad."

Audrey collapsed on the sofa.

"I just spoke to the five of them on the phone, one by one," the ex-regulator said. "None of them told anybody, but Angelo said that he spoke to his dad."

"I still don't get it. Why—"

"He thinks his dad has a girlfriend who works on K Street." She shrugged her shoulders. "So Angelo told his dad about the bill idea meaning no harm, and his dad told his girlfriend, and the girlfriend took some notes and ran it up the flag pole to Swag."

Audrey thought for a second. "Let's do nothing. We're not moving forward with this bill yet. It's just ideas written down on the page. Let's not do anything and let the dogs go back to sleep."

"Why don't we get some help with that?" Olivia took her phone out.

"Angelo?" Olivia said into the phone, "Yes, I know how strongly you feel about this. I think we can cure it."

She listened.

"Tell your dad that the idea is dead, that there are no interested parties in it. The American people won't accept it, and it's dead on arrival. It's not even going to go for final formatting."

She listened for a minute. "Well, he played you. It's time for you to return the favor. Okay. Bye. And, Angelo, thanks for your honesty."

She hung up and then turned to Audrey.

"Men being men, this will work."

"I've no doubt of that."

"Now, Audrey, tell me more about this Alcatraz," Olivia said, sitting.

"Time was when lobbyists acted independently of one another," Audrey said, taking a chair across from the ex-regulator. "For example, I would lobby for certain bills on my own. I was hired by private corporations to lobby on their behalf.

"It's so much more complex now. A team of lobbyists will get together and lobby for or against an issue. It may be an issue involving the environment, or maybe drug companies or telecommunications.

"But they work together as a team, Olivia, there are two things a great lobbyist must have, expertise in the scope of the bill and access to influential people.

"And," Olivia said, rubbing her face with her right hand, "one lawyer can't know everything about a topic and have good access anymore." She leaned back. "Want a drink?"

"Not me, but thanks. So a team of lawyers get together with different skills. Some of them have tremendous, detailed expertise,

"They share with other members who have access to important people," Audrey said. "They pool their resources and then pull together.

"But it's deeper than that. They can come after you."

"Well, I'm not breaking any law."

"No, but they can shut your access off where people don't return your phone calls anymore. They can also turn over your background again and again digging up what's needed to snap your credibility. They can't hurt you physically of course, but they can make you persona non grata in the offices of people who make a difference and the people to whom we need access."

"What should we do about that?"

"I don't know."

"I do," Olivia said with a smile, "and so do you. Remember, we can always rely on the pharmaceutical industry."

NOTE IN A SONG

Jubal jammed his hands into his jean's pockets. "So we have mathematics that help us listen to peptides bind to receptors and read the message the receptor is receiving."

"That's the stimulus. How do you measure the cell's response?" Jon asked.

"Ava's molmacs can measure a cell's global response, increased energy production, increased ribosomal activity, and general measures."

"Okay." Jon turned to the Polish scientist. "How are we actually getting this message from the cell?"

"Yeah, yeah. I have a molmac use an iron atom in combination with electrons to flick the metal from ferrous to ferric and back again."

"Goodness," Kevin said, "molecular Morse code."

"We should call it—"

"Don't even go there," Emily said.

"'MolMorse'," Jubal said with a smile.

"Have mercy," Jon said, laughing.

"That would be molmercy."

"Please somebody get the mathematician out of here."

"Yeah, yeah. So a molmac is a communication chamber."

"Yes," Emily said, "but it also needs to be close to the cell membrane for it to transmit."

"Like walking to get a good cell phone signal," Kevin said. "I know I'm going to regret asking this, but just how does the molmac get there?"

"Yeah, yeah. I added a rotor to the machine."

"So," Jon said, now standing, "this rotor attached to the molmac powers carrying its way through the cytoplasm to near the membrane, where, another molmac serves as what, an amplification device?"

"A mini cell phone tower."

"More like Bluetooth. Yeah, yeah."

"Dios mio," Luiz said. "Can I listen to it on my headphones?"

"Cell song?" Emily asked. "Like whale song?"

"Since it is near the membrane it can signal out?" Jon asked.

Ava nodded, smiling, almost trembling.

"And that signal is."

"Simple for now, one means success—"

"Meaning that the peptide reacted with the receptor. or that cell activity is up, depending on the machine."

"Zero means failure."

"This fine tunes my function," Jubal said, standing up by the white wall. "The more ones I get, the stronger the peptide's ability to not just react with a receptor but also excite the cell's reaction, and the more credence I give it in providing a . . . a word in the language?"

"More like a note in a song," Kevin said with a smile.

"But you know, we really don't learn a language by listening. I could listen to Farsi all day and be clueless the entire time."

"You're clueless anyway."

Everybody laughed.

"Fair 'nuff, but the one way I'm going to really learn this language is to try to speak it. Make a chemical sound and see what the biochemical reaction is."

"Yeah, yeah." She put both feet on the table. "So learning the language that Jubal taught us by receptor counting and cell reaction is one thing, but the one way to be sure that we know what we're doing is to speak the language back and get the desired effect again and again. Then we've learned how to communicate with the cell."

"Emily and I have started down that path," Jubal said.

They all gathered around the table. "Some of the peptides we gave had no receptors waiting for them, meaning—"

"The cell didn't understand the protein, I mean the message," Emily said as Sparky did a figure eight around and over her boots.

"Right. But other peptides that we gave did find receptors in the cytoplasm," Jubal said, sitting. For some there were hundreds. But I'm troubled,"

"What bothers you?" Kevin asked, seated with eyes closed

"Every protein I get from Ava to translate begins with the same three amino acids. Alanine-glycine-cytosine."

"Yeah, yeah, yeah . . . That is strange."

"N or C terminus"

"N side. The amine end."

"Well, " Jon said, leaning forward, "that's number one hundred sixty-seven on our problem list.

"It's late. Let's pick up tomorrow."

"Agreed," Jon said. "We can beat these issues. We just need time and rest. We're getting there."

EYES WANTING TO BE BLIND

"We made good progress yesterday."

Kevin turned in the parking lot to face Jubal.

"How so?"

"Emily has been a godsend for me," the young scientist said, hands jammed into the pockets of his sports jacket. "Really helped me with this notion of translation."

Kevin basked in the face of his youthful exuberance. "Emily's good people. Hard shell covers a heart of gold. And," Kevin said, "Jubal, I think that Jon made a fine choice in choosing you as our mathematician."

He watched Jubal swell at the compliment. Envying him, he watched as Jubal turned and headed back inside. Working with this group, the mathematician was in the thrill of his lifetime.

Kevin turned to his car. The mornings were cooling off now that it was November, but the afternoons were still warm. He loved it, seeing that he was as lucky as Jubal.

Except Olivia. She filled the niche in him, and he knew it. The death of his wife had left a hole in him, and Olivia had filled it to overflowing. He was full with her. He knew she had to do what she needed to do.

She needed to go.

But he needed her here.

There by his car, someone was standing tall with full long black hair.

She turned to face him. She was pleasant-looking despite the scar, filled in but easily visible, running down from her right eye to her cheek.

Raven. Had to be.

Kevin inhaled.

"We should talk," she said in a strong but haunting voice.

"Let's . . . let's go back inside," Kevin said, pointing.

She didn't move.

"I think your car will be okay, maybe even better."

Kevin, at a loss, let her in.

●

"Raven?"

She looked at him forcefully.

Like she's made up her mind, he thought.

"I just . . ." he started to say. "No. You talk."

"You are Jon's best friend."

He shrugged. "Well, I'm a friend."

"No," she said shaking her head in deliberate motion. "You are his best friend. He speaks of you. He relies on you."

"Okay," he said, keeping his tone down. He noticed that while her voice too was low, her hands were tight in her lap.

"Jon is strong. He saved me without knowing who I was."

"He knew."

She turned. "I didn't know that."

"He was stunned that day at the carwash. He didn't think that he'd ever see you again."

"Yet he looked out for me."

The CEO inhaled.

"I could never be smart like Jon," Raven said, head down, "or intelligent like him or have his vision. But he is weak in some areas. You know this, don't you, Kevin?"

Kevin nodded, now looking at her. *What was this? A warning for Jon, delivered to a trusted friend?*

"And one of those things is not seeing trouble coming."

"Go on." Kevin turned to face her.

"He is consumed by emotion but doesn't see its effects on him, like he's telling you how a train engine works without seeing the locomotive bearing down on him."

"I see this too."

"He told me about this woman in his life."

Kevin nodded. "You mean Rayiko."

"I think he was injured by her."

Why is she saying this? He nodded.

"He's not been the same, Raven, until he met you."

He watched her face turn to face him. The stoicism was gone. He instead stared into eyes that showed they had seen too much and cried too much.

Eyes were yearning for blindness.

He looked away.

"I have nothing, a wind-blown shadow. But, Kevin," she said, head now down and shaking, "I've come to know my purpose now."

She turned to him again with a face now warmed by conviction.

"Jon."

Not a warning, she was being . . . protective.

His eyebrows rose.

"Jon is a drained battery, running from socket to socket for a connection. I am the connection for him."

"Raven, I thi—"

"You are his friend. So I say to you. Jon DeLeon has become my life for me. I will become his. You should know because you protect him too."

"I . . . Can I drive you somewhere, please?"

"No. I'm okay."

She got out, leaving him in the car, overpowered by pure, raw devotion. He sat still, basking in her purpose.

Then he picked up the phone.

"Jon? Let's get some dinner in a couple of hours."

•

The two friends met at Texas Roadhouse on Gilbert and were seated.

"Jubal's really pleased about how things are coming along."

"He has good grounding," Jon said, sitting across the table from his friend. "He just needed some structure."

"Well, he's found it with Ava and Em."

All of a sudden, Kevin was famished. "Let's do some ordering."

"Okay, I'm all in for ribs."

"Steak for me."

"Kevin," Jon said after the waiter left with their orders. "I haven't asked you for a while, but how are you doing without Olivia?"

Kevin sighed. "I can't tell you how much I miss her. Without her, I'm an old man. With her, I'm young."

"I know she's working on something important in Washington but don't know anything about it."

'Olivia found her purpose in life, for right now anyway, in DC. And it is—"

"Here are your orders, gentlemen," the waitress said.

"Jon, Raven came to see me today," Kevin said after she left.

His friend froze in mid-rib bite, staring at him.

"Umm. Why?"

"The impression that you made on her runs deep."

"She said that to you?"

Kevin nodded, looking at his friend.

"Well, she's made a difference in mine," Jon said, picking up a second rib.

"She came to me because she knows I am your friend. I think she meant to convey to me, 'I'm not Rayiko.'"

Jon dropped his rib on his plate.

"I have to say," Kevin said, looking across the table at his friend, "it was one of the most poignant, emotional conversations that I've ever had. I was reluctant to talk to you about this because your relationship with Raven is, well, your relationship with Raven. But you're also my good friend, and I want nothing to be between us. So I wanted to share what she said."

"Do you like her?"

"Like her?" His hands went up in the air. "After today, I adore her."

Jon wiped his hands on his napkin. "I'm trying not to fall too hard for her, but—"

"The heart knows what the heart knows. And as for the rest, you and I can talk anything through."

Jon smiled. "Friends speak, but good friends take good actions. Thanks for yours today."

Kevin leaned back, laughing. "You sound like Raven."

"Good for me." The scientist laughed. "Will you stop hiding the dessert menu over there?"

ZIP CODES

"Yeah, yeah. The thing is, how does the body keep all these messages straight? If Jon is right, and all of these peptides are messages, then there must be some structure. I mean, a peptide arrives at a cell. There are trillions of them. How does the cell know the peptide is meant for it and not some retinal or skin cell?"

"So a cell needs to know that a peptide is made for it." Jubal put his elbows on the desk, resting his chin in his hands. "There are far too many different new peptides and cells would be overwhelmed with them."

Jon watched his team struggle with one more immense problem. His head started to pound.

"Yeah, yeah, yeah. It's like everybody's mail goes to everybody's house."

It became quiet.

"There needs to be a something like a post office," Jubal said in low tones.

"No," Luiz said, standing, "not a post office. Zip codes."

They all looked at him.

"Well, I mean, the zip code allows a letter to be delivered to a specific local community, right?"

"And what?" Jubal asked. "These zip codes sit on or in the peptides?"

"Maybe," Jon asked, now standing and walking the conference room, "In fact, over eons, these peptides could have developed a short protein tag that serves that purpose."

"You mean a short string of amino acids that lets the cell know what its destination should be?" Jubal turned to Ava.

"Yeah, yeah, yeah. And the cell reads that code. Or the membrane reads it. And if that code is for the cell, then—"

"The cell admits it, clips the code off, turning it into another protein—"

"It opens the message."

"And if the peptide doesn't contain the code for the cell, then—"

"Yeah. Then it just destroys it."

"Hence all the killer lysozymes. They kill the messages not meant for the cell."

"Seems wasteful."

"So is a 39 percent efficiency rating in glucose metabolism," Jon said. "But it works, and we're alive for it."

"Yeah, yeah. How do we find out where the zip code is and how long it is?"

"Well, that's pretty easy," Jubal said. "All of the short peptides that go, for example, to chief cells in the stomach should have the same code prefix. It's just a question of commonality of amino acid prefixes in the tissue that we're studying."

"Jubal what was the three code sequence you found?" Jon asked.

"Alanine-glycine-cytosine."

"Well, let's crack on," Luiz said.

NOTE TO SELF

"The subpoena duces tecum arrived," Meredith heard Leanne say over the phone.

She watched the snow fall into the lake in front of the trees whose reigning leaves had the last of their splendid glory shattered by the weekend's icy winds. "We now have a date for the deposition.

"Friday, January 18, 2019."

"Approximately two months away." As an afterthought, Meredith asked, "How many do I have to sit through?"

"Just one. If we were part of the MDL, then well, they may argue that they'd need a few more to—"

"What's that?" *This gets more complicated by the week.*

"MDL stands for multi-district litigation. It's a way to collapse hundreds, if not thousands, of cases into an organized structure that can be managed by a much smaller number of lawyers."

"Hmmm."

"Rather than bring all of those cases to trial and exhaust the different jurisdictional court systems, the cases are all combined into one broad movement, overseen by a single judge, plus a small number of plaintiff and defense attorneys."

"This case, as a single case, is just going to state court. Just one jurisdiction is necessary."

"In Iowa?"

"Yes, Iowa City."

Meredith took a deep breath. "MDL sounds interesting. I'm sure there's a downside. Why aren't we part of the multi-district litigation?"

Leanne was silent. "Well first, there are not many of these Ascension cases yet. Second, even if there were, multi-district litigation is very complicated. For example, we don't control the cases coming to trial. It's a selection process. Plaintiffs choose say five cases. Defense chooses five cases. Then the presi—"

"What?" Meredith said, sitting down in front of her fireplace, long, dark, and cold. "How does the defense get to choose any cases at all? They're all plaintiff cases. How could there be anything else?"

"The idea is to choose both strong cases and weak cases for plaintiffs to take to trial. They're called bell-weather cases. Verdicts in those cases set the value of all of the untried cases."

Meredith rubbed her brow. "I know this makes sense to you, Leanne, but it makes little to me. How could a weak case in say San Luis Obispo affect a strong case in Augusta, Georgia?"

"If two strong cases produce outright acquittals of the drug company, then that finding reduces the value of all of the cases, weak or strong."

"I see. On the other hand, of course, if the weak cases are big wins for plaintiffs then—"

"That increases the value of all of the remaining cases."

"Right, that leads to a formula—"

Goodness. Nothing but the money, Meredith thought.

"That places a settlement value on each case. Defendant pays, plaintiff attorneys retain about 40 percent and the injured get the rest."

"You're right. It's complicated."

"There are other efficiencies. There is a huge reduction in court time and attorney travel just hearing four cases. Yet there's plenty of wrangling among the lawyers over money. I try to stay away from the MDL cases because the facts in these drug cases are complicated enough without adding the sometimes toxic MDL environment."

Meredith shook her head free of these new concerns. "Well, I plan to spend the holiday season preparing"

"Good. First we have to make sure that we turn over all documents that we're going to use in court to the defense."

"Oh why? I mean most of the documents I have, the defense already has and besides, why should we tip our hand to them?"

"That's why it's called discovery. The point of the deposition is to tip our hand. Both sides, both defense and plaintiff witnesses, including you, have to share what we know and what we're going to talk about.

"You will be asked questions about what you're going to testify to. You have to answer those questions honestly and completely as long as you stay within the scope of the question. This way, the defense knows what it is we're going to do in trial."

"And their witnesses do the same?"

"Yes. All witnesses have to come clean, both with evidence and with testimony. In this fashion, we as well as the judge can see the strength of each of our positions. The relative strength of one versus the other can push one side for settlement without having to go to trial."

"What's wrong with going to trial?"

"Two things. First and foremost, you never, ever know how a judge will rule on procedures and evidence in a trial.

"Second, you never, ever know what the jury's going to do with that evidence.'"

"In addition, court time is expensive. It's expensive for the citizens of the state who have to foot the bill, for jurors who spend their time there, for some witnesses, and for the attorneys. If all those expenses can be reduced by settling, then that can be considered a win for everybody."

"Okay, why not just settle it up front?"

"That's what we want to do. And in fairness, that's pretty much what plaintiffs always want to do. Plaintiffs work without pay as they prepare the case. So the earlier they can settle, the sooner they get money to pay their bills.

"Defense counsel gets paid on a running basis. So as the clock ticks, the discovery process begins, depositions proceed, and motions get filed with the court—"

"And their billable hours climb."

"Yep."

"So the defense council wants to settle late."

"It's when the defense counsel has received the billables they need and they recognize that plaintiff's case is good that the defense counsel settles. I've seen several cases that have literally settled in the hallway outside the courtroom the morning of trial."

"Trying not to be cynical here, Leanne."

"It's a lot to process. The judge, if she thinks that both sides have been stubborn, can require a settlement conference, but oftentimes that doesn't work."

"Why?"

"Ego, I guess, lawyers overestimating the strength of their own case."

"Well, are we better off going to trial?"

"I look at the facts in this case. Here, a healthy child is stricken by a drug that was newly approved and fast-tracked by the FDA with a disease from which they're not going to recover. It's a disease that so far has just been seen with the use of this drug.

"So there are no intervening factors, no other possibilities of other drugs causing this. We have experts who testified to this effect. I think we have a strong case.

"But in the end, it depends on the judge and the jury. Judges can have good and bad days. Juries can be attentive or inattentive, generous or hostile. One jury held for the plaintiff in a multimillion-dollar heart valve case and then awarded that same plaintiff just one hundred fifty dollars to cover the cost of a single heart test."

"Sounds malignant," Meredith said, now lying on the plush red leather sofa. "Even mean-spirited. Anyway, I don't see how any individual can be hostile to the plaintiff here who is a dead child.

"Doesn't matter. Defense can raise so many objections that it throws the plaintiff's case off its axis. The jury is confused. Experts and witnesses can be thrown out at the last minute. In one case where the bailiff had a seizure, my expert stepped in to render aid. When the hoopla was over, the court accepted the defense's motion and declared a mistrial."

"Good God, why?"

"The jury saw my expert in action. It would prejudice them against the defense."

"Court sounds like a madhouse."

"In an adversarial process, insipid decisions are required to keep a spirit of fairness."

Note to self, Meredith thought, *keep your business out of court.*

She gritted her teeth. "Tell me more."

EVIDENCE

"**B**y the way what are you going to study over the holidays?"

"Well," Meredith said, working to gather her strength at this point in their long phone conversation. "I have all these adverse events reports that I received from . . . a newspaper. Plus, I have the documents that Cassie sent me."

"You mean the ones that you received just before the executive committee meeting the day of the blast? That described the activity of legal counsel at Triple-S?"

She heard Leanne sigh. *Here we go,* the ex-CEO thought, steeling herself.

"Well, there are problems right out of the shoot. Take Cassie's statement that I reviewed. Defense will challenge these. How do these relate to this particular case?"

The ex-CEO was still.

"Meredith?"

"I don't know how to answer that."

"Well, was our client the specific and direct object of these, as you described them, 'unethical attorneys'?"

"No."

"Was our client's family the object of this unethical behavior?"

"No."

"Then what is their direct relevance of Cassie's note to this case? And also, I know that this a sensitive area for you. You didn't speak directly to the attorneys specifically about these acts, right?"

"No."

"You didn't interrogate them, right?"

"No." *Here we go,* she thought.

"Then, how can you vouch for their validity?"

Meredith gripped the phone hard. "Well, Cassie wrote them."

"An attorney who you fired, and is now dead? What credence does that have? It may be tossed by the court as hearsay."

"We can enter it during discovery, and you'll be asked questions about them during your depo, but a defense motion to exclude will likely win."

"Then I have just the adverse events," Meredith said.

"Now I've not read those, but let me ask you, do any of these AEs relate specifically to our client?"

"No."

"Then . . . well, Meredith . . . by this time you know where the questions are going, right?"

"Yeah."

"Okay, I've been rough on you tonight. What would you like to do with the AEs?"

"They support the notion that the company is sloppy with managing adverse events. They miss reporting deadlines. They misrepresent the AEs to the FDA."

"And what else?"

"Damn it, Leanne," Meredith said, now sitting up. "Hard evidence doesn't count? Does simple human decency not count in court either? I mean, Jesus, what's the point of a process that finds one excuse after another to toss clear evidence of malfeasance.?"

"They are part of the foundation of your moral outrage."

"Absolutely right."

"Well, what do we do with that?"

"I have a thought."

NEW YEAR'S EVE, 2019

"No New Year's Eve party for us."

"Maybe the . . ." Jon's voice trailed off as he sat in the conference room. Kevin stood next to him, Jubal and Emily to his left. Ava with long leather boots on the table as always was sitting to his right.

"This is the party. Listen up. Jubal and I confirmed that the alanine-glycine-cytosine sequence resided on 98 percent of the proteins that enter the chief cells of the stomach and were not destroyed by lysosomes.

"Yeah, yeah, yeah. This is phenomenal,"

"We also found the zip code for the skin epithelial cell we've been working with," Jubal said. "Alanine, tryptophan, aspartic acid."

"How do you know?" Kevin asked in a low voice.

"Did the same analysis on the peptides entering the dermal cells."

"Yeah, yeah. The peptides with the Ala-Trp-Asp sequence have their own receptors. We estimate that there are fifty million receptors in the cell wai—"

"Wait." Kevin put his hand out. "Fifty million? Million?"

"Yes," Jubal said, "some mammalian cells have as many as ten million ribosomes, and these little receptors are much smaller and far more populous than those huge protein-building factories."

"And these receptors are just floating in the cell cytoplasm waiting for a message. How many messages for an epithelial cell must there be if there are fifty million receivers?"

"Yeah, yeah. Over five hundred million per day," Ava said.

The room was quiet.

"Well, if a receptor translates a message a second, then the cell has adequate capacity for the message load."

"Again, a ribosome spits out two hundred amino acid sequences a minute. The peptides we're talking about are shorter, ten to twenty amino acids long."

"And how many different messages are those?"

"Well, assuming the chain is twenty amino acids and subtract off the thee Ala-Trp-Asp precode sequence, that's . . ."

They all stared at Jubal, waiting for the answer.

"Carry the three."

"Jubal," Emily said, kicking him playfully.

That's twenty to the seventeenth or 1.31 times ten to the twenty-second power."

They stared at him. "That's slightly less than the number of stars in the known universe."

"Serious throughput, and that's just a single cell."

"Well, "Jon said, "the bottom line is that there are a lot of possible messages, the skin cell receives hundreds of millions a day and it can translate and act on them."

"That's . . . that's intense."

"So uh, what . . . most messages get translated?"

"But many of these messages may not be operational, right?" Jubal said, coughing into his jacket sleeve.

"Why?"

"Well, this is a three-and-a-half-billion-year language, right?" He looked at Jon.

"Yes, that's right, and going with that metaphor, doesn't it stand to reason that much of this language contains words that are no longer used? Dead dialects."

"You okay, Luiz?" Jon whispered over his shoulder.

"Never better than this," the cell scientist responded. "Never."

"Words sent to an organ that no longer exists?"

"I don't think I can stand it," Kevin said as his phone rang.

"Guess you don't have to."

"It's Olivia." Jon watched him step away.

"We'll save a ribosome for you," Jubal called out.

"Anyway," he continued, "with Ava's help, we learned that the receptors clip off the precode sequence and in many cases push the shorter peptide to messenger RNA producers.

"And what does this mRNA do?" Kevin asked, reentering the room.

"It goes to the ribosome. And there the message information is translated into a new peptide. We just did that."

"Yeah, yeah. What did you find?" Ava asked.

"Dunno, we're still sweating it out."

THE LIGHT OF LIFE

"I've never been here."

"Neither have I," Jon said, "but I heard the food is magnificent, plus they have storytellers—what?"

He watched Raven stare down at her phone and then look up at him, showing him nothing but pain and anguish.

"What happ–"

"Will you come with me?"

"Of course."

•

"So what do you think of my Raven?"

It was thirty minutes later, and Jon was sitting next to the bed containing the oldest man he'd ever seen—bald, had wrinkles on wrinkles, brown skin, and no fat. His arms looked like a picture from an anatomy text. Yet with bright eyes, he was a man still in control of his life.

He was a man who insisted on a high death, dying with dignity.

"Mr. Sorrell, she has poured herself into me. I don't know where I end and she begins."

"She cares for me every day," the old man said, coughing. "When I am gone, she has nothing left."

"I di—"

"Let me finish. She never speaks of it. She was badly damaged, uh . . . twenty years ago, involved another man, another man who had money, a man who was rich. She got involved with him. They had a child.

"Soon the man tired of her and took the child. Raven was beside herself with grief. Some of the light of life left her eyes, never the same. Who would be?

191

"I don't know her future. I do believe she can't survive that again. So if you're not serious, it is time to respect her by leaving."

Raven walked in for a second.

"Dad, how are you doing?"

"I don't have much time left, but what time I have I will enjoy with my daughter."

Jon watched the father and daughter talk, play, and dote on each other.

"May I speak to you, Ms. Sorrell?" a voice called from the hallway.

She and the doctor stepped out.

Jon said, "One thing I am not committed to, Mr. Sorrel, is money. I've done good work, and I get paid for it. But I'm not money's slave."

"She told me." The man tried to rise up from the pillow and fell back. "Money makes people do things they hate."

"I enjoy my life," Jon said, leaning closer, "and I want Raven to enjoy it with me. We have money now. We may not have money in the future. Who knows, and really, who cares. We are devoted to each other. Letting go of Raven would be like letting go of myself."

The man's labored breathing now filled the room.

Jon turned to look out of the window. The warm January air was sweet, cooled by a north breeze.

The room was silent.

Jon turned back and saw that he was accompanied by just a lifeless body.

Raven came in and stopped at the foot of the bed as Jon stood and walked to her.

"For years he was my world."

"I know you need time alone with him."

She began to cry.

"I hate relationships, but I can't stand being alone."

He'd never seen anybody so open, so honest, so vulnerable. She turned to him collapsing into his arms.

"I am yours, he said. "You belong to me. Together, we face the world."

NEW WORDS, NEW WORLDS

"**C**an somebody please summarize for me what we have accomplished here?" Kevin said several days later.

"Well," Jon said, "I'll try. We started by simply trying to learn the language of intercellular communication. We've learned that small proteins, in fact, are made by one cell with the expressed purpose of communicating with another. The receiver or target cell knows to follow the instruction—"

"To open the mail."

"Based on the three code prefix, affectionately known as the zip code."

"We've learned how to duplicate these messages, sending a message from a cell that ordinarily might not send that message. And sending that message to another cell, the target cell operates on that message.

"The problem has been to figure out what message each of these proteins is conveying. Some of these messages might be an ancient dialect, attempting to communicate with organs we shed millions of years ago."

"Now, Jubal has been able to decipher many of these, but there are hundreds of trillions of them, and a random search for important ones won't cut it," Emma said. "So he did something ingenious. He decided to try to talk to the cells that is, make a peptide that he and I have built, introduce it to the cell with molmacs, and see what happens.

"What did we get? Receptivity and cell response."

"But it's easier to get the cell to react to its own mRNA, the specific structure for a particular protein and then to a peptide that may convey the same message but that we can't be certain about."

"So we fashioned a message to tell the cell to produce mRNA to generate a small protein like, say, insulin, insulin or a large protein like carbonic anhydrase. Since we know the structure of the large protein, we can back-solve to get the sequence of amino acids codes needed in the mRNA and deliver a molmac to tell the cell to make the mRNA for that protein. So we can make proteins as large as we want."

"Or we can stop the manufacturing of proteins."

"Yeah, yeah. That's one logical step, isn't it? Suppose somebody has amyloidosis, for example. They make huge quantities of useless protein that get into the heart, sometimes into the GI tract, ruining the organs in the process. We could now learn to interfere, even target, and destroy the disease-producing mRNA.

"Same things with Alzheimer's, right?" Luiz said.

Jon sat back down. "I just wanted to discover a language. Now, I feel like I'm peering into a new universe."

ENDOGENOUS PRODUCTION

"We really ready for this?"

"Sure. We can take skin cells, and see if we can get them to produce insulin," Emily said.

"Yeah, yeah, we know the structure of insulin. It's a very short molecule. So, Jubal and Emily, give us the three amino acids' three-code sequence for the skin and the code needed to instruct insulin-messenger RNA construction in the cell.

"Remember that I need the instructions for rat insulin, not human insulin. But I can give you molmacs that will figure that out and transit them from the rat cell to you."

"Agreed."

"Quite right."

Then I build the molmacs for delivery and assembly. We inject, the skin cells take delivery of the molmacs targeted for them, then we watch what happens."

"What could happen?" Kevin asked.

"Insulin levels go up, or go down, or nothing."

"So," Luiz said, "if I were pancreatic cell, I would be jumping for joy knowing that I had backup, that is, insulin production wasn't all on me."

"Why wouldn't the pancreas know that?" Kevin asked.

"Because its cells never got a message," Jon said, stretching.

"I like the idea, but there is another point?" Kevin said, lifting Sparky up into his lap. "You are getting heavy," he said, scratching the dog's ears. "He seems a little down recently."

'He's missing Olivia.'

"Me too," Kevin said without looking.

"We all do," Jon added.

"What happens if a patient with type one diabetes can no longer make insulin in their pancreas?" Kevin asked. "Would this not be a way to produce insulin that they could use, that would be produced . . . How do you say 'in the body' . . ."

"Endogenously?" Emily said.

"Yes," Kevin said, pointing at the computer expert, "what she said. And be effective? Like a backup?" Kevin stopped pursing his lips.

Kevin's worried, Jon thought, breathing deeply. *I should be too.*

"So," Jon said, strolling around the room, "let's go through the steps here. We are claiming that we can essentially have a cell communicate with us. And in addition, we can eavesdrop on the communication it is having with the body"

"You make it sound like a crime."

"Not yet."

"That's because there're no lawyers here."

"What. You think intra-body communication should be privileged?"

"And," said Jon said, raising his voice, "by intercepting this, message, we can produce a response that the body understands."

"Yeah, yeah."

Luiz turned to Ava. "Does the skin cell actually make insulin?"

"No."

"Could we induce it to?" Jon asked.

All heads turned to her

"Yeah, yeah, sure. Every cell has the same DNA. So theoretically, every cell can make insulin."

"Well, that's a question we need to answer," Emily said slowly. "If the skin cell is not reactive to the request then—"

"Maybe we shouldn't be asking it," Kevin said.

"Okay," Jon said, running his hands through his head.

"Hey," Kevin said, shaking his head. "I am easily confused with this molecular technology, but I think that I know that the ramifications of this go beyond anything we considered."

"Yeah, yeah. What do you mean?"

"I'm not really sure I know yet."

MISSION CREEP

Jon got to work early the next day.

"Hi, Kevin. You couldn't sleep either?"

"Guess not."

Jon frowned. "Hmmm, well, something's got into you. I've been watching your face tighten up yesterday and now this morning. Can't believe we have money problems."

"We're all good there. How're you and Raven? Ah, there it is," he said, pointing at his friend. "You smile when I bring her up, not like you did with Rayiko."

"So much different when I have no expectations."

"How so?"

"She calls me Lion."

Kevin backed up a step. "Noooo. No way."

"Square business."

"Why?"

Jon shrugged.

Kevin laughed. "Bowling, I bet."

"It's a long story. Anyway, nothing is a disappointment. Everything is somewhere between good and wondrous."

"Welcome to the real world."

"Thanks, Morpheus. Now, what's up with you?"

"Well, let me first ask you how long these molmacs last."

"Don't know. I should talk to Ava about that."

"Let's talk in my office."

Once in Kevin's office, Jon watched Kevin sit next to him rather than across the desk.

"You gonna hit on me or what?"

Kevin laughed.

"What are you thinking, my friend?"

"Well, if our work is to have human implications, then the molmac lifespan—I mean how long they exist in the cell–is a natural question." The president wrung his hands.

"Ava would know, but," Jon sighed, "molmacs are relatively small proteins, and proteins get digested in the cell cytoplasm all the time."

"So they likely would be wiped out, and we would need to think about replacing them. To do that on a continuing basis would be prohibitive."

"It sure would." Jon nodded. "An individual would need trillions of them. Costs and distribution would be enormous." *No wonder he's serious.*

"I guess you could deliver them like IV therapy. You know, as needed, but . . . this is a big hole in our bucket."

"What if they can reproduce?" Jon asked.

"If molmacs reproduce, then we don't have to worry so much about replacing them. And since they make mRNA, Ava can get them to make mRNA that codes for new molmacs that the cell's own ribosomes can reproduce. Goodness," Jon vision blurted with excitement.

"Then, my friend," Kevin said, nudging Jon with his elbow, "we are at a point when we should rethink what it is that we are doing."

"Why? I thought it was clear what we would doing."

"So did I," Kevin said, placing his hand on Kevin's arm. He stood up.

"When we started this. The idea was all about understanding a 3.5-billion-year language, right?"

"Yep," Jon said, stretching out in the chair.

"But now we have mission creep on our hands. We understand the language, but aren't we now beginning to manipulate that language, essentially get cells to do what they were not intended to do to make products that other cells could be making?"

Jon nodded.

"But that was never our purpose. I am not saying that we have crossed some kind of ethical line learning the language, but I feel that we're edging toward one now."

"I'm not quite following you. Kevin," Jon said turning around in the chair to face him. "But this is a good conversation. Let's talk this out."

"For example, look at the implications of molmac reproduction. If they can't reproduce, then I have no doubt that Ava can get them too, along the lines you laid out a minute ago."

"Sure, they'll be churned out by the millions, maybe by the billions in each cell."

"And they'll be building proteins or signaling other cells."

"Uh . . . yes."

Kevin turned to his friend. "Isn't that what viruses do?"

Jon froze. Then, breathing deeply he said, "I think viruses are different in the . . . in the main. But—"

"Let's say molmacs reproduce. I would like to think that these molmacs stay within their cells. But in fact, they populate other cells, right? We've shown that."

"And what instructions will the new ones follow?"

"Ava's."

"Now, yes. They slavishly follow the instructions provided by our team. But why couldn't they make their own instructions." Kevin shook his head. "Call it a mutation or aberrant behavior, but what are the implications of that?

"Now I'm officially nervous."

"We didn't plan it this way, but we are inadvertently making the perfect virus."

"Well, we would need to find a way to inhibit them," Jon said, raising his hands

"One thing I've learned from working with you, Luiz, and the others is that inhibition fails. Cells and their structures find a way around them. I can't describe how they would do it. I'm no molecular biologist or a molmac specialist or whatever you call them. But I do know that anything that we do to try to inhibit them would likely lead to a molmac-driven work-around. And then what do we do?"

Jon nodded. "Kevin, you're right. First of all, this has been mission creep, and I've been caught up in this like everybody else. Now it's our tendency to follow the science wherever it leads. But it does pay for us to stop and think through this. Maybe there's a way to avoid the kind of problems you're suggesting.

"But as we sit here now, these problems are real problems and we can't go blindly forward. We have to think through the implications. If engineers has talked about the implications of emails in the early 1990s, I wouldn't have a spam filter.

"I know it sounds like navel-gazing, but—"

"Well, it does sound like navel-gazing. But if scientists had navel-gazed in the 1920s, then maybe there wouldn't be nuclear weapons. If they—I mean we—had navel-gazed in the 1950s, then perhaps we wouldn't have bacteriologic weapons now. Seems to me that navel-gazing every now and then, for our species, is a good—sorry, didn't mean to preach."

"Preaching's not bad either. What?"

Jon saw that it was Emily, Jubal, Luiz, and Ava.

"Better get in here guys."

•

"All of them?"

"Yes," Emily said, scratching her head, "all the experimental rats are dead, and the control rats that did not get the molmac injections to make inulin are alive and well."

Jon couldn't help himself. He looked down the row of racks, control rats interspersed with the molmac-treated ones.

Every single cage with the experimental animal had a rat that was unmoving. The control group rats scampered happily in their cages.

"What could have gone wrong?" Luiz asked.

"Yeah, yeah. It's always a possibility that my molmacs didn't do what we needed them to do. I'll have to recheck my programming."

Jon looked up, "You know, the experiment might not have failed after all?"

"What do you mean?" Jubal asked.

"If these skin cells all suddenly produced insulin, what would have happened?

Ava smacked the table. "Yeah, yeah. Of course."

"I don—"

"Yeah, yeah, yeah. Insulin shock. They produce so much insulin that they overwhelm the rat, making them hypoglycemic, then pushing them all into a coma and death.

"Maybe Ava, we could repeat this by producing 50 percent less molmacs and taking continuous ICF glucose readings?"

"Easy for molmacs to do."

"Yes, one for the cells at a lower count," Luiz said, already walking out of the conference room. "The other is for the ICF to monitor and send back insulin levels."

●

Three hours later, Jon received an email from Kevin:

> The repeat experiment was an absolute success. The entire experiment is a warning.
>
> Kev

WHAT HAVE WE DONE?

Two days later, Jon and Kevin hurried to the conference room.

"You guys look like 'The Wreck of the Hesperus.'" Jon said as they entered.

"Yeah, yeah. What is this?"

"Well," Luiz said, "it ain't no compliment."

"It means Ava that we need a good night's sleep."

"Yeah, yeah, yeah."

"So what's up today?"

"I'll tell you what we did, and I'll tell you what we found," Luiz said. "There's a hormone called erythropoietin that induces the formation of new blood. We know that this is produced by the kidney. We know of no other organ that produces this. So what we did was choose an organ that has no business producing this eryth—"

"And what organ was that?"

"The spleen," Emily said, yawning. "While the spleen is involved with collecting and sequestering blood cells, it's not involved in regulating the generation of new blood."

"That's right. So we generated a message to make erythropoietin and added the three-code sequence for the spleen."

"What organ sent the message?"

"The testicles," Jubal said.

Jon sat back in his chair. "Well, you wanted to choose an organ that doesn't feel the need to make erythropoietin. I'd say that you found one."

"Yeah, yeah, yeah. That's what we were thinking. So we set up molmacs in the testicles—"

"I'm not going to even ask you how you did that."

"The same way we do every organ. We just release these molmacs in the intercellular fluid around the cells—"

"Leydig and Sertoli cells in this case," Emily said.

"And they are absorbed?"

'How did you know that again?"

"Yeah, yeah, yeah. Remember, we get to communicate with these molmacs."

"We got a signal from the testicular cells that, in fact, there were molmacs there."

Like those cells don't have enough on their mind. Jon blinked twice.

The molmacs added the three code presequence for the spleen, and off they went."

"How many?"

"Millions. Spleen molmacs noted the reception, and Jubal confirmed it was the same message."

"Easy in his case because the peptides received had the same amino acid presequence as those sent."

"Yes."

"Shortly thereafter, we did a serum assay. Erythropoietin levels were up."

"How don't you know they weren't up already though?"

"We did a preexperimental assay. E-levels were barely detectable."

"So we augmented erythropoietin levels, a fantastic accomplishment. Did it produce new blood?"

"The blood count is not elevated, but that takes a few days."

"So there's just one thing to do at this point."

"Yeah, yeah. What is that?"

"Let's talk," Jon said.

●

They all walked to the conference room. Jon laid out the gist of his discussion with Kevin.

"Never considered this," Jubal said, almost in tears.

"Nobody did," Jon said, patting his back. "Kevin brought it to me and I felt like a molidiot."

"Even I didn't think of it," Kevin said, head down. "Olivia asked me a related question and the problem just appeared before us."

"Well, what's the best solution here?"

That molmacs function as machines and don't function as living things, reproducing, growing, etc."

"How long do they function now?"

"Yeah. Forty-eight hours at most."

"You sure."

"Yeah, yeah, yeah. By that time, the lysozymes gobble them up."

There was silence.

"Well, how does the body handle this problem?" Luiz asked.

"The body lets lysosomes kill the molmacs, and it just produces more. The key," he said, "is not to let them reproduce—"

"And for right now, that's regular external reinjection.

"Or a time release—"

"Yeah, yeah, but reproducing is such a natural solution. And so easy to program."

"Ava," Luiz said, putting a hand on her shoulder. "What you just said is exactly the problem. And once we know how to reproduce them—"

"Others will too. And they may not be as moral or courageous as you," Kevin said.

She shook her head. "Yeah," she said in soft tones, "you're right. What we create, others pervert. That must be stopped." She sat up straight in her chair. "Yeah, yeah, yeah. I agree. No natural reproduction."

"But how do we stop it once word gets out about what we've done?"

Kevin folded his hands on the table. "I think that I may—"

Jon's phone rang.

Kevin looked at him, watching his eyes grow. Then blink once then again twice more.

"No,. Then they narrowed as he listened.

"What's up, boss?"

"Raven. She's been hit by a car, maybe not bad, but I've got to go."

"I can stay here or come with you. Your call."

"Let me do this. You stay here and manage this."

"Okay."

As Jon hurried by Luiz, he kissed his friend on the head.

BEATING HEARTS, BEATING HEARTS

The sun was sinking fast behind the Sonoran Mountains when Jon pulled up to the Banner Gateway Hospital entrance, heart pounding.

There, sitting in a wheelchair was someone tall in white pants, jacket, and sandals.

"Raven," he said, bending over.

"Nobody like that in this chair," the man said, flicking cigarette ashes on the concrete.

"Sorry," Jon stood and whirled around.

"Looking for me, Lion?"

He whirled.

Behind him, she was standing wearing a brown jacket, black slacks, and bright white sneakers.

"Where did you come from?"

"Nowhere." She entered his open arms, and he hugged her, kissing her forehead as he gently stroked her back.

"Come on, let's get you someplace safe."

He opened the passenger door of the Cherokee and helped her up and in. She was limping on the left side, struggling to lift her left leg up to get into the car.

Jon supported her on the right as she grimaced, crouched, got in, and inched into the center of the passenger seat. Jon closed the door, went around, and sat behind the wheel.

"Glad you called me."

"I'm not hurt bad," she said, rubbing the top of her thigh. And I feel better now, but I am stiff."

"What happened?"

"I was in the Fry's parking lot, and without warning, a car pulled out from my left, catching me on the left side."

205

His fingers pressed down hard on the steering wheel.

"She stopped and offered to help."

"And?"

"I said no. I thought I was fine."

Jon exhaled. "But you're uncomfortable now."

He turned to see her nod once.

"Well, what do you feel like? Resting? Eating?"

"I've been in the emergency room for several hours. Let's eat."

"What do you feel like?"

"Chinese food?"

"I know a place"

"Okay."

He drove for ten minutes to a Chinese bistro in central Gilbert, the darkness now everywhere.

After the plates, heaped high with vegetable fried rice arrived, they ate for twenty minutes in silence.

He saw that sometimes she used a fork, sometimes sticks.

Jon threw this out of his mind. *Not here as an etiquette observer, that she eats well and is safe is all that matters.*

"I think I'm ready to go to sleep."

"I bet you are. They give you any pain medicine?"

"They told me where to get some."

He shook his head. "I have some at home that aren't dangerous.

She looked at him

Dammit.

"Raven, I don't know where you live, but I do know that you live far from here, somewhere west of Alma School Road, close to the reservation. I live much closer here in Gilbert."

He sat up. "Now, there are lots of things you might think about me. One that doesn't cross my mind tonight is sex.

"Not now, not tonight. You need sleep and rest, not me chasing you around the bed for heaven's sake."

She smiled. "I'm tired."

"Let's go."

In twenty minutes, they were pulling into Jon's garage, and they entered his home.

"Nice kitchen."

"Not a cook, so I don't use it much. Come on with me now.

"Here's your bathroom," he said a few minutes later. "Feel free to take a bath if you want. I'll lay some clothes out for you. They won't fit but they'll be warm. And you sleep here," he said, turning and opening his hand to the double bed.

"You stay with me tonight."

Jon looked around the bedroom, its dim light barely illuminating the room.

"Raven, I don—"

She had turned and walked to the bathroom.

"Well," he said, with a sigh of relief when she came out a few minutes later. "What did I tell you, too big but warm."

"Lion, I just want to lie with you."

He sat on top of the comforter, clothes untouched, and lied down. Leaning over from the left, she rested across his chest.

"I—"

"Say nothing, Lion. Let's just let our hearts beat together."

She was asleep in a few seconds.

Jon followed.

TOMCAT

"Do you have any final questions for me?" Leanne asked, in a small preparation room down the tiled hall from where the deposition would take place.

"I don't think so," Meredith said.

"How do you feel?"

"Confident and wary."

"I bet you have those adverse event reports memorized."

Meredith laughed. "Until I'm sick of them."

"Okay. Remember, you're here to answer questions. Defense had a right to know what you're going to say in court. They have a right to ask you questions that are relevant. By being here, you're obligated to answer them."

"Yes."

"Answer truthfully and honestly. Always tell the truth. Don't be in such a rush that you don't allow them to finish their questions. And before you answer, give me time to object."

"Uh-huh," the ex-CEO said. *I'm ready for this.* Her heart pounded.

"Now, Meredith, I'm not going to lie to you. These lawyers are cannibals. They are here to keep you from testifying in open court about what you know concerning Triple-S behavior. They have all the information that you gave me. I know you're well prepared."

"You bet I am."

"But be ready for anything."

How do I do that? Meredith thought. She asked, "How long do you think they will go?"

"Well, under Iowa rules, they have seven hours to depose you."

"But just this one time, right?

"That's right. Just on—yes?" Meredith watched the attorney turn her head.

"We're ready to start," a voice said through the thin panel door.

"Let's go."

"Yes, boss," Meredith said, smiling.

●

"Clay? You know who this is?" The voice came through the cell phone.

"Yep."

"We need to do everything we can to keep her testimony out of court."

The deposing attorney paused for a second then smiled.

"I'm going to fuck her like a tomcat."

●

Comfortable chair, she thought, now seated at the end of a long glass table in the conference room, but there were so many people.

There had to be twenty at the conference table and another fifteen people in the chairs that lined the conference room walls in front of her and to each side. Plus there was a videographer for heaven's sake who was now walking around the table toward her.

I didn't know I was going to be videotaped. But then again, she didn't know to ask. She had been videoed many times for Triple-S. She didn't imagine this would be any different.

The videographer came up to the ex-CEO, put a lapel microphone on her, and said, "I will need for you to look straight at the camera as best you can. Think you can do that for me?"

To Meredith, for a moment, the videographer's clear smiling face, olive skin, wonderful smile, and gentle fragrance were the kindest experience she could remember. Suddenly, the ex-CEO felt alone and wanted to embrace the young woman as she adjusted her mike.

As the videographer walked away, Meredith glanced to her left. There sat a big bald man about ready to burst out of his suit in a white shirt with two stains on it, a blue jacket, and definitely a nonmatching blue tie. His wire glasses seemed ready to fly apart as they struggled to hold his face together. She concealed a smile.

The man didn't look at her but was busy looking through notes on his legal pad in front of her. A box filled with papers sat at his feet, between the two of them.

"I'm going to go on the record and introduce myself," the fat man said, looking over at the court reporter, sitting to Meredith's right. "My name is Sephus Clay. I represent Triple-S Pharmaceuticals, and I will be conducting this deposition. Here is my card." He took a small business card out of his pocket and just slid it across the table to the court reporter.

As all the other lawyers introduced themselves. Meredith forced herself to settle down. She recognized three lawyers from SSS, avoiding their glares. *I've forgotten everything.* Her heart pounded. She took a breath, knowing that her memory would return when her pulse rate dropped.

You're just new to this.

"Do we know what kind of transcripts we want for this deposition?" the records asked.

"Let's worry about that at the end, shall we?" Clay said, waving a hand at her. "Just swear the witness in."

"Very well," the court reporter said, a man who Meredith guessed was in his twenties, with a full head of hair and a goatee.

"Ms. Doucette," Leanne said sitting on the other side of the court reporter and now seeming far away, as if in another world, "Are you ready?"

"Yes," Meredith said. *I'm ready to get out of here.*

The ex-CEO watched the court reporter turn to her.

"Will the witness please raise her right hand?"

Meredith turned to the right to face her, raising her hand, her upper and lower arm making a perfect right angle.

"Do you swear to tell the truth, the whole truth, and nothing but the truth, so help you, God?"

"I do, sir."

"Please state your name for the record."

"Meredith Doucette."

"Let the record reflect that the witness is sworn in at 9:03 AM."

9:03 AM

"**D**r. Doucette, I am Se—oh its Ms. Doucette, right?
"Yes."

"Not Dr. Doucette?"

"Correct? I am not an MD." *Shouldn't have said that. I'm just starting this thing and already screwed up.*

"Did you say . . . no, we'll come back to that. I am Sephus "Clay" Clayton. I represent SSS Pharmaceuticals. That is where you used to work, isn't that right?"

"Yes."

"Have you ever been deposed before?"

"No." *Starting out friendly enough.* She took a deep breath.

"Well, let me just lay a couple of ground rules out. Although no doubt, your counsel has spoken to you about these.

"I'm here to ask you questions related to this case of Leighton Standover versus SSS Pharmaceuticals. Are you familiar with the specifics of this case?"

"I am."

"Please understand that. Strike that. Let me just ask, is there any reason that you cannot give me full and complete answers today?"

"No."

"Are you taking any medicine that would interfere with your giving full and accurate testimony here today?"

"No." *This guy must be joking.*

"Have you completely recovered from the many hospitalizations that you have had last year?"

"Yes." *What a jerk.*

"Mental and physical problems require attention, don't they?"

She gritted her teeth. "I can answer your questions."

"Thank you, I will ask my questions as carefully as I can. Please think carefully before you answer."

"Yes."

"And if you have any questions about the question I've asked, please ask me to clarify. When you give an answer, I am going to assume that you understood my question completely and you're giving me a truthful answer."

"Yes."

"You have the right to take breaks. You can take as many breaks as you need. I would like to wrap this up today . . ."

So would I.

"And not have it roll into tomorrow. But nevertheless, you can take the breaks you need.

"I would just say that please do not take a break when I have asked a question and you have not yet answered, you can ask to take a break after you've answered any question that I ask you. Do you understand these rules as I have related them to you?"

"Yes." *Can we please get on with this?*

"Do you have any questions for me about this proceeding today?

"No."

"Did you bring anything with you today?"

"No."

She saw his eyebrows shoot up. "Nothing?"

Uh-oh. "No."

"Okay. Please state your full name for the record."

"My name is Meredith Doucette."

Where do you live?"

"Here in Dover."

"Your complete address please?"

Why do they need to know where I live? Well, they know at SSS.

"At 2317 Odem Place."

"Now, you were telling me that you are not an MD?"

"I am not an MD."

Clay paused, looking at her.

Sizing me up.

"Are you even a nurse?"

"No."

"Are you a PhD? There are a lot of those, right?"

"Objection as to form," Leanne said.

Meredith was silent.

"You can answer, Ms. Doucette. May I call you, Meredith?"

Horrid. "Let's keep it proper, shall we, Mr. Clayton?"

"As you say."

"I am not a PhD."

"But I asked if there are a lot of those?"

"There are many fields in which one can get a PhD."

"And you don't have a PhD in any one of them, not a PhD in chemistry or physics?"

"No."

"How about epidemiology?"

"No."

"Now you know . . . strike that. Do you know that Leighton Standover is suing SSS Pharmaceuticals?"

"I know that his parents are."

"Yes. Have you reviewed this case?"

"I'm familiar with it."

She watched him study her.

"Yes or no, please."

"Yes."

"Have you reviewed the medical records in the case?"

"No."

"Do you know when he started taking the medication in question?"

"Yes. Two months ago."

"And do you know how long he took it?"

"No."

"Do you know when he first presented with symptoms?"

"No." *I told him I'm not a doctor. Why all these questions?*

"Despite your not knowing the details of this case, you are to present facts relevant to it?"

"Yes."

"Do you know the plaintiff personally?"

"He is three years old."

"Please answer the question, Ms. Doucette."

"No. I do not know him personally,"

"I see. Now, is it your understanding you are here to provide fact testimony, in this case?"

"Yes."

"Can you tell me what that means to you?"

"That means that I can speak specifically about facts that have occurred that I think are relevant to this case that I have knowledge of."

"You are not here as an expert, is that right?"

"Object to form."

"That's my understanding."

"Again, Meredith, yes or no please."

Again with the name. "No, I am not."

"Well, then that means that you're not here to provide opinions. You are here to just provide facts. What you have observed, is that right?"

"Yes."

"What have you observed in the Standover case?"

"I . . . nothing."

"Hmmm. Let's talk about the facts of your education." He removed some papers from the box that Meredith saw he could barely reach. "I'm going to move to mark this document entitled 'Meredith Doucette, Resume' as exhibit 1."

Meredith saw him give a copy to Leanne. "No objection," she said.

"Now, Ms. Doucette, do you recognize this as your resume?"

"Yes."

"You prepared this?"

"Yes."

"It contains all of your relevant—strike that. It contains the universe of your professional experience?"

"It does."

"Can you describe your education for me, please?"

Relieved, Meredith described her high school and college education.

"So you only went to college, is that right?"

"Objection as to form," Leanne said.

Meredith watched Clay ignore Leanne.

"You can answer."

"I wouldn't say I only went to college as if that's deficient."

"I'm just trying to clarify. You went to college, is that right?"

"That's right."

"What was your major?"

"Classical music."

"I see. And you thought that was appropriate training to be a CEO?"

"Ob—"

"Easy, Counselor. I'll withdraw it." Then, turning to Meredith, he said, "And then you went into the navy."

"Yes." *You son of a bitch*, she thought.

"And then in the navy, you rose to the rank of petty officer in let me see, four years, is that correct?"

"No. I was in the navy for six years and finished as a petty officer, second class."

"Where in that training did you learn anything about being a chief executive officer?"

He's baiting you. She took a breath. "Nowhere in that training did I learn about being a CEO."

"Okay. Why did you not finish your career in the navy?"

"I got married."

"Hmm. I see. So you married a vice president at Triple-S, correct?"

"That's right."

"Is it fair to say that you became a corporate wife?"

Careful, Meredith. "I became my husband's wife, Mr. Clayton."

"And he was a corporate vice president, right?"

"Yes."

Clay paused. "I do not want to spend more time on this than I absolutely have to, and I want you to know that I appreciate the delicacy here. You lost your family during 9/11, is that correct?"

"That is right."

"I am sorry for your loss. I just want to establish when your husband died. Unless you want to add anything, I will say nothing more about this."

"Let's move on." *Civil enough.*

"Fine. Subsequently, how did your relationship with the company change?"

"Well," Meredith began, relaxing, "after 9/11, I was asked to assume a leadership role."

"I see. And ultimately you became the chief executive officer, correct?"

"Yes."

"Didn't that seem—strike that. Can you tell me how that happened?"

"There was . . . well, uncertainty in senior leadership at Triple-S.'

"About what?"

"Who its leader would be?"

"What do you mean by uncertainty?"

"I simply mean that people were confused about who would be the new chief executive officer. There were different points of view, strongly expressed. No consensus merged."

"So they just asked you, a dead vice president's wife, to be CEO?"

I really hate this guy. "I would say that I was asked to be a stand-in CEO, a temporary CEO until they decided on who a permanent CEO would be?"

"And you agreed to this?"

"They needed my help, so yes."

"Without any training for the position, and with no experience, you agreed to just step in and pretend to be the CEO of a company? What's wrong? Did classical music start to bore you?"

"Object—"

"Withdrawn."

"I did not pretend anything," Meredith said, voice rising. "I was asked to be CEO."

"But you really had never trained to be a CEO?"

"That's right."

"How long did this temporary situation last?"

She thought. "It lasted three or four years."

"Well, if you just look at your resume, it shows four years, right?"

Well, it's on the resume in your hands, what are you asking me for? "Yes, four years."

"And all during that time, they were unable to name a replacement?"

"That is my understanding,"

"Again, Meredith, yes or no."

"Yes."

"And so how did you manage to stay in the CEO position beyond a temporary standing?"

"While I learned a lot, I also had good teachers there at Triple-S."

"So these people there supported you?"

"Yes."

"They answered questions that you had?"

"Yes."

"They came to your help whenever you were in trouble?"

"I had . . . there were some decisions that I was asked to make that I didn't think I had the knowledge to make, and they provided the knowledge for me."

"So you realized that you were unprepared for the job, and they helped you?"

"They gave me on-the-job training."

"Oh yes, I like that, an OJT CEO."

"Objection."

"Withdrawn. So it was a collegial relationship you had with leadership, Ms. Doucette?"

"That is right."

"And then, approximately four years later, which would be 2004?"

"Yes."

"You became CEO."

"Yes. *I'm tired of this.* May we take a break?"

"Of course."

"Off the record at 9:59 AM," the videographer said.

●

Meredith saw Leanne stand, stretch, and point to Meredith. They both left the room finding a quiet stretch of hallway.

"So strange—"

The ex-CEO saw Leanne look up.

"One rule he did not tell you," she said, touching Meredith's arm," is that we should not talk about the deposition proceedings during this break."

"I didn't know."

"How could you. This is kind of cool for January, isn't it?"

"Certainly is. Maybe in the teens tonight."

"Well, let's go back in and move forward with the depo."

"Of course."

"Back on the record at 10:04 AM," the videographer announced.

BACK ON THE RECORD AT 10:04 AM

"Now," Clay started. "You just had a break, Ms. Doucette, right?"
"Correct."

"And you went out with your counsel, is that correct?"

"Yes."

"What did you talk about during the break?"

Nosy asshole. "We talked about the weather."

She watched him stare at her. "That's all you talked about was the weather."

"That's correct."

"You realize, don't you, that lying in a deposition is the same as lying in trial? That is perjury. And sanctions could be imposed on you."

You'd be surprised what petty officers know. She choked it back. "Yes."

"Okay. Now you have submitted to us through counsel several boxes of adverse event information, correct?"

"That is right." *About time we got to this.*

"And this adverse event information was collected initially by you, correct?

"No."

"No? Then how did you get this?"

"The adverse event information was managed by Triple-S. This information was given to me just before the accident at Triple-S."

"By the accident, you mean the terrorist attack against Triple-S?"

"That is correct."

"So let me just ask you if I can raise the issue about the terrorist attack. I know you were physically injured as well as emotionally scarred."

"Yes." *Where is this going?*

"What were you doing at the time of the terrorist attack, Ms. Doucette?"

"I was in a discussion with SSS's executive committee."

"And the executive committee consisted of an executive vice president, correct?"

"Yes."

"Senior vice presidents?"

"Yes."

"And people from marketing?"

"Objection to the form," Leanne interjected.

"Yes."

"And senior members of your clinical team, is that correct?"

"Yes."

"Have you seen this before?"

Clay handed a single piece of paper to Meredith.

"Yes," she said.

"Let's mark this as exhibit 2."

"What is this?" Clay asked.

"It's an invitation to the executive committee meeting."

"On what date?"

"April 4, 2017. That's the date of the terrorist incident, right?"

"That's right."

Clay said, "Okay. So you are at this meeting. Oh, I should say. Attorneys were at the meeting as well. I don't want to leave them out."

He smiled, revealing hideous, twisted yellow teeth in a tortured mouth.

"Attorneys were there, correct?"

"Yes."

"Now, these were all people who reported to you, right?"

"Yes."

"You had worked with them over the years while you were CEO, right?"

"Yes."

"Some of them you hired and others worked at SSS before you were hired, right?"

"Yes."

"Some of them helped you as you began your tenure as CEO?"

"Yes."

"Now, did you call this meeting?"

"No. They called it."

"Was that unusual?"

"Yes. It's the only one where that happened."

"Well, what was the purpose of this unusual meeting?"

"It doesn't say on the agenda, but I believe the purpose of the meeting was to replace me as CEO."

"And how do you know that?"

"Because the discussion focused on concerns about decisions I had recently made and whether they were justifiable grounds for my resignation."

"I see, they wanted you to resign. I guess after all of these years, they finally found someone competent to take the helm from the temporary classical music CEO? Withdrawn. Did they identify someone?"

"The explosion interrupted the proceedings."

"What were they concerned about before the explosion, specifically?"

"They were concerned about the development of a product, then known SNW-17012 but now known as Ascension."

"You were interested in going forward with Ascension?"

"No, I was not."

"I see." She watched Clay pause for a second.

"Among all these vice presidents, executive vice presidents, attorneys, marketing people, did anybody agree with you about Ascension?"

"I don't think so."

"Did anybody in the company agree—strike—did anyone on the executive board want you to remain as CEO?"

"They did not want me to stay, and they didn't want—"

"Please," Clay said, looking over his glasses, "I asked you a question. Did anybody want you to stay? You may have feelings about why they didn't want you to stay. I'm asking you, did they or did they not want you to stay?"

Meredith swallowed hard, her fists balled into hard knots. "They did not want me to stay."

"And is it true that they didn't want you to stay because you objected to moving forward with this medication?"

"That is true. Yes."

"Is it true that they were counting on the approval of this drug to help the company's critical state of finances?"

"That is correct."

"Is it not a CEO's responsibility to help ensure the financial stability and growth of the company?"

"Yes, but only in certain—"

"Again. I'm just asking you to answer my question directly."

Enough.

"Mr. Clay, I understand that I'm here to answer your questions, but I am also here to describe my testimony. This is called a deposition to elicit testimony. My testimony. You are in my way, blocking me from providing what I am going to testify to my opinions here that I will give in court."

"Ms. Doucette, you can talk with your attorney about what you want to say. You can talk to your attorney about what her direct examination will be in court. But I must have answers to my questions."

"I'm not denying you answers to your questions. I'm trying to give you context."

"Keep your context, lady. I simply want answers to my questions."

Meredith felt like she had just been strapped to a bull's eye, and the archer was five feet away.

"Now. Can the recorder please read my question back?"

The recorder read the question back. Meredith put her hands in her lap squeezing them to calm herself.

"Now, please answer my question. Is it your responsibility to look after the financial well-being of the company as CEO?"

"Yes."

"That's a good girl, Meredith. And wouldn't the approval of this drug lead to an increased flow of revenue to your company, everything else being equal?"

"So would making nerve gas."

Meredith stared hard at Clay who was leaning forward.

She leaned over into his face and said, "Withdrawn."

"You don't get to do that."

"I just did."

"Answer my question please."

"Yes."

"Many people in your company thought Ascension would be a blockbuster drug, right?"

"Yes."

"But you refused to approve it."

"Yes."

"Why?"

"Because we needed more data"

"Really? More data? Ms. Doucette, are you a biostatistician?"

"No."

"What is a sample size calculation?"

"It . . . it is a calculation that produces the number of patients required for an experiment."

"Have you ever done a sample size calculation, Meredith?"

"No."

"What is the difference between type 1 and type 2 errors?"

"I don't know."

"Now that we have established your prowess with statistical calculations, let's turn to safety. Do you think Ascension was unsafe?"

"Objection to the form."

"You may answer the question," Clay said, ignoring Leanne.

"I said we needed more data."

"Yes yes, we heard that. But that's not what your safety team thought, was it?"

"No."

"In fact, your safety team approved the drug, right?"

"Yes."

"The FDA was interested in reviewing this drug with the view of approving it."

"I don't know if that's true or not."

"In fact, you said, and I quote, 'Those people sometimes approve drugs that they shouldn't. They can be weak.' Do you remember saying that?"

"Yes."

"They in your statement referred to the FDA, correct?"

"Yes."

"But they ultimately approved the drug, did they not?"

"Yes."

"And when the FDA approved the drug, strike that. And the FDA's mission is to provide drugs that are safe and effective, correct?"

"Yes."

"So when the FDA approved this drug, they are essentially saying—no—they are affirming that a drug is safe and effective, correct?"

"Yes."

"And in fact, they write a label that lays out in great detail how this drug should be used, helping to ensure that it could be used safely and effectively, isn't that right?"

"That's right."

"So in the face of the FDA conducting its review, strike that. The FDA conducts its review independently of what Triple-S did. In fact, it was going to make a decision about whether this drug was safe and effective, is that correct?"

"Yes, bu—"

"But you decided to have your company pull this drug from the FDA before they could make their decision, isn't that right?"

"That is correct."

"So you denied both you and your company access to what the FDA's thinking was simply because you didn't like this drug."

"Because we needed more data to assess safety."

"Because you didn't like this drug because of your own personal safety concerns, right?"

"The drug needed to demonstrate a clear safety record."

"Ms. Doucette, just what is your training in safety?"

More than yours, moron. "I've gone through the safety course that all employees have to go through at Triple-S."

He laughed. "That's a web-based course? When did you last do that?"

"Fifteen months ago?"

She watched Clayton shake his hand. "I don't understand. Your HR policy requires annual testing, right? I can dredge up the document, but isn't that your recollection?"

"Yes, I was a couple of months behind."

"So your safety certification had lapsed for ninety days, correct?"

"That's one way to put it."

"Yes or no, Meredith. Had it lapsed?"

"Yes, it lapsed."

"You were out of compliance, right?"

"Yes."

"So not having an active safety certification and acting just on your sense of safety, you decided not to move forward with Ascension's approval, right?"

"That's right."

"And you decided not to approve this drug even though your safety team, with active safety certifications, wanted to move forward with this drug."

"That's correct."

"Even though the FDA was in the process of determining whether the drug was safe and effective, you and you alone pulled the drug and stop them from deciding, right?

"Yes."

"Okay, let's go off the record."

"Off the record at 11:05 AM," the videographer stated.

"I don't think I'll need the entire seven hours. I just intend to go at about noon. I just want to let you know that as you think about breaks, Meredith."

●

When the plaintiffs left, Paler Roe approached Clay from behind.

"That will be the last we see of her, Clay," he said, slapping his boss on the back.

"Man, oh, man. How I love tearing into fresh ass in the morning."

●

Meredith, trying not to bolt, walked out to the bathroom alone.

She knew she was taking a beating. She also knew she wasn't going to hell over it.

She checked her smartphone, then exited.

She felt a hand on her shoulder.

"Meredith," Leanne said in low tones, "ready?"

"Sure am."

LET'S PLAY THREE

Meredith walked down the side of the long conference past all of the murmuring lawyers. She saw Clayton leaning over her chair, digging through his box of papers.

"You know, Clay, I thought you were the kind of man who loved sniffing seats."

He started to stand up. "Wha—"

When he reached her height, her right hand lashed out, catching his larynx in the web between her thumb and index finger.

He staggered back into the corner of the conference table from the blow's force, hands going to his throat.

A brutal right cross caught him under his left eye, and he went sprawling over his chair onto the floor, face up.

She took the glasses from his face and placed them on the floor, grinding them with her heel until they were twisted plastic and shattered lenses.

"This is what petty officers, second class do," she said, "look at me."

He tried to twist his head up to bring her face into view. She helped him, grabbing and pinching his fat chin, lifting the drooping skin.

"I am and will always be Ms. Doucette to you. Don't dare address me common again."

She stepped over him and returned to her seat.

There was death stillness in the room.

A woman in a black suit and white blouse stepped forward. She leaned into the mike that sat on the table to Meredith's left. "Can we go on the record please?"

"Uh sure, on the record at 11:48 AM."

"I am Jen Evans, representing SSS Pharmaceuticals today. Defense has no further questions for this witness."

"Deposition ends at 11:49 AM."

●

"That's a first for me," Leanne said, ten minutes later.

"Did I break any laws?"

"Technically yes, assault. More likely they will file against you."

"No, they won't."

"How do—"

"Because I looked Clay's record up during the break. He has a long history of insulting and abusing witnesses. There are many complaints against him."

She watched Leanne relax in her seat.

"Then I doubt he's going to try to get sanctions after that performance this morning. The fewer people who know about what happened to him, the better from his perspective. Meredith, how are you?"

"Better now." Meredith turned to her attorney and winked.

"This has been a mean day for you. Every witness's first deposition goes something like it although it's usually not as brutal as this was."

"Why so rough?"

"Simple. They don't want you to testify. And so they went out of their way to be disrespectful and yes, hurtful.

"Now, if the witness is a brutal thug, like somebody in organized crime, we all rejoice to see these tough people reduced to sniveling humility.

"But some men and women enjoy hammering anybody, everybody for the sadistic pleasure. They go after them for the expressed purpose of tearing them down. This is what you experienced today."

"Yes."

Leanne lowered her voice. "And the question is now, how do you want to continue? If you withdraw from the case, and witnesses sometimes do, then nobody will think the worse of you."

Meredith turned, facing her counsel. "I liked Ernie Banks as a kid. When he was returning from an injury, he was asked whether he could play a doubleheader. His answer was 'Let's play three.'"

"Well," Leanne said, snorting, "remind me not to fuck with petty officers, second class."

WYPOĆ TO

"The insulin result gives us a jumping-off point for a new experiment," Jubal said to the team.

"So, Jubal, are there any more peptides that give you a message that you can translate?'"

"Yes," he said, head down in thought, "but it's a real reach. We want to take a shot at the liver cells."

"Why?" Kevin asked.

"Because liver cells are complicated. They are in the process of detoxifying substances all the time. Plus," Luiz said, "they are making proteins the body absolutely requires. For example, proteins that control blood clotting, proteins that help control how much water stays in the intravascular compartment."

"And of course, many functions that we can't imagine."

"Bottom line. The liver sends lots of messages and receives lots. Let's see if our molmacs can keep up."

"Okay," Jon said, "what's the plan?

"Yeah, yeah. Right. Through the molmacs, we determine the three-code sequence, add a proteomic with a message Jubal and Emily agree on, inject the molmacs in the ICF, and then—"

"Wypoć to," the mathematician interrupted.

Kevin smiled. "Meaning—"

"Sweat it out," Jubal said.

"And the destination is?"

"The lungs," Emily and Jubal said at once.

"What will the message be?"

"Something more generic this time. I translated a more general message. It simply means protect."

Jon and Kevin looked at each other.

227

"Let's go," Jon said.

●

"Let's convene now," Jon said, eight hours later, checking the white and brown clock on the wall at 5:30 PM. "Emily, what do you say? Tell us."

Everybody was quiet, leaning over the table, all eyes on Emily.

"Based on the activity of the bronchial tree epithelium, our message induced the liver to tell the bronchial tree to produce a thick proteoglycan that, as far as we can see, helps protect and lubricate the bronchial track."

"So you're saying that the liver produced a message with destination lungs? The lungs received that message and produced something that we think may be of value to them. I guess that begs the question, why does the liver know what the lungs need?"

"Because the lungs send peptides to the liver and other organs all of the time right?" Kevin looked up. "That's what we're learning? That every organ knows what other organ needs although they may not respond?"

"Yeah, yeah. You go, Kevin."

"So," Jon said, running his hand back and forth over the smooth tabletop, "let's see if we can produce a message that induces another organ to produce something that we know the target organ does not make. If we can do that, then we now have a mechanism by which we can provide chemical knowledge to an organ about an unmet need that it can fulfill."

HAWKEYE

"Well, it's been a bear of a winter, Susan, but we've managed to ache our way through March. And I, for one, really appreciate the warming temps. Thanks for the pleasant weather forecast. We're rarely so lucky in the Cedar Springs part of the state."

Hector Sifuentes looked up at the camera with his usual smooth and effortless grace. He knew the teleprompter was just a glance away, but he wanted the KICS station audience, his audience, to know he was focused on them. He resisted the urge to cough, a pain-in-the-ass remnant of a late winter cold that had knocked him around for two weeks now.

"And this now is a new story, covered by our own Sowaka Owens. It's getting real traction, Sowaka?"

He watched the camera turn to the Asian lady standing fifteen feet to his left, both hands gripping papers that she held down in her lap.

"This story is coming right out of our East Iowa viewing area," she said, with perfect pitch, "and it looks like it's got important consequence for many parents.

"Hector, we have just learned from our local public health group offices that Eastern Iowa is experiencing the sad and troubling death of her children. As of right now, there are four families, each experiencing the death of an offspring. The four children were less than five years old, and have come down with the same catastrophic illness.

"This illness is neurologic collapse disorder, known by a few as NCD. This essentially means that all of the muscles of the body become, as the doctors say, flaccid. They are no longer able to contract. They can't support the weight of the otherwise healthy child, and the child ultimately dies.

"The first case occurred two months ago, and in the past five weeks, there have now been an additional three cases. This is a disease that is

229

extremely uncommon, and so gruesome to watch that we can't show you a video of it. And unfortunately, nobody knows how to treat it.

"The initial clue that we have was that this resembles a disorder that was seen in some of the children tested in the program for Ascension, the new blockbuster drug that is believed to prevent autism. In fact, I'm told that there are court cases going forward where the relationship between Ascension and this NCD disorder is going to be made on the record."

"Well, Sowaka, this is really a concerning story. I'm certainly glad that you brought this to our attention. Do you have any idea how many parents have given their child Ascension?"

"Great question, Hector. You know, we always have to keep in mind that there are two ways to look at this. One way is to look at the four deaths. The other way is to look at the death rate of children taking Ascension. But for that, we would need to know how many people took the drug and neither SSS nor the FDA has been forthcoming. A back-of-the-envelope calculation shows that there are proximately one hundred fifty thousand Iowans less than five years old, but we don't know how many of them have been given Ascension, so we can't do a helpful computation."

"So we don't know how common this is?"

"No, not yet. But we do know that if you're a parent with surviving children, you are in two groups. Either you have already given this drug, and you're, well, sweating it out, or you haven't treated your children, and your fingers are crossed that they will not get autism.

"Of course, our hearts go out to the Iowa families who have lost a child and are so devastated by this."

"What does the FDA say about this?"

"Hector, the FDA has not been forthcoming. I called their public relations office and was told simply that they are monitoring the situation, which of course we are doing in Iowa."

"Well, one would hope that they are looking at their data and trying to make some determination that would guide them and the CDC on this. After all, they are all over us about influenza, and this is far more important."

"You're right, Hector. Local physicians are at a loss as to how to manage this disease."

"And as you said, Sowaka, or maybe you didn't, this disease kills every child affected."

"My sources tell me that every child who comes down with these symptoms dies.

"And Triple-S has said nothing?

"Interestingly enough, Triple-S Pharmaceuticals has been mute. No one in any authority is saying that parents should reconsider the use of Ascension. Parents naturally turn to their local doctors, who have prescribed this drug because the FDA has approved it as safe and effective."

Hector was outraged, his pulse pounding. He put her on the spot. "This could be the biggest threat to our children since polio. What do you think is next?"

"Well, public health authorities here are contacting public health authorities across Iowa. And actually now throughout the Midwest. We had a hearing about cases occurring in Nebraska, the Dakotas, east to Illinois, Indiana, Ohio, and west to the mountains. But again, these are not formal reports, so there isn't much detail.

"Parents are really caught between a rock and a hard place, Hector. Every parent with a young infant is concerned about autism spectrum disorder. No parent wants to be responsible for their child having autism. However, no parent wants their child to die from NCD. It's a very delicate balancing act. And they go to their doctors, and as I said, the doctors rely on the statements from the FDA. And now there are new concerns raised about the drug's safety."

He saw her take a deep breath, and he held his.

"Hector I'm going to go out on a limb here. It seems prudent that in the face of this uncertainty with some families already facing tragic consequences, that families rethink the use of this drug."

Hector knew the risk this young reporter had just taken. "Make some room on that limb, Sowaka. I am out there with you, and I will add my voice to yours. Hawkeye parents, please rethink the use of Ascension until we are closer to understanding what's going on. If your child hasn't taken it, don't let them start."

He saw his colleague notably relax.

"Now we're going to hear from our regional weather reporter, Domino DeBecca, on location in Saskatchewan, telling us about novel ways to remove snow. Dom?"

•

"I was nervous about my last statement," she said to him at the station later that evening.

He looked at her. "You needed support and it was an honor to provide it. But it may not matter. I smell a lawsuit coming over what we just did, for us and the station."

The young reporter's hands flew to her mouth. "I never even thought of that."

"You did what you had to do. Let them sue us. Hawkeye children are at stake. And, Sowaka, if you don't stand for something, you lie down for everything."

DOMINATION

Vannesa Seymour, ex-executive vice president and now CEO of Triple-S Pharmaceuticals scowled, scrutinizing the gloomy management team.

"I assume that you have all seen the reports coming out now about this damn neurologic condition?" she asked the management group. "How did the Iowa yokels get this story?"

"They just dug it out from doctors, public health officials, and of course, parents."

"Yes. And the common denominator for all of them is that they have been given Ascension by their par—"

"I get that, Donna. Let's get that broadcasting station a couple of mean letters and file a restraining order that they should stop giving medical advice on TV. The question is how are we going to manage this?"

"That's why I asked Mr. Clayton, our outside counsel in on this meeting."

"It's not going to be long before people put two and two together and realize that, in fact, this dirty problem has washed up on our shores," Clay said. "However, we do have a friend in DC, however reluctant they may be. The FDA."

"How is that?"

"Because the FDA approved this drug. Specifically, they knew about neurologic collapse disorder. They knew what the potential problem was, and they approved it anyway. All we did was follow their direction."

"It's not going to be as easy as that," Vannesa said.

"We're the ones who collected the data. We're the ones who reported NCD to the FDA. People will ask, 'Wasn't it your responsibility to see what patterns were developing in the data stream and stop the drug before approval?'"

233

"Well, I know you'll probably throw me out of the room for this, but that's exactly what Meredith was talking about," said Jen.

"Who are you?" Vannesa asked.

"Jennifer Evans. Triple-S attorney."

"What do you do around here?"

"I'm the one who ended the Doucette deposition."

"Okaayyy . . . well," Vannesa said, looking around the room. "Meredith is not here now, but we're going to have to do a culpability analysis, at least for public consumption. I look forward to conversations with each of you.

"In the meantime, let's set up a meeting with the FDA."

Donna shook her head. "I think—"

"We need to go after them now," Vannesa said, holding her hand up. "The reason that they haven't come to us is that they are not ready. This problem caught them napping. Now is the time to dominate their arguments."

Vannesa stood to leave but saw one person remain seated.

"Yes, Jen."

"I think I can do something for you."

"And that would be?" she said, holding her hands out. She watched Jen glance at the other participants.

"Everybody else, goodbye. Go get us out of this."

With the room emptied, Vannesa sighed and then looked at the tall, attractive attorney. "What do you have in mind?"

"A story."

EATING OUR OWN

Moses on a bike. How do these people get hired? "Well, I don't really want to hear a story now,"

"It's a pretty good one. You should listen."

"Alright," she said, sitting. "Take a seat, Jen. I'll listen to anything that will help get us through this damn mess."

Jen nodded. "It's a disaster alright. The outrage will be almost unbearable. And I hate to think about the litigious consequences."

"So say we all. What's the damn story?"

"I was not alive when this happened, but I'm told that after the conclusion of the Cuban missile crisis, First Secretary Khrushchev was forced out of leadership of the Soviet Union. After the infighting, Leonid Brezhnev was named to replace him.

"Now, nobody liked Khrushchev. He was brutish, an earthy man, prone to lash out savagely at his opponents. So Brezhnev was startled when Khrushchev called the new first secretary up to his office.

"Brezhnev assumed that it was just an opportunity for the two old men who had known each other for generations to rough talk it for one last time, and perhaps to get his old friend and adversary's blessing.

"But before Brezhnev could sit down, Khrushchev stood up and with an outstretched arm, said, 'I am giving you two letters. When you get into trouble the first time, I want you to open letter number one. When you get into trouble the second time, I want you to open letter number two.'

"Brezhnev, shocked then puzzled, said goodbye, but Khrushchev had already walked out the door.

"Of course, it didn't take Brezhnev long to get into trouble. And after he had tried everything he could think of in a desperate attempt to keep his job, he remembered the two letters. So he went up to his office and opened the first letter."

"What did it say?" Vannesa asked.

"'Blame everything on me, Nikita.'"

"Brezhnev's head snapped up, and he went about blaming all of his troubles on Khrushchev. And it worked like a charm. The Politburo forgave him, and he was able to go on with his leadership.

"But of course, the time came around when he was in trouble again, years later. Again, he could not figure out how to get out of it. Again, he remembered Nikita's letter. He found it, sat at his desk, and ripped it open.

"It said, 'Leonid, sit down. Write two letters. Nikita.'"

The CEO shook her head. "Not sure that I'm reading you, Jen. You think I should write these letters?"

"No, ma'am. Don't write two. Just open the first."

Vannesa just stared at her.

"We can survive this problem by blaming it all on Meredith, Ms. Seymour. After all, wasn't she CEO during the time of Ascension's development? Did she really do everything in her power to stop the drug from being released?"

"Many people would say that she did," Vannesa said, now rocking in her chair.

"But the fact of the matter was that it was approved on her watch. Nobody can deny that. However, the threat of the letter is that we can just use it once, so the timing has to be perfect."

Vannesa leaned back and closed her eyes. "Meredith was sincere, maybe even right." She opened her eyes. "But this is survival, and we have to eat our own, one of them anyway.

"Get the word to legal to hammer Meredith, but before that, tell them to sue the hell out of Iowa. Let's reconvene in two days."

SCREAMS

"Everybody seated? Good," the CEO said forty-eight hours later, not really caring if butts were in chairs or not. "We have two threat vectors we need to deal with."

"The FDA," the senior vice president said.

"Are you asking me or telling me?"

"Uh, I mean, I was just sug—"

Sniveling weasel, if there's a SSS house left to be cleaned in a month, she goes out in the first dustpan.

"And the other one is, what's going on in the Iowa court system," Vannesa said. She sat back in her seat. "Let's talk about the FDA first."

•

"You boys better hurry up on in here."

Sam, the seven-year-old came bounding through the door, his five-year-old brother Peter behind him, just as the thunder rumbled through the valley.

"Don't worry, Dad. We weren't going to get wet."

"Right," Stu Rinapee said, messing his seven-year-old's hair up.

"Well, maybe just a little bit," the younger brother said.

"Now," their father said, laughing, "that I can believe. He bundled each in his arms and the boys erupted with peals of laughter.

•

"The FDA should recognize how perilous their situation is," Vannesa said. "While they didn't make this drug, they certainly approved it. And by approving that drug, it makes them complicit in what's going on across the nation."

"They could reduce their culpability by demanding Ascension be removed from the market."

"And we should argue that they not do that," Clay said, coughing. He rubbed his tender throat.

●

"Somebody better go get your three-year-old brother and see what he's up to."

"I'll go," Louise said

The eight-year-old girl pushed her way through the male mess and ran upstairs."

"Girl's getting strong, Cindy. What's for dinner?"

"What they love and you hate."

"God, Sloppy Joe's."

"Well, they love it, and you'll get to love it too."

"In years."

Well, I'm certain—"

"Mom, can you come up here?"

"What's wrong, Lou?"

"It's Stan."

●

"Autism is a serious disorder. And there's no question that our drug reduces autism. In fact, I've seen a new data set, which shows how much more effective this drug is than we originally thought," Jen said.

"Keeping the drug on the market prevents autism. Like other drugs, it has serious benefits and serious harm like Adriamycin, " Clay added, removing his glasses to rub his eyes.

"Like what?"

It's a useful tool in breast cancer but also produces heart failure."

"Well and good, Clay," Jen said, "but Adriamycin is used infrequently in breast cancer patients, a.k.a. adults. Ascension is for children, lots of children, not just a few, exclusively children."

"Children who will not get autism."

"I'm not convinced by the cancer argument," Vannesa said.

"Really, so what?" Clay said, turning to her. "It's an argument we can use, whether we believe it or not."

Lawyers. And I chose to surround myself with them. I'll need a bigger dustpan. Vannesa shook her head.

●

Stu and his wife turned from the kitchen table, ran through the short corridor, and bounded up the steps.

"You boys stay down here."

The boys followed them into the small bedroom with its single overhead bulb.

"Look at how he's sitting on his side."

"Well, he just fell over," Stu said.

"But he can right himself. He's done it lots of times by now."

Cindy rushed over, scooping Stan up into her arms. Rather than hug her, his arms just collapsed, and his legs fell down in front of him.

"Cindy, he's in trouble. Let's get him to the hospital."

●

"I know at least one SSS employee who has lost a child to NCD," Jen said.

"How many children does she have?" Vannesa asked.

"A set of twins who are two years old, in addition to the four-year-old who died."

"Will she make a statement, along the lines of 'My husband and I grieve for our son but have agreed that autism is so life-altering, we will give it to our other two children?'" Clay asked.

Vannesa watched Jen stare at Clay. "Would you?"

"What's her number?"

"I have to get into my contacts," Jen said getting her phone out.

"Not her telephone number. The dollar amount she would need to make our statement."

Jen stood. "Well, Clay, maybe you should ask her. And it's your statement. It's not our statement."

"It is now," Vannesa said. "Clay, make the call. Jen, sit down."

"What's wrong folks?" Vannesa said, raising her voice. "In case you haven't been keeping up with current events, this is an all-hands-on-deck situation. I don't like all of these ideas either, but we have to employ them to survive. And that's what this is all about, survival of Triple-S."

•

"I'm going to call Mom and have her come over to look out for the boys while we're here, and you and I go to the hospital."

Stu drove them toward town, heart now pounding.

"After they closed Community, we have a longer drive to Samaritan Hospital." Cindy clutched the baby tight.

"Talking won't get us there. Let's hustle up now." He leaned on the gas pedal.

"Stu, you ran that light."

"Just trying to make some time up." He squeezed the wheel tighter.

"I don't want all of us to die going to the hospital."

"And I won't kill you, just focus on Stan."

"Jesus. No no no, he won't respond to me." Her voice was loud and sad.

•

"Speaking of the navy, what do we do about Doucette?" Clay asked.

"We're putting her face on it," Vannesa said.

"How can you possibly do that?"

"She was CEO of the company. What happens at the company under her watch is her responsibility."

"People are sympathetic."

"People may be sympathetic with her, but people have been sympathetic with all of those who were injured in the blast. The fact of the matter is, this all happened on her watch, and that needs to be publicized."

"You know, she's going to fight it."

"I think Meredith is unstable," Jen said. "She got into a little bit of an altercation with the attorney at the end of a deposition, right, Clay?"

"She assaulted me."

"On video?"

"No, off the record."

"Can't we charge her?" Vannesa asked, staring at Clay.

"Best not to."

Vannesa raised her arms. "In heaven's name, why?"

"It will make her look like a martyr. Better to just release it to the public."

"So," Vannesa said, "you're saying that Clay pushed her hard at the depo and deserved it." The CEO took a deep breath. "Anyway, release a statement about our concerns for our ex-CEO's stability."

"I don't like the statement idea," Jen said.

●

"Okay. Call the ER, Cindy."

"What do I tell them?"

"Tell them we have a three-year-old who can't control his muscles."

"You mean like a seizure?"

"Yes, but a quiet one."

"Nobody's answering."

"Don't worry. We're just a block away anyway."

When they got there, Cindy jumped out, took the child, and ran into the hospital.

"Can you help us?" Stu said to a nurse. "We have a three-year-old who suddenly is not able to control his muscles."

She looked at him, then over at the child in his mother's arms.

"Take him right to bay 2, second on the left there." She pointed.

Stu felt her hand on his arm. "Sir, can I talk to you?"

As Cindy left, the nurse asked, "What medicines has he been taking?"

"Well, he doesn't take anything. The only thing we gave him was that medicine to keep him from getting, what's it called? Hambur—"

"Autism."

"Yes, that's right."

●

"You don't have to like it," Vannesa said. "Just show that Meredith was out of control, and therefore let a bad drug through. People don't want a complicated story. They just want a face."

●

"You're going to have to be strong, sir, for your family."

He just looked at her, mouth open.

Then he heard Cindy scream. It was the worst sound in the world.

BLEATING

Sebastian Jenkins, deputy director of FDA-CDER, stood outside of the Bethesda Hyatt Regency, jerking a cigarette out of his shirt pocket, then feeling along the bottom of each jacket pocket. "Know I have a—"

"Hey, boss."

Jenkins dropped the match that he just pulled out. "Damn it. Where have you been?"

"I didn't get a call to come back to DC until yesterday, April 4. I busted records to get here from Salt Lake City," Sam Morrison, assistant deputy director, added. "Why are we here? We didn't call this meet—"

"Triple-S wanted to meet with us, Sam. And scuttlebutt has it that they are furious."

"Furious?" Sam said, moving aside for an attractive woman exiting the hotel. "They should be down on their knees begging the American people's forgiveness."

"No, my friend, they're furious at us."

"What a surprise," Sam said, kicking at something on the floor.

"We're supposed to meet with them in the conference room downstairs."

"Why aren't we at Fishlawn?"

"Triple-S wants this confidential."

A setup. Sam shook his head.

Neither had noticed the same woman who was exiting had turned around and now followed them from a distance.

•

Jenkins hustled down the steps from the lobby to the collection of conference rooms on the lower floor, then walked the long hall to a closed door.

Turning the handle, he entered.

"My god," he whispered.

There had to be thirty people in the room, some he recognized. The CEO Vannesa was there. She sat next to a big man with wireless glasses. They sat in the center.

"Guess we should ask the hotel to slap some more burgers on the grill, boss," Sam said.

"We've got these seats for you," Vannesa said, pointing to two chairs at the head of the table.

"Uh, Vannesa," Jenkins said. "I was under the impression that we were going to have a private conversation."

"That's what this is, Deputy Director. There's no public presence here. All I have here are my senior people and my lawyers."

Ambush, Sam thought, watching his boss grimace. *Well, then let's get to it.*

"Fair enough," Jenkins started. "I understand your drug is associated—"

"You mean, allegedly associated with," a high-pitched voice came from somewhere.

"No, I mean associated, specifically associated with a large and growing number of deaths of children in this country due to neurologic collapse disorder. I assume that we all know what the neurological disorder is. I'll just refer to it as NCD. Do you dispute any of this, Vannesa?"

The CEO sat still and silent.

"At this point, we have as far as we can tell at the agency, over eight million children less than five years old who are taking your drug. Those numbers come from public health teams as well as from physicians. Severe adverse event reporting tells us that approximately 0.08 percent of these children are now dead. That's sixty-four hundred children dying in this country. In add—"

"Does that report also tell you how many of the eight million children didn't get ASD?" someone called out.

"Interesting point." Sebastian pulled some papers from his suit coat. "Based on your recent efficacy data, we expect that one of the eight million children, sixty-five hundred children would have gotten autism who now will not. That means that there are over 7,993,500 who would not have gotten autism anyway, and approximately sixty-four hundred will die. If you want to weigh this, it costs sixty-four hundred deaths to prevent sixty-five hundred cases of autism. We know that."

"That's one-to-one, an intolerable ratio," Sam said, looking straight at the CEO. "And we know that adverse events count undercount deaths."

"But what about the sixty-five hundred children who we saved," Clay asked in a booming voice. "How about those families?"

"Those families are fine, right up until one of their siblings taking Ascension dies," Sam stated, heart pounding. "Then they're not so fine anymore."

Sam glared at Clay who stared back, unmoving.

"That's 64,000 deaths versus 65,000 living with autism prevented? Looks like you're in a pretty bad fix, Vannesa," the deputy director said.

"What did you say?" Clay asked, leaning forward.

Jenkins swallowed. "I said you're in a pretty bad fix—"

"Well, in case you haven't noticed, you're in it with us."

Sam watched his boss shake his head. "I'm not following you. Keep in mind that people are looking for somebody to blame for these deaths, forgetting about the number of children who've actually survived."

"Well, let me help you, Deputy Director," Vannesa said. "Think they blame us? We had a rogue CEO who was responsible for all this but has since left the company while continuing to exhibit unstable behavior. Nevertheless, we complied with all the FDA's rules, and you approved the program. So don't deliver these deaths to our doorstep. You own them as well."

"Now wai—"

"You studied this drug. You asked for additional data. You got additional data. You decided to go forward and approve the drug. This is on your head as much as ours. You want to be a partner with pharmaceutical companies? Welcome to partnership.

"Now," Vannesa said, "I suggest that what we do today is stop throwing dead bodies at each other and focus on how we are going to survive this."

Sam saw his boss flush.

"I don't have to tell you," Clay said, "how ugly this is going to be for you, Sebastian. Triple-S will be fine. The culpable person is gone. Worse comes to worst, we will have to withdraw this drug. That's a shame because we still think it's a good drug. But we'll survive it.

"However, you and your agency are going to be called before congressional committees. And you're going to be hammered by congressmen and women who have been going to funerals, who have been getting phone calls from all of their constituents, all complaining about this drug, and want to know why you're not doing anything. They will demand to know first why you even approved it and second, why you're not moving against it with haste and energy."

Clay brushed some dust off his suit pants. "I'd be surprised if more than a handful of you still had your jobs when this was all over.

"We'll keep ours. You will lose yours, and you know something, Deputy Director? SSS will keep going. So why don't we all just help each other out here and skip the bullshit?"

Sam saw that his deputy director was sweating. "Well, what do you propose?"

"Making more money and killing more children," Sam said, starting to stand. "That's all they care about."

Clay said, "I was talking to the deputy director."

"Did you talk to him about the last effectiveness dataset you sent us, Mr. Clayton?" Sam asked, pulling his chair closer to the table. "Did you tell him that much of it was simulated?"

Clay shrugged. "He knows."

Sam turned to see Sebastian looking straight ahead.

"Simulated?" Sam said, voice raising. "You mean you made it up?"

"We did some computations using Poisson-Gamma model and exponential time to ASD event—"

"Right, so you did make it up." Sam shook his head.

"It supports our position that the drug is effective."

"Yep. Made-up data will do that."

"Yet the FDA accepted it, right, Deputy Director?" Vannesa said.

"It was a state-of-the-art dataset," Sebastian said. He turned to Vannesa. "So you propose to continue to use this drug, continue to let the number of deaths from this drug climb, and just remind people that this drug prevents autism?"

Sweating now, he reached for Sam to sit.

"Well, people don't understand the risk of autism."

"Maybe we need to treat this drug like thalidomide," Jenkins offered.

"What?" Vannesa asked. Sam noted her hand clutching a Kleenex.

"Here me out," Jenkins said. "Thalidomide was removed years ago but is back on the market now, governed by new restrictive rules. Patients have to sign detailed informed consents to receive it."

"This drug is not like thalidomide, Deputy Director," Clay said, waving a hand. "Sure, thalidomide produces terrible defects just like Ascension is alleged to. But thalidomide is only effective in a small number of leprosy and AIDs cases. Ascension is overwhelmingly effective in a very prevalent disease. The benefit-risk is so much greater for Ascension. The two are not comparable."

"Yet just as deadly, Vannesa," Sam said.

"Not a very helpful comment," someone said from the back.

"But accurate," Sam said, his hands balled into fists. "Just want us to keep our focus. The ASD prevention arm of Ascension is overwhelmed by the deaths that it produces," Sam said. Then he looked at the CEO. "It should be off the market."

"We like the supplement approach," Clay said, turning from Sam.

"Supplements like what?"

"We've really focused on the B vitamins. We think that the B complex vitamin supplement will help to reverse NCD."

"What?" Sam stood, raising his voice. "What data could you possibly have to support that claim, more simulations?"

The room was silent.

"Just what I thought. And while Triple-S carries out the studies to learn B complex is as useful as Brylcreem, you'll have thousands more deaths on your hands."

"Sam, you're excused. Please return to your office."

Sam whirled. "There will be the devil to pay if we roll over for—"

"Thank you, Sam. Please return to your office."

Sam stood, swallowing the hot curses he had for the group, then turned and left.

●

"That's what we'd like to go on, Deputy Director," Clay said. "That and the phenomenally reduced ASD incidence produced by our drug. And frankly, we would really enjoy your support here. You have everything to lose by working against us, and everything to keep by working with us. You haven't gotten to your position by being stupid."

"I think we will move forward based on your approach," Jenkins said.

•

"Thanks for all your help, Clay," Vannesa said as the meeting broke up.

"Sure. Know how you can tell you're in an FDA meeting?"

"How?"

"The bleating of the sheep."

They both laughed, brushing by Audrey, who uninvited and unrecognized in the tense meeting, also left.

CHARADES

"What? Even if we win, we lose?'"
"They can always appeal."

The ex-CEO ground her teeth, standing in her living room on a May day.

"But there will be a verdict in the Iowa State Court, right?" Meredith asked.

"Yes," Leanne said on the phone, "but remember that there's an Iowa appeals court, then the Iowa Supreme Court, and then the US Supreme Court. And if I know Triple-S, they will take it up the ladder, one level of appeal after another. That's what happened in the Havener case."

"What was that?"

"It's a famous Texas lawsuit. The Haveners felt that they had been hurt by a drug named Bendectin. There was a large settlement that the civil court reduced. It was appealed, and the appeals court cut it again."

"Then, the state supreme court vacated the entire penalty."

"Well, Leanne, why are we doing all of this work if lawyers and judges turn the jury decision inside out? Why go through the charade of a trial if not the juries, but the attorneys and judges call the shots? Goodness, what's the damn point?"

"Easy, Meredith, I get how you feel. There are some checks. For example, judges themselves worry about how their decisions will be reviewed by other judges. A harsh, pro-defense judgment can be reversed as well, insisting on a retrial."

"Great," Meredith said, hanging her head, "more testimony?"

"Not really. Most appellate courts just review transcripts of the trial and relevant evidentiary rulings that the lower court made, as well as the law. Their involvement can help to keep the lower courts in check because no lower court judge likes to have a ruling reversed."

"So a counter-balance?"

"Yes. Appellate judges can modify judgments or throw out verdicts wholesale and require a new trial. This in and of itself can lead to new settlement discussions.

. "Then, even though each side may choose not to appeal, there are several reactions in the nonjudicial community that can be compelling."

The ex-CEO sat down. "You mean in the real world."

Leanne's laughter came over loud and clear over the phone. "One is from the stockholders who recognize that this company is in trouble and then bolt. Perhaps the company doesn't have to pay big dollars to plaintiffs, but it will no longer be an attractive investment.

"The next is the insurance industry. They can insist that a company sued must hold money in reserve."

"That money comes from their operating costs."

"That's right. The company must hold that money aside in escrow. They're not able to invest it and therefore can't grow the way they want."

"God forbid that SSS be asked to sacrifice some of their advertising or lobbying costs to pay for the human damage that they caused," Meredith said, shaking her head.

"And that's why some companies are settling cases for sums that are larger than they'd like but less than the cost of having huge sums in escrow that may not be available to them for years."

Meredith drew a deep breath. "Somehow, that doesn't seem like a big enough penalty."

RANCID BUTTER

"A debacle, Vannesa."

Vannesa leaned over the conference phone in her office at SSS Pharmaceuticals.

"I don't need you to tell me that. JJ, I simply need you to tell me what Alcatraz is going to do?"

"We had ten operators ready to go. But that's no match for the over sixty-five hundred deaths due to your drug in children, Vannesa. My neighbors have just lost their daughter. It's awful."

"This is not awful. It's hell. What happened in the House?"

"Let me tell you, there's no amount of lobbying that could have stopped that bill from going through the House of Representatives as fast as it did."

As JJ babbled on about Alcatraz's failure to block the passage of the bill, Vannesa reviewed the explosive surge in NCD cases. Nobody could understand why the deaths started in the deep Midwest, but they rapidly took off following prescription use patterns greater in California and then of all places, the DC area.

There were firestorms everywhere.

"We are tracking the cases of autism that are prevented."

"You can track that the livelong day, Vannesa, but there is no way you'll convince America that child death is a good price to pay for autism prevention. Why not prevent car theft by wrecking your car? Come on."

'You mean you and Alcatraz haven't convinced America. That was your job."

"Ascension is flying into a wall."

"We have no parachutes here."

"So you're not pulling the plug?"

"No, and the FDA supports that decision."

The line was silent.

"I expected that the House would support the bill," the CEO continued. "They're wingnuts, consumed by emotion, busy running into walls. The question is, can we choke this in the Senate?"

"Vannesa, I have to say, I don't know. I've got Smithhorn on it. The senator is, you know, a good friend of the drug industry and can be a brutal questioner. He may not be able to kill it—"

"So he may be rancid butter, but he's on our side of the bread."

"Right. He may be able to stop its progress, put it on hold, or bottle it up in committee so that it never sees the light of day. I think that's our best tact here, especially since deaths are declining some."

"Deaths are declining because parents stopped giving it to children." She wondered for a moment whether Ascension might be good for adults. She could see how some personality disorders might be improved with Ascension. But that was for another meeting, another time.

"I want this bill destroyed, JJ."

"And I want to wake up next to Beyoncé and a bowl of Viagra. Look at what's practical and accept the pragmatic approach, Vannesa. Alcatraz, I think, can deliver the practical.

"Then get to work."

She called her assistant on the cell. "Can you convene our research team? What's left of it anyway."

LITTLE FELLA

"Yeah, yeah, yeah. It worked." Ava kissed Jubal and Emily. "Jon said we now go on to cancer, oh." She stopped.

"So maybe you can tell me why we're not using chimpanzees for this next one?" Jubal asked.

"Because they, by and large, don't get cancer," Emily said.

"You lie. Seriously, I didn't know that," Jubal said.

"Yeah, yeah, yeah. How DNA is methylated in chimpanzees is different than in humans. It allows them to switch genes on and off in different patterns than we do. Anyway, they avoid cancer." Ava smiled.

"Well, I guess I'll look at chimps with awe now. Anyway, we're forced to use rats?"

"Well, rats really do have a solid cancer propensity," Jon said. "And the cancer we're looking at is mammillary cancer. It's spread throughout the skin of rats.

"Man, that's way too sad."

"Anyway, "Jon said, standing before the group at the conference center. "Let's just talk through this experiment again. We can provide molmacs that construct mRNA that itself will lead to the cell's ribosomal production of a protein.

"What we're going to try here is to take cells that are cancerous and get those same cells to manufacture chemotherapy to kill the cancer, essentially to ask the cells to commit suicide."

"Well, how do we know that we are injecting the molmacs into cancerous cells?"

"We don't really know. We're just injecting into all the cells throughout the cancer."

"And since they are in the mouse's skin, that's easy to do.

"Umm."

"It's a big step, Jon," Kevin said. 'What we're doing is providing instructions to the body to kill this cancer using a specific chemical that we tell it to create."

"Yeah, yeah, yeah."

"Em and Jubal, you have the instruction set ready."

"Yes. We have it,"

"And where you're going to inject the molmacs, I leave to you, Luiz.

"I circled a collection of lesions that we want to inject." Luiz turned the mouse over exposing its underbelly. The mouse squealed delightedly in his hands

"Don't worry, fella, we're gonna try to cure you," Luiz said.

"How long before we see the effect?"

"Yeah, yeah. It won't be long. It's a relatively high concentration of chemotherapy, right where the cancer is. That's exactly the circumstance we want to be able to produce."

Jon thought for a minute, reviewing all of the steps required for this process to work, his mind numb from stumbling through the complexity of this experiment. *What am I missing?*

"And these molmacs can't reproduce?"

"Yeah, yeah. Like we all agreed. They cannot."

"Well, guys," he said. "I'm fresh out of excuses not to do this. Let's go."

BEEHIVE

"Invited, me?"

Olivia read the letter again. Her breath came raggedly. Then dropping her hands by her sides she said, "I can't do this."

"Hey," Audrey said, guiding her friend to the vacant part of the hotel lobby, "most individuals are pleased to be invited to testify before the United States Senate, believing it to be an opportunity to get their views out on a question of public policy. You're the progenitor of this bill. It would be odd if you didn't show."

"I've been spoiled," Olivia said, playing with her fork. "The House passage of our bill was so easy last month."

"It was a snap in July. The publicity from the rise in NCD cases energized Americans." Audrey looked around, then lowered her voice. "Members of the House were deluged with emails. The bill was rushed through committee and onto the floor before the company had a chance to respond."

"And now, the empire strikes back. But the Senate?" Olivia asked.

"They want a hearing."

"Which committee?"

'It was a real fistfight between the chairs, but commerce, science, and transportation got it."

"Is that good?"

"No. The chair, Sen. Jackson Smithhorn is in the drug company's pocket."

"Swell." Olivia swallowed hard. "Public?"

"I think I know what you mean. Most are public, this one will likely be televised."

"To the nation?"

"And beyond. It's inevitable," Audrey said as Olivia watched her friend hold her hands open to her. "Ascension has generated a public health crisis. Almost seven thousand children in this country are dead now because of Ascension. People are out of their minds about it.

"Many people argue that death is worth the prevention of ASD but so many?" Audrey clasped her hands. "Your bill's release tapped into that rage. Congressman Pitts' timing was excellent. The House wanted concrete action and your bill gave it to them. The groundswell of support overcame all resistance. It has influence—"

"And publicity."

"Even notoriety now. The world is interested. People know Big Pharma wants to fight, and well, you're in the middle of it. Senator Smithhorn will likely take the lead on questioning."

Olivia's stomach rolled over. *The leadoff hitter. And I am the ball.* "So how does this work?"

"Hearings are just information gathering."

"Not based on what you just said. This will be a bloodbath."

"Or a battle royale, depending on how you play it."

Olivia stared at her friend, who looked back calmly.

"This will be a legislative hearing for the committee to study the bill and ask questions."

"I'll have to prepare."

"I will help, and also it may be best to get your young bloods reengaged."

Olivia was dizzy. "Bloods?"

"Rashida, Sharra, Julie, Angelo—"

"Yes. Good idea."

"Committee members and staff usually plan extensively for hearings. They prepare backgrounds on you, dossiers on you, all public statements that you have made."

"So they can ambush me or overwhelm me."

"Or for you to ram this bill down their throats."

Olivia studied her friend.

"I'm sorry, Audrey. I'm just surprised is all. Please go ahead."

"Anyway, with good prep, most hearings can be expected to proceed smoothly as silk. Plus you have a right to counsel."

"Like a mafioso, that's encouraging." She smiled.

"Although keep in mind that debate time in the Senate is generally unrestricted."

"So they can question me as long as they want."

"Hey. Remember that you kicked over the beehive, Olivia. You can expect some stinging."

Olivia stared then sighed. She knew what to do, had known it since Smithorn's name came up.

LET WHAT YOU WANT TO BE, BE YOU

Jon and Raven looked northwest out over the mountains the next day. "I've never been here before." Raven pulled the shawl over her shoulders.

"How funny," Jon said. "You've been here all your life and never been to Payson. I've been in this state for just three years and come up here all the time." They both looked out again over the heavily wooded mountainous terrain. He put his arm around her. She sat close.

"I'm scared, Raven."

"I know you are."

"I don't know how this experiment is going to turn out."

She looked at him.

"We have come so far and dug so deep." Jon turned to face her. "Two years ago, we weren't even thinking about this project. Now we're able to work within a cell, manipulate its protein production apparatus, and produce new molecules."

"And you do that with small machines?"

"Well yes, the team does. I actually don't do any of the manipulations. It's Jubal, Luiz, Ava, and Emily, who do the heavy lifting."

He shook his head. "It's so . . . credible now. It seems so easy. Two years ago, this was really beyond imagination."

"So what's your role in this?"

"Right now, to be scared." He looked straight ahead. "I used to look at the narrow vision of scientists and feel . . . rancor. How could they not see that the chemistry of nerve manipulation would lead to the making of nerve toxins or that bacteriology would lead to germ warfare? Or that behind the promise of the internet laid poisonous disinformation, invective, and pornography.

"Now I know. They were too afraid to look. And I don't blame them. The future doesn't blossom. It threatens. And we are not ready."

Jon saw Raven stare straight ahead.

"You want a god's eye view?"

"No," he said, " just a bigger view, a broader view of how things work."

"You mean a god's eye view."

He smiled. "Yes."

"I don't know how you do what you do. There's no end to it."

He looked at her.

"New failure, new experiment, new success, new questions, new experiment, new failure, on and on."

She turned to look at him, head on her bent knees, wind bringing her hair alive.

"The sky, you look into it, but that's all you can do, no beginning, no end. You are part of it. This is what it will always be for you and your questions, neither beginning nor end in sight."

Jon looked out over the clear blue, on and on.

"I want to be that."

"Then, let what you want to be, be you. Hungry?"

"Sure. What do you want?"

"Pancakes." She smiled.

●

They drove fifteen minutes to Denny's. It was 7:00 PM and the sun was still visible, filling the fading blue canvas with reds and oranges.

They sat next to each other in the warm booth and ate.

"Who's worse off because of your work?"

Jon looked at her.

"I mean, I know you're better off because you enjoy this work. I think that your team at CiliCold is better off as well, because they enjoy working with you, and they enjoy the work. But who is worse off, Jon?"

After a moment, Jon remained quiet.

"Are there companies that make what you're getting cells to make?" she asked. "What is left for them to do if you succeed?"

He inhaled.

She leaned on his shoulder as he sat closer.

"You are better looking out than looking in, so it takes you time, but don't worry when you finally see it, you'll walk it."

He kissed her, inhaling her. She opened her warm mouth, and his tongue entered.

"Take me back to our hotel, Lion," she whispered gripping his thigh. "I want to feel you inside me."

APPROVAL

"So you couldn't sleep either?" Kevin said into the cell that told him it was September 2, 1:37 AM.

"I don't know if I'm up to it."

"Well, if you don't get any sleep, you won't be. You need to rest, Olivia."

"Yes, I know. My testimony doesn't start till ten. So I have some time to sleep later this morning, but I just wanted to hear you."

"Well, you're screwing up my plans. I have an early flight this morning."

"What do you mean?"

"I'm actually at the airport getting on my plane to DC."

"What? I didn't know that they still had overnights."

"This one's private."

"Kevin."

"And at just $6,200 an air hour, I'll be there in no time."

The relief in her voice washed over him. "I would love to see you again. Kevin,"

"I can't stand to be away from you anymore, and I won't let you be alone in this."

"I've spoken to Audrey for quite a bit after she showed me the invitation two weeks ago." He heard her sigh. "It's a ton. I've where I need to be with mastering it, but, Kevin, these are US Senators."

"I know that. Rely on that part of you that few see that I always see. Siphod didn't see it, and you were ready to destroy him."

She was quiet. "He was going to rape and then kill me after he killed you."

"No. You were going to kill him. Don't forget that. You were ready, that's what counts.

"Courage, sweetheart, give yourself permission to fight back in the Senate, fully expecting to be hurt in the process.

"Accept, and not just accept, but accept with approval that they will rough you up."

"Accept with approval that they are going to criticize your background."

"Accept with approval that they will try to destroy your reputation."

Kevin took a deep breath. "There comes a point, honey, where silence doesn't matter anymore. Differences don't matter anymore. Where negotiation, modulation, and moderation do not matter and being hurt doesn't matter."

"I need luck."

"If you keep your courage, your luck will hold well enough.

"Be pleasant, but if they hack you, hack back and hack back hard. Give yourself permission to fight for yourself. Leave the demure Georgia lady that I love so much in the hallway. They want to fuck you? Fuck them first."

LET FLY

"**S**enator, I would just like an answer to my question."

The ornate room was dead still.

Olivia sat perfectly poised, hands in front of her, looking at Senator Smithhorn.

"I don't have to answer your questions, ma'am."

Olivia had been quiet and compliant during the early part of the proceedings, delivering her opening statement in a pinched but unhurried style.

She was relieved that Kevin sat behind her with Julie, Rashida, Sharra, and Alonso next to him. She endured questions about her background and most importantly, where she made her money.

Now she unfurled and let fly.

"Well, you don't have to answer to me, Senator, but you have to answer the American people. You've given a full and complete summary of my background. As I've told you, I am not making any money from any institution right now. I am on leave from my employer CiliCold—"

"Yes, a comp—",

"Which is the research organization for which I work. I think it's fair that people know who I work for just as they should know that I make no money from them for this. I'm just reflecting on the funding question back to you.

"Is it not fair for you to say to the American people that you get money from drug companies, as you question me? As you criticize me? This way, Senator, people know and can have some perspective on why you're asking me the questions you are."

"Like I said, I don't have to—"

Olivia waved her hand, dismissing the audience's gasps. "Senator, save your strength. As you and I are debating this point, people have their smartphones and their computers open, and they are checking who contributes to you and your campaign. So the question has already been answered."

"You know, Ms. Steadman, I can't say that I care for your tone. We have you so-called experts here all the time and they are not as insolent as—"

"We have children dying every day from a defective drug. Maybe it's time that you err on the insolent side of things.

"And by the way, Senator, is it illegal for me to be an expert? Because I get the sense from your questions that you don't think much of experts. Is it illegal to be an expert?"

"There was no question before you."

"I am putting the question, Senator. I am asking a question to clarify. Am I breaking the law by seeing here? I need to know that. Is it illegal for me to be an expert?"

The Senator stared. "No, it's not."

"Is it immoral for me to be an expert?"

"No, it's not, Ms. Steadman."

"Is it unethical for me to be an expert?"

"No."

"So I am breaking no laws, creeds, or ethos by being here as an expert. Thank you."

"What you have done, Ms. Steadman, is to make all of your money in an industry that you are now besmirching."

"Senator, that is absolutely not the case. I am simply saying that the model we have for developing, approving, and following drugs produced by the pharmaceutical drug industry is broken, and it needs to be repaired."

"Well, the FDA does a fine job doing that without your help."

"Just so I can be clear, Senator, are you talking about oversight."

"Of course."

"Would it surprise you to know that Triple-S leadership met with the FDA in secret two weeks ago to plan a joint strategy for managing this Ascension debacle?"

"I . . . I did not know that, but isn't that their job?"

"I have it from a witness that there was a meeting of leadership on both sides, where they discuss specifically how they were going to survive this problem.

"And I will represent to you, Senator, that during that conversation, there was no discussion of public interest. There was no discussion of how to decrease the number of children who are affected by NCD. There was no discussion as to how to provide guidance to the parents of children who they fear will get autism and how to reduce the likelihood of an NCD. There was no discussion of that.

"It was simply a discussion of how they could protect themselves.

"And I will also represent to you, Senator, that most of the driving in that meeting was done by the drug company."

"The committee would like to see such a summary and a transcript, Ms. Steadman."

"Read the *New York Chronicle's* website today, Senator. And this goes right to my point about the broken oversight model. There is no longer oversight. There is collusion. And we pay a great price for this collaboration."

She watched the senator shrug. "The number of drugs that are withdrawn continues to grow? Isn't that evidence that the drug oversight process is working?"

With blood boiling, Olivia's anger drove her. "Senator, you can't be that naïve. You are like the man who, catching his wife in bed with someone else, believes her when she says, 'Oh, don't worry, honey. I may be in bed with him, but I didn't fuck him.'"

The room was dead still.

The senator flushed. "I would ask you to show some deco—"

"We are not here to score debating points while children die. We are here to solve this problem. The American people demand it of me and of you. What are we to say," she said, holding her arms out to him, "accidents will happen?

"No, sir, that is unacceptable, intolerable, un-American, and inhuman. I am here to fight back, and I've come here to ask for your help."

The room exploded with applause and whistles.

"The room will come to order," the senator called out.

"Now, Senator, I give you the benefit of the doubt. I know that this was not the intent of your working closely with the industry. Neither was it the intent of the FDA. But we must deal with the result. And the result is that we have a broken system now."

"And I take it that your bill is a cure?"

Olivia shook her head. "Cure? No, Senator. But it's a good start. And the principal theme of these steps is to remove the FDA from all but enforcement and put them under the purview of the Justice Department. Allow the National Science Foundation to oversee the conduct of these clinical trials and to collect all adverse event information nationally and beyond."

"Well, you know," the Senator said, chuckling, "there are people who say that the most terrible words in the US. lexicon are 'I work for the federal government, and I'm here to help.'"

"Very cute. Next to the screams accompanied by the words, 'My child is dead,' those words that you uttered pale in significance.

"Senator, you seem to forget that while we are having these erudite discussions, children in this country are dying. And they are dying because neither the FDA nor the drug companies, Triple-S in particular, have chosen to recall the drug. They have not pulled it off the shelves. And in fact, the company is still asserting protection against autism."

"Are you denying that this drug is effective against autism, Ms. Steadman?"

"Senator, it is my said duty to inform you that its effectiveness is a lie."

"What do you mean?"

"As I said, it's a lie."

"Then, what's the truth?"

Olivia leaned forward. "The truth is that a document was submitted to the FDA by Triple-S Pharmaceuticals and promulgated by the FDA to the American public, purportedly strengthening Ascension's protective strength against autism. The fact is that the new database was fabricated."

"By who?"

"By Triple-S Pharmaceuticals, sir. Their purpose was to strengthen the argument, however nefariously, that this drug is beneficial when, in fact, it is not."

"You are presenting evidence to us that is new to the committee," Smithhorn said, motioning to his aides.

"I take no comfort in doing this. I do take comfort in revealing what the truth about this company in particular, and about the sad state of drug company regulation.

"I will also state that our law has no impact on drug companies that follow these new rules. But the companies that violate them, and just the companies that violate them, will be punished.

"And given the urgency, the public health urgency, the emergency that we now face, I would urge that the full Senate support this law as forcefully as possible, so it becomes the law of the land. And Americans can protect their own again"

"Thank you, Ms. Steadman, for your testimony hear today. You have given this committee a lot to consider. I would ask the Senate sergeant of arms to arrest you, but I fear you would talk him out of it."

She smiled. "Let's not put that one to the test."

UMPIRE

"What?" Dr. Samantha Tennyson, PhD, said. "The judge just . . . just threw my expert report out."

Leanne shook her head. "I'm sorry, Samantha, but yes, she did."

"Does she not know that this is the one research on record that demonstrates how NCD might develop from the use of Ascension?"

Leanne touched her expert on the arm. "Don't really know what she knows, but she has decided that because your work is not the standard of science, she shouldn't admit it as evidence."

Samantha shook her head. "Not the standard of science? My god," she said, voice rising, "What do you—"

"Let's step over here," Leanne said, as defense lawyers exited the courtroom.

"Mean?" Samantha said, face flushed and eyes wide with astonishment. "This is a completely new disease with little precedent to guide us. Standard tools missed the clues that point to the effects of Ascension on the nervous system. Ascension operates on the brain using a previously unheard of mechanism, undiscovered until this new technique was applied."

'Yes uh . . . she also said that she was not entirely convinced that you had . . . had the expertise required of an expert."

The forty-year-old blonde flushed. "Leanne, I'm completely confused here. I wrote a complete report providing my expertise. I'm a pediatric neurologist. I also have an active and ongoing research program in degenerative neurological diseases in children. For heaven's sake, my team published a paper in *Research Now*, which is the premier journal in biological sciences. That's not qualification enough?"

Leanne shrugged. "She didn't see any epidemiology background and wondered whether you could tell cause and effect from your experiments."

The attorney shrunk back as Tennyson closed in on her. "Well, I have some questions for her. How many histories of children has the judge taken? How many physical exams has she done? How many lab tests has she interpreted? Can you explain to me what paper she's published in this field? How can she possibly judge what I've done?"

"The law says she can. I'm sorry."

"The law said Dred Scott was property, too. Oh, damn it all to hell." The scientist paused, taking a deep breath.

The two were quiet for a minute.

"Well," Dr. Tennyson said, exhaling while pulling the handle of her roller out, "I'm heading home. Sorry that I was so tough, Leanne. I shouldn't get depressed over this. Why feel bad when you're called out on strikes by a blind ump?"

PARIAH

"I still don't understand why I couldn't just sit in trial before my testimony," Meredith said, sitting in a chair just outside the courtroom of the District 6 Linn County District Court in Cedar Rapids.

Leanne shrugged. "The court won't permit that. They don't want anyone's witnesses' testimony to be influenced by what they happen to hear from other witnesses who testified prior. It's a rule that applies to both sides. Anyway, you'll go in about an hour, right after lunch."

"How're things going?"

"Well, as of today, September 15, we're on a losing trajectory."

"What?" the ex-CEO said, now standing. *I just don't get this.* "How can we possibly lose?"

"Triple-S won some pretrial motions, and earlier today, they excluded Dr. Tennyson, one of our causation experts. We have to build a causal argument to show that Ascension excites the production of NCD in her absence."

Meredith saw Leanne, her head down, run her shoes again and again over the same patch of wood flooring.

"But," the lawyer continued, "the product is so new that no definitive research has been carried out on it. I think, though, that we might still get there."

"How so?"

"NCD is seen just after Ascension use and that's a strong plaintiff's point. However," she shrugged, "their experts are pretty good. I just don't know."

"Well, we have more experts too, don't we?"

"Yes, we do," Leanne said, touching Meredith's arm. "But the battle of experts is commonly a battle to the draw. There's no one side or the

269

other that gains a clear advantage based on the experts unless the jury really likes one over the other."

"So, Leanne, what you're saying is that it comes down to me?"

The attorney looked up. "That's pretty much it."

Meredith inhaled. "How does this work?"

"I'm going to go back in there when court convenes. Unless there are some afternoon motions, I will come right back out and escort you to the witness stand. You'll be sworn in, and I take your direct testimony."

"All right then."

"Let's first review some ground rules though."

Oh boy. "Such as?"

"The direct examination will be easy. You and I have practiced enough that I'm sure you all but have it memorized"

"That's right."

"Cross-examination is different. It can be a field of landmines. You must, and this is absolutely essential, you must listen to the questions very carefully and just answer the question.

"Sometimes judges allow you to expand on your answers. Other times, the judge requires you to simply say yes, no, or 'I can't answer the question.'"

"That's pretty restrictive."

"It's cross-examination. It's not supposed to be fun. The defense attorneys will do everything they can to discredit you. I toss you softballs right down the plate. They throw rocks at your head. We do the same to their witnesses. That's just the adversarial process.

"However," the attorney said after a moment, "trial testimony is different than a deposition."

"How so?"

"In a deposition, there's no judge and no jury, so the defense can come at you hard. Nobody's watching, so the audience's feelings don't come into play.

"It's different in trial. There, the jury and the judge are watching. If you're making clear, articulate, arguments in an affable way, then the jury may like you. It's very difficult for the defense experts to destroy an expert if the jury likes them. The jury winds up hating the attorney, something that the defense wishes to avoid."

"Leanne," someone called from the open courtroom door.

"Yes. I'm coming." Meredith watched the attorney turn away, then turn back to her.

"And no sarcastic answers, Meredith."

"May be difficult."

Leanne approached her. "I don't doubt it. But kill the sarcasm. You know, sarcasm sounds well and good when you say it, but when you read the transcript, it comes across as snarky and small-minded."

"Well—"

"Meredith, show that you're open to other points of view. Be the kind and assured executive I know that you are. I have to go."

•

"Leanne, can you join us up here?" Judge Ramona Coppers said, motioning with her hand for the plaintiff's attorney to approach the bench.

Leanne joined the gathering conference. "Ms. McCreedy has a motion for us to consider. But before I manage that, can you please, Ms. McCreedy, introduce this new participant to our conference."

"This is Judy Stanton," the defense counsel stated.

"The judge turned to face the new attendee. "And why are you here?"

"I'm an appellate lawyer, Your Honor," the short woman with close-cropped hair said. She took out her yellow pad and clicked her pen.

The judge was quiet. The appearance of an appellate attorney in this conference was superfluous. There would be a record of the conference's discussion that could be used in an appellate brief whether Ms. Stanton was there or not.

Neither was the plan of an appeal surprising. Defendants appeal verdicts as a matter of course.

However, she thought, the physical intrusion of the appellate attorney was a threat. Anything now that the judge said, any facial expressions, and any body language would go into the appellate attorney's notes.

It was intimidation, pure and simple.

But she had to endure.

"Thank you and welcome, Ms. Stanton," Judge Copper said. Now turning to Ms. McCreedy, she asked, "What is this motion?"

"We understand that the plaintiff is going to proffer a document as an exhibit. It was shared with us properly. It is a document that describes the activities of our client's in-house counsel. Unfortunately, we have not been able to either serve interrogatories on the author or take their deposition testimony because the author is dead."

The judge leaned forward. "Dead?"

"Yes. You may remember, Judge, that Cassie Robson was involved in the suicide death of a safety officer at Triple-S that my client was interviewing. She was present at the suicide."

"May I speak, Your Honor?"

"Of course, Leanne."

"Although the author was not injured at the suicide and did not commit suicide herself, she died several months later due to conditions unrelated to the death of the safety officer."

"What did she die of?"

"Mercury poisoning, Your Honor."

"Isn't that a form of suicide?"

The judge saw McCreedy roll her eyes.

"Yes," Leanne said.

"Well, I'm sorry to hear that," the judge said.

"Judge," McCreedy said raising her voice, "since we could not depose the witness—"

"Low tones, please."

"We are asking that you exclude this document."

"On what grounds?"

"On hearsay, Your Honor, and also relevance."

"Leanne?"

"We are anxious to enter this document as an exhibit. It goes to the argument that Triple-S has been involved in immoral activities for years. Allowing this document permits us to show that this one case before us does not stand in isolation, but instead is just picking the surface of what's a giant moral abscess at this company."

"You are not arguing to the jury, just to me."

"Sorry, Your Honor. This document goes into the necessary detail demonstrating that what happened in this case with this drug is simply part of a long habit pattern of Triple-S doing whatever it takes to get its drugs approved, silencing any concerns about their product."

"And I would have no problem with any of that, Your Honor," McCreedy stated, stepping closer to the judge, "if, in fact, we had the opportunity to depose its author. Plus, we don't know what the chain of custody is for this document. And we're not willing, with all respect to plaintiff's counsel, to accept their representations of authenticity."

"And the relevance argument?"

"The document does not discuss Ascension or the plaintiff."

"Do you agree, Leanne?"

"Yes."

No choice, the judge thought.

"I'm going to exclude this document on the grounds of relevance as Ms. McCreedy suggests." She looked at the lawyers. "Anything else?"

"No."

"No, Your Honor."

"Thank you. Then step back and let's proceed with the afternoon's testimony. Bailiff, please call the jury in."

•

Meredith sat alone in the hallway chair as people walked up and down the hall, running their errands, ignoring her.

She felt like a pariah, way out of her element.

So what. She had felt this way throughout her life. In the navy, after 9/11, and during major SSS decisions.

Life still counted.

"Meredith, it's time," Leanne said, standing over her.

"That took a while."

"The judge excluded Cassie's document."

"Figures."

The ex-CEO stood and walked to and through the courtroom door, fingering the flash drive in her pocket.

It was time indeed.

TWO HOURS LATER

"And that's what I did," Meredith said. She was in command of herself, answering Leanne's questions clearly and smoothly.

Just a little chilly though, she coughed, starting to sweat.

"As CEO, I understood the problems with this drug. The nerve and muscle changes were tragic and obvious. But it was impossible to know the truth about Ascension, good or bad, absent more data. So I refused to send the drug to the FDA.

"That decision was like an explosion that rocked our company, but I still refused to support it—"

"Objection," Ms. McCreedy said, standing. "I know that this witness is prone to speeches, but we are in a courtroom, and there at least needs to be the semblance of a question-and-answer dialog."

"I will ask a question, Your Honor," Leanne said.

"Thank you. Objection sustained. Please ask a question, Counselor."

"Please tell us what happened next."

"When I was replaced as CEO, the drug was sent on to the agency. When I learned it was approved, I resigned."

"And wrote this editorial?"

"That's correct."

"Objection, leading."

"I will rephrase, Your Honor."

"Very well, objection sustained. Please proceed."

"What did you do next?"

"I wrote the editorial. This drug could not move forward without more data—"

"Objection. There is no question before the witness, Your Honor."

"I'll end now, Your Honor," Leanne said. "Thanks very much, Ms. Doucette."

Leanne turned to the defense table. "I pass the witness."

Meredith felt herself slipping away. The fog was descending.

"Your Honor, may I ask for ten minutes?"

McCreedy jumped up at once. "Your Honor, I object. Plaintiffs, through this witness, have hurled false and dangerous charges against my client. Surely, the defense has the right to cross-examine this witness while the plaintiff's arguments have not yet been absorbed by the jury."

"The jury has already received instructions to not come to conclusions until all testimony has been presented," Leanne said, standing.

"The judge turned to the defense counsel. "The request is a reasonable request, Ms. McCreedy. I'm going to grant it. Ms. Doucette? Ms. Doucette?"

"Uh, yes?"

"Is ten minutes sufficient?"

"Uh, yeah."

"Let's break for ten minutes. The jury is excused until . . ."—the judge studied her watch—"three oh five."

Meredith, lost in her fog, recognized little now.

●

"I have three right here," Leanne said a minute later.

Her pulse rate dropped, watching Meredith down two of the Cokes. Meredith cracked open the third. "Thank you. Thank you,"

They sat still for five minutes.

"How's the fog?"

"What fog?" Meredith smiled. "Let's get cracking."

She walked back to the stand.

●

The judge arrived a moment later.

"Is the witness ready?" the court asked.

Yes," the ex-CEO said now sitting on the stand.

"Counsels ready?"

"Yes, Judge."

"Yes, Your Honor."

"Bailiff, let's get the jury back in here."

As the jury filed back in, Meredith watched the short woman wearing a grey suit over a white blouse.

What is her na—McCreedy. That's right.

"Ms. McCreedy, you may proceed with your cross-examination of this witness."

She had expected Mr. Clay.

It must be a remnant.

Fog fragment.

She smiled.

"Ms. Doucette. I am Alice McCreedy. I represent Triple-S Pharmaceuticals. How are you?"

Meredith watched the opposing counsel carefully. Having a man cross-examine a woman who lost her family on 9/11 would not be a good look to the jury. So of course, they were going to have a woman do the damage. They'd have another CEO do it if they could get away with it.

Better answer.

"I am fine,"

"You're not going to hit me, are you?"

"That dangerous thought had not even crossed my amicable mind today."

"Well, I'm glad because during your depo—"

"Objection. Relevance and hearsay."

The judge put her glasses on to study the screen with its rolling real time transcript of the proceedings.

"Overruled, but, Defense Counsel, please move on."

Meredith appreciated Leanne's interception of the line of questioning. She also knew that McCreedy had made her point with the jury, planting the seed that Meredith was unstable.

"Yes, Your Honor. Now, as I understand it, Ms. Doucette, you were trying to correct the company's direction, is that right?"

Keep it short. "Yes."

"You presented to the jury a collection of adverse events that occurred in the early 2000s that in your view demonstrated my client's nefarious behavior?"

"That's right."

"Well. It's just fair to take a look at them again. I have gone through and counted thirty different adverse events."

"I've never counted them."

"Well, I did, Ms. Doucette, and I will represent to you that there are thirty. Would you disagree with that?"

"Not necessarily, no."

"Well, then let's move forward with my count, shall we?"

"Yes."

"Well, I've these sorted chronologically from 2007 to 2015. How would you describe these adverse events?"

"I would describe them as representative of the proposition that Triple-S was not managing its adverse event collection and reporting responsibility well."

"Okay, and it is a safety team that reviewed these adverse events, correct?"

"Yes."

"Ah, let's take the first one. I think this is already marked as the plaintiff's exhibit 12. Can you please tell me what your concern was about this adverse event?"

Meredith studied the document, instantly recognizing it as an adverse event that was reported to the FDA late.

"It was not reported in a timely fashion."

"So the adverse event was reported to the FDA, but it was reported late in your opinion?"

"Yes."

"Well, what were the reporting rules at the FDA in 2007,"

She thought. "They have reporting rules that are based on the severity of the adverse event."

"Do you know what those reporting rules were, Ms. Doucette?"

"I don't have them memorized."

"Did you ever know them?"

"Yes."

"Did you know them when you reviewed this record?"

"Yes."

"So how far out of the time guideline was this adverse event reported?"

"About a month?"

"So this was reported to the FDA a month later than the FDA would have liked to have seen it, is that your testimony?"

"Yes."

"And as CEO of SSS, when you heard about this safety infraction, what did you do?"

"Well, this was 2007. I didn't hear about this until I received these records this year."

"And you got these records from whom?"

"*The New York Chronicle?*"

McCreedy looked up. "So the newspaper had these records?"

"Yes, somebody sent them to the newspaper."

"Do you know who sent them to the newspaper?"

"I believe it was a safety team member."

"But you don't know who that member was? Was it Cristen Sanders?"

"No, Ms. Sanders worked for Tanner Pharmaceuticals."

"Yes. Cristen Sanders is the safety officer who worked at Tanner and committed suicide in the presence of two of your senior attorneys."

"That is correct."

"Well, we'll come back to that. But let me return to the original question. What did you do to the SSS safety officer who reported this adverse event lapse?"

Meredith swallowed. "I didn't do anything."

McCreedy stood up straight. "I'm confused. Didn't you just tell this jury that you were working vigorously to change the direction of the company?"

"Yes."

"Now, you've taken an oath to tell the truth, correct?"

"Yes"

"Before God, right?"

"Yes."

"Do you know what perjury is?"

"Yes."

"So which is the lie? That you were trying to change the direction of the company by correcting these lapses or that you did nothing to correct the direction by refusing to follow up on these so-called reporting lapses."

"I didn't know about this event till this year. But it occurred in 2007."

"Well, you were CEO in 2007, right?"

"Yes, but I didn't know until recently."

"We will deal with the absence of your attention to your job back in 2007 later. You didn't reprimand the safety officer who reported this late?"

"I did not."

"Did you talk to the safety team this year expressing your deep concern and explain to them that FDA rules had to be followed?"

"I did not do that."

"Why not? You were the CEO of the company. This adverse event reporting delinquency, which you bring forward now, occurred while you were the in a leadership position. And you took no corrective action. Let's go to the next one, shall we."

And on it went, Meredith feeling more strength drain with each and every review.

●

"So during the last three hours, we've gone through all thirty adverse events that you have brought forward. And in not a single case with you as the CEO did you know anything about the adverse event at the time of the infraction."

"That is correct, Ms. McCreedy."

"You didn't make it your business to learn about these, did you?"

"I did not."

"Do you think you were derelict in not knowing about these adverse events?"

"Well CEOs commonly don't know particulars about adverse events."

"I am not asking you about CEOs in general in the pharmaceutical industry. You're not an expert on CEOs, are you?"

"No."

"You haven't taken any special education courses involving CEO training have you?"

"No."

"You didn't bring any particular knowledge or experience to being a CEO when you became one, correct?"

"No."

"So you really can't testify about what other chief operating officers would or would not do because as we pointed out earlier, you are not an expert on CEOs, isn't that right?"

"Correct."

"But one fact we do know is that you as the chief operating officer did not know anything and did not educate yourself about any of these adverse events in real time."

"I did not."

"You could have easily said to your safety teams, 'I want to know about deficiencies reporting adverse events.' That was in your purview, correct?"

"Yes."

"But you didn't even do that, did you?"

"No."

"And yet you come here now, saying that after the fact, you're outraged about it."

"Yes, that is why I am here."

"You were in the navy, were you not?"

"Yes."

"In fact, you said in your deposition that was taken for this case that you had reached petty officer, second class?"

"Yes."

"And you had been in the navy for six years?"

"Yes."

"What, Petty Officer, is your understanding about the chain of responsibility in the navy?"

"Objection, Your Honor, argumentative."

"I'll rephrase. Where does the chain of command on a ship end?"

"The captain of the ship bears ultimate responsibility for what happens on their ship."

"So you are the captain of Triple-S, are you not?"

"I was a CEO."

"Let's please not quibble about words. You were the leader of Triple-S Pharmaceuticals, right?"

"Yes."

"And these deficiencies happened on your watch?"

"That is correct."

"And you didn't make yourself aware of what was going on. And because of that decision, these deficiencies were allowed to continue. Isn't that right?"

"I don't kn—yes, that's right."

"Tell us, Ms. Doucette, what would happen to the captain of a ship if they knew of infractions in ship operations but did nothing about them?"

"They would be court-martialed and would lose their command."

"Well, isn't that what happened to you?"

"No."

"No? Did you say no?"

The defense attorney, eyes narrowed, approached the ex-CEO.

"Isn't that exactly why the executive committee met? Because they were tired of your incompetence, your inability to manage the company professionally, and your stubbornness in insisting that the company not do what it needed to do to raise money.

"Isn't that why they fired you, kicking you out of the meeting for . . . for radiant incompetence while you admitted your own wrongdoing, begged, and pleading to stay? By that reasoning, this entire debacle is your responsibility, isn't that right?"

"By that faulty reasoning, that's correct."

McCreedy looked up. "Why do you call it faulty?"

"Because that's not the way it happened. I fought to change the direction of the company in that last meeting."

McCreedy shook her head. "Your Honor, I'm going to use the defense exhibit 14 to impeach this witness."

"Please proceed."

"Ms. Doucette, here are the transcripts of the meeting. Do you deny that these transcripts describe what actually took place? Please take a moment to look them over."

Meredith studied the documents, then handed them back, pulse now racing.

"Is this an accurate transcript, Ms. Doucette?"

"No."

"What?" McCreedy stood up straight. "On what basis, is it not accurate?"

"On my recollection."

"And why do you trust your recollection over these black-and-white transcripts?"

Meredith reached into her pocket and placed the flash drive on the short table in front of her.

"Because, Ms. McCreedy, I have an audio file."

McCreedy looked stunned. "Your Honor, objection. May we approach?"

"I think you'd better," the court said. "In fact, let's go to my chambers. Witness and court reporter as well, please. Bailiff, please release the jury for thirty minutes. Thank you."

CHAMBERS

Five minutes later, Judge Coppers with the two attorneys of record and Meredith listened to the audio file in the judge's chambers with the court reporter.

> "We all heard about the debacle with the FDA and the autism drug. Many smart people lay the blame squarely at your feet."
>
> "Blame for what, Denise? For saving the lives of children who would never have come down with Asperger's? I'm happy to take the blame for that,"
>
> "You know what he means."

The judge stop the playback.

"Was that your voice, Ms. Doucette?" she asked.

"Yes."

"Can that be corroborated?

"Yes, my ex-CFO Nita can confirm."

"I'll get an affidavit for her to sign delivered here," the judge said. "What address should I use?"

"May I have a piece of paper please?"

Meredith wrote out the address. Handing it to the judge, she said, "Whoever you send will have to be patient with her."

"Oh? Why is that."

"She was blinded by the blast."

The judge studied the ex-CEO for a moment.

"Let's continue."

> "I don't know what you or he means. Why don't you just get it out on the table for once."

"Okay. This was an opportunity for us to recoup the losses of our past drug failures and make money, finally."

"You're confused about your job."

"I know my job."

"You do not. You simply know how to keep it. You think you're here to care for a money-making machine. You are here, Denise, to help preserve people's health."

"Please."

"Say please to children with vitamin D deficiency in Arkansas, legs twisted by rickets, or the poor who are unvaccinated for measles in Missouri, or those struggling to restart their anticancer treatment after killer Louisiana storms have devastated their communities. You want to say please? Say it to them, dear, but you'd better shout because their deathbeds are a long way away."

"How dare you lay these problems on me, and on our company."

"And how dare you not rise to the challenge, Stella. I don't blame you for the inception of these issues. You didn't choose these health battlefields. But like it or not, you are in the fray now. And you choose not to fight when you have the financial weapons in your hands. The extent that you don't stand and push these problems back is the degree to which you are responsible for these health debacles."

"Meredith, we are here to make money for our shareholders."

"Above all else?"

"And for our big investors, the banks."

"They can make money coincident with our goals. Our mission 'to protect and preserve' predominates."

"I am an investor and I disagree."

"Then sell your shares back to me. You seem to think our highest goal is shoveling money to shareholders. I think it's treating customers in accordance with their high value."

"We all want to do that."

"No, you don't. Sure, you all say that when caught in the bright glare of the public light, but when that light is off, we fall back to a shockingly low standard. Once we reject the value of people, we disconnect ourselves from the best that our community, our civilization offers."

"I don't need to hear this."

"My experience is that people who cannot bear to hear this are precisely the ones who need to."

"Are you blocking me?"

"Only if I have to. Please be seated."

"So, ladies and gentlemen, maybe you should read the SSS mission statement because that is now our north star."

"Meredith, you talk about weapons. Wasn't our anti-autism drug one of those weapons and you yourself pulled it?"

"SNW17012 had the promise of being that drug, but it was just too dangerous. I am glad that I killed it based on the latest data."

"But why didn't you leave the decision to the FDA? They may have said yes."

"That is what I was afraid of."

"What?"

"Those people sometimes approve drugs that they shouldn't. They can be weak, and I wanted a safe drug. This wasn't it."

"Enough. Please, let's move on. Here's a letter," that the board would like you to sign,"

"Belay that."

"I need you all to sign these."

"I'm flabbergasted."

"Well fortunately, Denise, since you won't be here, you need not be upset for too much longer."

"You can't force us to resign."

"No, but I can make life hell for you,"

"We can do that to you as well."

"Please proceed. I'm used to it."

"This is a good company you are ruining,"

"Then God damn good companies."

"You shouldn't be CEO,"

"And you were born to be slaughtered—"

"That's the end of it?"

"Yes," both Meredith and the court reporter said at once.

"Your Honor," McCreedy said, "you can't poss—"

The judge put her hand up. "Ms. Doucette, what can you tell us about the chain of custody here."

"There is an audio-taping system at Triple-S for all leadership meetings including those of the executive committee. If you listen at the beginning, there is a faint identification made by the SSS IT person authenticating the file with date, time, and recording device."

"I can verify the file marker," said the court reporter.

"Why wasn't this file destroyed by the blast," the judge asked.

"The mikes were destroyed. Those last words were mine before the explosion. The file itself was on a server in the building's basement."

"I am just staggered, Your Honor," McCreedy said, rising from her chair, "that we are just hearing about this from plaintiffs now at the end of their presentation to the jury."

"Well, it's your client," Leanne said, turning around in her chair to face the defense attorney. "They didn't tell you that they had a taping system?"

"Plaintiff's counsel has a good point," the court replied. "And what's the source of the false transcript? Perhaps you can help us with that document's chain of custody, Ms. McCreedy?"

"Your Honor, if you admit this into evidence, this will be grounds for an appeal."

"Perhaps."

There was silence.

"Thank you very much. I'm going to extend the recess for thirty minutes as I consider playing this in open court. Oh, Ms. McCreedy and Leanne, can you stay for a moment please?"

I'LL MAKE THE CALL

"Tell your story walking, Counsel," Judge Coppers said, turning away from the defense attorney to sit down behind her desk after listening to yet one more appeal threat. "Anyway, you look at it, this is not a good development for you."

"Yes, Your Honor," McCreedy said.

"You're now looking at this jury holding for the plaintiffs, plus the addition of a considerable punitive judgment. Sure, you can appeal, but keep in mind that the court does not control all copies of this file. You can plan on it getting a public airing, TV, web, what have you before your appellate brief gets filed."

"We can manage that."

"You are also looking at your client being brought up on new charges of manufacturing evidence with that phony transcript you proffered in my courtroom. Your own firm may be liable for that charge as well. And of course with every passing day after this story rolls out, SSS stock takes a hit. What is it worth to your firm to make this case go away?"

"Thank you, Your Honor," McCreedy said. She stood up, and the judge was pleased to see all fiery indignation drained from the tired woman's eyes.

"I'll make the call, Judge."

PASSED OVER

Jon shook his head in astonishment. "We have induced a cell to generate a complex molecule that it otherwise would not do, and that led to the destruction of cancer in rats?"

"Yeah, yeah, yeah, the rat produced its own chemotherapy, killing its own cancer. Mark this day, December 1.

"So what do we do with this?" Jubal asked. "Do we just turn the cells into, for example, antibiotic-producing machines? Have then produce lots of antibiotics, and that antibiotic we then draw from the patient's bloodstream. Distill it or whatever and have it available for other patients."

"No," Kevin and Jon said together.

"We have done this so the patient cells, properly stimulated can help to heal themselves," Jon said in a low tone, heart pounding.

"We in fact do what drug companies do without the external work and effort."

"Costs drop," Kevin said. "Molmacs can now be made on a dime, right, Ava?"

"Yeah, yeah. Your dime."

Everyone laughed.

"Yes, a cancer chemotherapy agent used to treat breast cancer will not cause hair loss because cells in the capillary cell walls will have molmacs that inactivate it."

"New drugs will be made by NIH scientists, who discover many of them anyway," Luiz said.

"It goes farther than that," Kevin said. "Suppose we can develop a compound elaborated by coronary arteries and is a natural inhibitor of coagulation, coronary artery blockage, and heart attacks. The same thing for strokes. So we're now talking not so much about disease treatment, but we're talking about disease prevention."

"Yeah, yeah. Patients make their own drugs?" Ava said. "What then happens to the drug industry?"

Jon shrugged. "They either change or they're passed over."

VISIGOTHS

Vannesa put the phone down. "Wait," she said, stretching her arms out. "Are all of the recorders off."

"Yes, ma'am."

"Okay, the president will sign the damn bill later this month."

"I don't know how that could have been avoided," Jen said. "After the live Senate testimony, the political fallout would put his own administration in jeopardy."

"Were there any passages stricken?"

"No, there are some minor differences between the House and Senate versions, but they got ironed out pretty quickly. All seven points will be law."

"Well, "Clay said, "could be worse. We could be FDA employees."

"We'll see how long your smile lasts," Vannesa said. "Can someone please review the implications of the Iowa case settlement?"

"It's hard to see how we're going to avoid bankruptcy," Hev Streeves said. "Plus the insurance companies are now balking at paying the settlement due to our, what did they say, 'recalcitrant, incompetent, and malfeasant conduct.' More lawsuits are circling like vultures overhead, and the insurers, well, they're going to require a heavy collateral preamble before they provide any new insurance for us."

"Banks?"

"Treating us like one of our ears fell off from the plague."

Vannesa shook her head. "Visigoths. This is a nightmare."

"You can't wake up yet, Vannesa," Clay said, handing the CEO his phone.

Vannesa took a look at Clay's phone turning the volume up.

"Thanks, Simi. We rarely see a day like today."

"In just a month, life in the pharmaceutical industry has been upended. The president will sign into law the Fair Medicine Act, which enables seven new rules that have to be followed.

"The FDAs has lost its independent autonomy and has been put under the Department of Justice.

"As you know, this bill has been hotly stalked, hunted, and shot at by the pharmaceutical industry. Not one single company wanted to see it passed, or if they wanted it passed, they wanted to gut it. But after the surprising revelations in the live testimony of Olivia Steadman, recently, the president felt that he had to act, reacting to the overwhelming response of the US public to the depredations that companies have inflicted on them. The president said that he had no choice but to follow the public's will.

"Then there was a stunning announcement of Iowa where a seven billion settlement was found against the Triple-S drug company for their drug Ascension that they claimed prevented autism.

"New information revealed that Triple-S Pharmaceuticals, the maker of this drug and in a position to make millions if not billions of dollars worldwide, filed fraudulent data with the FDA fabricating a drug success story that was no more than a lie.

"The drug company has yet to respond to this finding, but our experts tell us that this is the knockout blow to a drug company that has a less-than-stellar reputation.

"And then, if that's not enough, finally, word out of Arizona that a small company named CiliCold has been able to induce cells that produce medicines themselves. There would be . . . wait . . . let's, let's go live to the press conference where Kevin Wells, the CEO of the company is giving a briefing.

"It's with great humility that we respectfully present these preliminary findings to the international healthcare community at large. Our goal was to explore the admittedly controversial notion that cells communicate in abundance with themselves, and with each other. Cell signaling has been studied by several prominent researchers. It was our initial goal to treat this as a language and to try to understand it using computers and mathematics.

"We have been able to decipher some of it. There is much more work to be done. However, with our new knowledge, we have shown that it is possible using what are called molecular machines to actually have cells produce medicines that combat disease. We have already demonstrated our ability to produce hormones. And most recently, we have shown that we can, in a rat with cancer, have those rat's cancer cells produce anti-cancer medication that kills the disease.

"We recognize that there are stupendous implications for this breakthrough. We recommend the following. First, all scientists of interest will have access to all of our worker materials. We have only our work to show, and nothing to hide.

"Two, most importantly, that there be a new international ethics committee and panel that would control the initial use of this technology. For every five hundred scientists who want to do some good, there's a pernicious one who will want to turn our product to harm. The Ethics Committee's responsibility is to control and monitor the use of this tool. Two of our own eminent scientists, Drs. Ava Sivova and Luiz Sandoval will sit on this committee. We have some ideas that would be most helpful to this committee for which they might do this.

"This is an important step forward, but it has to be taken with deliberate care. We are happy to work with any and all nations and government bodies to help ensure that this product is used safely and effectively. Thank you."

"Back to you, Simon."

"Jesus, that's what we do."
"Not anymore it's not"
"It's an industry disaster."

Vannesa sat back in the thick leather chair. "Hey, Clay?"

"Yes."

"Regarding that transcript, it's your business, but if I were you, I'd get an attorney."

"You'll need one too."

Quiet filled the room.

"Jen?" Vannesa called out.

"Yes ma'am. Right here."

"Two things. First and, everybody, hear me clearly. I want Ascension pulled from the market now."

The room erupted

"You can't do that"

"What about our plan."

"That would be a disaster."

"Better," Vannesa said, raising her voice, "that we do that now before the DOJ commands us to. At least we'll be able to harness some . . . some degree of street credibility out of this horror story.

"All pills are to be removed from the shelves. Health care providers should receive text messages and emails to that effect. Second, I want a press release sent out today, and a press conference by 5:00 PM this evening stating our reasons for the drug's removal."

"Which are?"

"Problems in our application that was developed for the FDA's consideration, the website should reflect this change by noon tomorrow. Also, let's move to settling these court NCD cases.

"Next thing, Jen?"

"Yes?"

"Remember, Nikita?"

"Yes, ma'am."

"Get me a piece of paper so that I can write that second letter."

NON-UTILIS

"What's going on," Sebastian asked, stepping into the elevator with Allen the CDER directors administrative assistant at the FDA.

"I guess we're going to meet with Tom,"

"At 7:00 AM on December 12, 2019? We close on a house today, Primo real estate." He winked.

Sebastian saw Allen hesitate for a moment. "Sound's good, I guess."

They walked into the CDER director's office.

"Sebastian, you and Allen have a seat," J. Thomas Dawson, CDER director said.

"Sir." They both sat at once. Sebastian noticed that there was a stenographer present.

"I just got off the phone with our commissioner. You heard that the US Senate passed the bill. My sources tell me that the president will sign it at noon today. By 12:01 PM everything will change.

"We can expect a full listing of demands from NSF by 1:00 PM."

"How could they have a list alread—"

"Because they saw the handwriting on the wall, Sebastian," the director interrupted. "They've been working for weeks on the transition. My sense from the National Science Foundation is that they're making some serious housekeeping changes up and down the line.

"I understand that in six months we are going to lose our clinical research review teams."

Sebastian stirred. "That will hold up the ongoing drug applications. They should at least allow us to con—"

"You're not hearing me, Sebastian," Dawson said. Sebastian stiffened at the raised voice. "That is how we used to do business. That's not what the NSF or apparently the American people want. They want rapid-fire change and that is what we will provide, however disruptive."

"Then let's withdraw Ascension on Monday," Sebastian suggested.

"Triple-S withdrew it yesterday."

"What?"

"Why they have always been a step ahead of us is a worry for everyone."

"Maybe," Allen said, shaking his head, "it's because we treat them as partners and tip our hand to them. They, on the other hand, treat us as enemies and skewer us if it helps their cause."

They were quiet for a moment.

"When can we plan on FDA personnel transfers to NSF?" Sebastian asked

"No one is looking to take us in."

Sebastian's pulse rate jumped. "How about the Department of Justice?"

"No room in the inn at the DOJ for our employees either. Justice may want to talk to FDA leadership about the standard for drug approval to give them background, but DOJ will be relying heavily on NSF."

"What time do we have?"

"Six months if I can swing it," Dawson said, pulling his chair closer to the desk. "Then two weeks of base pay for every year after ten years of service. Of course you can appeal, but don't hold your breath for a long, drawn-out process with a positive outcome."

"So what are we supposed to do, go outside with our hands up? Do a perp walk?"

"For the rest of us, that comes in six months. For you, Sebastian, the time for that is now." Dawson stood.

"What?"

"As I understand it, Dr. DeLeon came to talk to you about concerns he had last winter involving Ascension?"

How did he know? "Yes, he did come to talk to us . . . to me. And he talked to me specifically about matters to which I gave little credence."

"The American people, Congress, and in five hours the President of the United States will disagree with you. Why did you not make a record of the conversation?"

"I didn't think it was worth memorializing."

"Again, Sebastian, someone disagreed with you. Allen?"

Sebastian stepped forward, took the page from the administrative assistant, then looked at it, and walked back to his seat.

It was an email.

I deleted this.

Scanning the header, he saw that it had been sent to multiple people, both inside and outside the agency, including the director.

"My initial read of this is that you had the opportunity to stop this FDA disaster on the ground floor," Dawson said. "We could have told Triple-S to remove their drug and take aggressive, decisive action that would have saved us,"

'You all got this email," Sebastian sputtered. "Why am I being singled out here?"

"First, you were in the chain of command to manage this issue. Second, you took the meeting with DeLeon. You were there. Nobody else was.

"You are fired effective immediately," Dawson said, walking over to the new ex-deputy director. "There are terms that govern our ability to fire for a malfeasance cause. You'll get the customary severance pay, but beginning at this moment, you have absolutely no authority in this building. I can't imagine you want to stay here under those circumstances, but it's up to you.

"CDER will be out of existence in three months. Other FDA centers will follow. The ax is not going to fall. It already has. We will assist if asked by the NSF or the DOJ. For the agency in general and you in particular, though, we only need to be guided by the term non-utilis."

"Meaning?

"No longer useful. Good day."

WHERE?

"Always late to your own parties, huh?"

"Merry Christmas. That's right, Luiz," Jon said, slapping him on the back. "How are you?"

"Good as can be. Nice gig and all."

"Nothing but the best for the greatest cell scientist in the realm. This private room's the ticket. Hope they have some ice cream."

Jon waved. "Hey, Emily, how are you?"

"Any better and it would be a crime."

They hugged.

"Whose this on your arm, Jon?"

Jon watched as Emily walked over to Raven. "We rely on him," the biologist said, "but he himself needs close watching."

Raven motioned Emily over, then whispered in her ear.

"And a poet, too," Emily said, turning to Jon. "Not a bad way to end 2019."

Jon turned to the new commotion at the entry door of the private room.

"My goodness, Olivia, we haven't seen you in months. And where did you find this guy hanging on to your arm?" Jon said, pointing to Kevin.

"You can't believe how cold it is back east," she said, hugging Jon. "So glad to be back out here in the warm sun with all of you." They laughed.

"And how are you, Kevin?" Luiz asked.

"Whole again," he said, smiling as he pulled Olivia close.

Jon saw Ava, holding a drink, talking with Jubal.

"Is that Polish I hear?"

"Stawiasz na swoim tyłku, szefie."

Jon laughed. "I don't even want to know what that means."

He turned when he heard someone else enter, then waved his hand so all could see. "You all have heard of Meredith Doucette. She gave testimony in the Iowa trial against Triple-S."

Everyone stopped to greet her.

"Very mean case," Kevin said. "I read the transcript. They came at you hard."

"And it was her very first one," Jon added. "With no experience, she went up against professional trial lawyers who, when they could not lacerate her arguments, lacerated her. They tried to break her."

"But I ain't broke yet," she called out, raising her left hand.

They all laughed.

As the group returned to their conversations, Jon turned and walked with the ex-CEO. She was thinner than he remembered, dressed in a gray skirt and black blouse.

"You look radiant."

"After years in a wilderness, I've found myself again."

He guided her away from the celebration. "You were a big help to this company. Your call to me in Indiana before we left there saved our asses. You put yourself at risk for us, and you didn't really even know me."

She reached out, touching his right arm. "My compass is rusty, but it still shows true."

"Need a home?"

She nodded.

"Know that you have one in Arizona. We do good healing out here."

"Thank you. I need a family again."

"Welcome to CiliCold," Jon said, touching her right arm. "You don't know Raven."

The tall woman stepped from behind Jon and shook Meredith's hand.

"I wouldn't have much mind left if it weren't for her," he said, smiling.

Jon watched Meredith study Raven.

"Raven, he saved me when I didn't know I needed saving. Now, you save him."

Raven smiled. "He is as close to me as my own heart."

"Let's all sit."

Jon stood, leaning over the round dinner table, with no speech prepared. Beckoning Raven to stand by his side, he let his heart rule.

"I want us all to enjoy dinner tonight. But first," he raised his glass, "to absent friends."

Everyone stood.

"To Dale and Robbie. To Breanna and Cassie and Rayiko. To Wild Bill. They were . . . no . . . they are part of what we have done. They're the boost phase of the rocket that propelled us to this point."

"Absent friends," they all said.

Everyone but Jon sat.

"Let's enjoy our fellowship tonight. This started with . . . no . . . it's easy to say that this started with a crazy idea of mine. It didn't. It started with the indignation of two of our colleagues, Olivia and Meredith, who felt that they could no longer stand drug company depravations. And so they took independent actions. My head was, as always, lost in the clouds."

"Don't you mean the ICF?" Kevin called out.

They all laughed.

"So I had little idea what they were planning. The fact that it all has come together suggests . . ." He paused.

"Destiny," she called out.

"Signed, Emily," everybody said, glasses in the air, looking her way.

"Fair enough. Let's enjoy our meals and talk."

A cell phone rang.

Jon looked around the room and saw Kevin reach into his pocket, pulling out his iPhone.

They listened.

He put the phone on the table and looked up.

"Kevin, what do you have for us?" Jon said.

"A call for you, actually."

"From who?" He held Raven's hand tighter.

"Nobody I know, but I know where it's from.

My phone says . . ." His voice dropped.

Olivia looked at him. "What? Wher—"

He looked up, shrugging. "Wuhan? Somewhere in China."

Printed in the United States
by Baker & Taylor Publisher Services